Praise for *The Lost Girls*

'A wonderfully unsettling novel about anger, loss and hope. Tightly written and compulsive, its twists had me frantically turning the pages.'
Emma Viskic, award-winning author of
And Fire Came Down* and *Resurrection Bay

'A beautifully compelling book that dares to not only ask "What if ?" . . . but to explore that question with heart-busting yearning, wry humour and masterful storytelling.'
Kate Mulvany, playwright and actor

THE LOST GIRLS

JENNIFER SPENCE

SIMON & SCHUSTER

London · New York · Sydney · Toronto · New Delhi

A CBS COMPANY

THE LOST GIRLS
First published in Australia in 2019 by
Simon & Schuster (Australia) Pty Limited
Suite 19A, Level 1, Building C, 450 Miller Street, Cammeray, NSW 2062

10 9 8 7 6 5 4 3 2 1

A CBS Company
Sydney New York London Toronto New Delhi
Visit our website at www.simonandschuster.com.au

© Jennifer Spence 2019

All rights reserved. No part of this publication may be reproduced, stored in a retrieval system, or transmitted in any form or by any means, electronic, mechanical, photocopying, recording or otherwise, without prior permission of the publisher.

A catalogue record for this book is available from the National Library of Australia

Cover design: Christabella Designs
Cover images: Colin Hutton/Trevillion Images; Shutterstock
Typeset by Midland Typesetters, Australia
Printed and bound in Australia by Griffin Press

The paper this book is printed on is certified against the Forest Stewardship Council® Standards. Griffin Press holds FSC chain of custody certification SGS-COC-005088. FSC promotes environmentally responsible, socially beneficial and economically viable management of the world's forests.

1

Whatever can have happened to the jacarandas?

This morning the street was awash with electric blue, fallen blossoms slippery underfoot after a welcome shower in the night, the air balmy and fragrant with promise. A woman sitting in front of me on the bus to the city had blue flowers scattered on her bowed head, sparkling with dewdrops.

Now all at once it's turned cold and the blossoms have gone, the branches stripped bare. Maybe there was an early summer storm while I was in the cinema, weeping through the new *Dunkirk* film. I found myself shivering in my light clothes at the bus stop and was disconcerted to see that everyone else was well equipped with coats and umbrellas. But I got a seat on the bus and it was warmer there as I half-dozed through the short journey home.

I sense without looking up the moment when the bus leaves the main road and starts winding into the narrow streets of our waterfront suburb. Richard and I have lived here for forty years – without children, with children and then once again without children. It's home to me now, the streets familiar and secure. This is our *shtetl*.

But the morning's jacaranda blossoms have inexplicably vanished.

Still a little sleepy, I walk the length of our street to where the grey bulk of the former engineering works looms over the water, its stark exterior giving no hint of the comfort inside. Most days I walk up the stairs to our beautiful apartment on the third level, but today I'm planning to take the lift, my body aching with weariness. I'm fighting it, but the ageing process is winning, and my idea of voluptuous pleasure is to get into bed with a book.

But there are still no electric blue flowers, not even on the ground, and there's something odd about the big double doors at the entrance. Why haven't I noticed this before? The paint is a faded green, not the glossy deep red it's always been. I can't imagine why anyone would want to do that, and why weren't the residents consulted?

More seriously, the keypad is missing. The only way into the building is to type in our code and wait for the door to swing open. Why would they move the keypad? I search around in vain. And why are the concrete steps cracked and stained?

With a growing sense of dread, I step back and look up at the building. Several of the windows are broken or boarded up. The open space around the entrance, where it's set back from the street, has lost all its lush green plants, and is now a discoloured expanse of concrete with weeds growing in the cracks.

I peep along the narrow side alley, to where I should be able to glimpse the smart town houses the developers built at the back, facing the water view. All I can see is some ramshackle old tin sheds.

It's possible that I got off at the wrong stop and came down the wrong street. But I know all the streets, all the buildings, and this one is not familiar; except that it is.

When I push at the doors they don't move. I reach up and hammer with my fist. The heavy doors muffle the sound, but a middle-aged man walking past with a scrawny little dog on a lead looks around and grins.

"You won't rouse anyone in there, love," he calls cheerfully.

I try to frame a question, but he's gone. The light is fading and I'm cold. All I want is to go home.

Home. Our beautiful quiet apartment with a view over the water, even a prized glimpse of the Harbour Bridge. Home, where it is always warm on these chilly winter days as the sun streams over the balcony onto the well-worn rug in the living room. Richard will be watching the ferries and fidgeting in his armchair opposite mine, waiting for me to get home so he can take the white wine out of the fridge and pass me my glass, anxious to tell me about his day.

We moved into the apartment as soon as the conversion was finished, bringing only what we needed. We shed our old lives with the old furniture, and the project steadied us and gave us a future.

Things have felt strange today ever since I fell into a reverie at the bus stop and looked up dreamily, my attention attracted by a noisy bunch of schoolgirls who were jostling their way to the front of the line. I recognised one of them, or thought I did: a solemn little thing in her too-long checked dress and private school hat, and I started racking my brain for her name. Vanessa? Veronica? She was quite friendly with Claire in the early years and I used to chat with her mother in the playground while they ran around shrieking. Samantha, that was it. I gave her a tentative smile, but she turned away, expressionless.

Then I realised how silly I was being. I'd spent too long browsing pointlessly through the city shops, then losing myself in the film, and my brain was fogged with tiredness. Any friend of Claire's would be in her early thirties by now, not a flower-faced schoolgirl.

When I got onto the bus the card reader was nowhere to be found. People were pushing past me and taking up the last of the seats. In desperation I thrust some coins at the driver and to my surprise he accepted them and even gave me an old-fashioned paper ticket.

On the journey, I didn't pay much attention to the world around me. When I glanced out the window to see how far we'd come the surroundings were familiar, but at the same time disorientating. I usually press the button to stop the bus just after I see the brightly-lit clothes shop on the corner, but for some reason this time I didn't spot it. But it was certainly the right bus. I remember passing the supermarket on the right, and feeling glad I didn't have to get off to buy food. Julian called me this morning to say that he and Françoise won't be coming to dinner after all. I would have loved to see them and their enchanting little girls, but I'll welcome a quiet night, and to be honest Richard gets a bit grumpy when the twins come on week-nights, tired from a full day at preschool and inclined to be naughty.

Richard. Whatever strange thing has happened to our building, I know he's at home waiting for me. He can come down and let me in. I pull out my phone to call him, but there's no signal.

A feeling of dread is growing inside me. I walk past our building to where the street finishes at a barricade with a view over the harbour lower down, and sit on the bench that's thoughtfully provided there, looking back up the street. Lights show in a few of the houses, but the windows of our building remain dark. There's something different about the street, but I can't put my finger on it. I have a feeling some of the houses are the wrong colour, and maybe some of the front gardens are not quite right – either too lush, or not lush enough.

This is what dementia would be like. Could it be that I'm much older than I think, and things have changed around me, but I'm fixated on the way they were in the past? In this unfathomable future our apartment building has inexplicably been abandoned.

If I'm demented, I wonder, would I think so rationally? I look at my hand to see if it's wizened and covered in brown spots, but it looks normal. If only I had a mirror. Oh, of course. I switch my phone to selfie mode and peer at myself on the screen. Wrinkles around my eyes and mouth show up in pitiless digital detail, and my hair is lightly streaked with grey, but I'm pretty sure this face is no older than the one that grimaced at me in the mirror this morning.

I'm still in my right mind. I know what day it is: Tuesday 7 November 2017. I switch my phone back to the home screen and glance at the readout, but oddly it reads *<date> 0:00 am*. Some sort of weird communication error, I suppose.

I just want to go home.

2

I walk up the street, looking for clues. Reflected lights shimmer on the wet road. The bins must have been put out last night, because half of them are still on the kerb, waiting for their owners to get home from work. They're not the standard red-topped wheelie bins, but an odd assortment of steel or coloured plastic garbage cans, all different sizes.

My apprehension grows and begins to take form.

The people on the bus were dressed normally, and some of their faces seemed familiar, but I couldn't have put names to them. They weren't all peering into mobile phones, I recall now. Some of them were reading books, even newspapers, and many of them had headphones.

I could go into the corner shop, and ask Karen or her husband if they know what's happened to our building. I'm pretty sure the shop was open when I went past. I turn at the top of the street and look along the road. Yes, all the lights are on and there are the usual tubs of flowers and a stand with a few varieties of fruit out the front.

But that's wrong too. The corner shop closed down five years ago, collateral damage in the battle of the two local supermarkets; and yet there it is.

Before we moved into our empty-nest apartment, when the factory was still an abandoned jumble of old buildings, we lived around the corner in our large, run-down family house. Lately I hate going near it, because the new owners have renovated all the character out of it and razed our garden. What will I see, I wonder, if I walk past it now?

The thought takes hold, and I couldn't deflect my steps even if I wanted to. The old house. Am I going to see it renovated yet again, or am I going to see something else, something even more frightening?

I'm standing on the other side of the narrow street, looking at the row of terrace houses, wide and tall, isolated by narrow side gardens from the smaller single-storey houses. The terrace on the corner, our house, is ablaze with light. The curtains are open at the upstairs French windows, and I can see right through to the Van Gogh print hanging on the bedroom wall. Richard picked it up at the Rijksmuseum when he went to Amsterdam for that conference, and he always assured me that it was true to the original. By the time we threw it out the colours had faded to a uniform bluish-grey, but I knew that when he looked at it he still saw the real painting in all its vibrancy.

We threw it out, but there it is.

The frangipani in the front garden, bare and fleshy, is just tall enough to clear the iron fence. They take a long time to grow, but by the time we sold the house it was glorious, strewing its flowers extravagantly all over the footpath. Dripping ferns surround the frangipani and hang over the front path, which we rarely used. A side door gives direct access to the lane that leads back up to the main street. I stand at the corner, looking.

This doesn't make sense. This is not dementia. It's Pincher Martin reliving his whole life in the moment when he's drowning.

My whole life. This house was my whole life. Other periods might be hazy in my mind, but memories of the years we lived here come flooding back in vivid colour.

Someone is coming down the road, a stooping figure. It's old Mrs Grainger, the eyes and ears of the street, usually glimpsed peering out through the lace curtains of the house she was born in. She squints up at my face and passes by without recognition.

We went to her funeral. Her son told her life story, revealing a woman none of us had bothered to get to know. I remember wishing I had talked to her more.

Now there's another flurry of movement, a shaft of light darts across the lane as the side door opens, and suddenly she's there, turning to go up the hill, calling something over her shoulder.

"Milk too? Okay."
She. Me.

I have never seen myself like this. You strike a pose in the mirror. You compose your face into what you think is your best expression. You look into your own eyes.

But she is there in front of me, not looking this way. I tentatively raise one hand, but she doesn't raise hers. Me, but not me.

She's young, slim, still wearing her work clothes, a ridiculous tailored dress with padded shoulders. Her honey-coloured hair is tied back at the nape of her neck, puffy over her ears. I was right, that hairstyle didn't suit me, I saw the light and changed it just before Lauren and Phil's big party for their twentieth anniversary. I want to follow her. I'm watching a movie and she's about to walk out of the frame. Without premeditation I step into the lane and call her name. My name.

"Stella?"

She stops and turns, frowning a little. She sees her own face gazing at her, every contour familiar, the colour of the eyes, the slightly parted lips over the carefully straightened teeth. The two front teeth! Surely she will recognise me.

"Hello?" she says doubtfully.

What she sees is the papery skin, the slight stoop, the wrinkles and blemishes. She sees a crone with frizzy greying hair.

A slippery thought darts into my mind. Didn't a strange old woman come up to me one winter's evening and tell me some garbled tale . . . what was it now? Why haven't I remembered this before?

"Stella," I say. "You are Stella, aren't you?"

"Yes. Can I help you?"

Let me in. I want to see everything, all the details of your life. Your home, your children, your husband, your cats.

A flash of inspiration.

"My name's Linda," I say. "Linda McCutcheon."

"Oh, my God," she says.

3

She brings me into the kitchen and it's almost unbearable. I want to stop and marvel over every object, and I hardly hear her nervous chatter.

"I don't believe it. Mum always said, but I never thought . . . My God, I can see that you're related to me. Look, I really have to get some bread for tomorrow's lunches before the shop closes. Please, sit down, don't go anywhere. I'll be back in a minute, then we can talk."

I sit on one of the hard kitchen chairs. When did we put cushions on those chairs? It wasn't long after we got them. The kitchen is cluttered as usual, schoolbags dumped on the timber bench, a chopping board hastily rinsed off, carrots and broccoli lying next to it. I'm startled all over again to see the cupboards. The colour looked nice in the sample piece and the name appealed to us – what was it? Something like *Ashen Rose* – but when the whole thing was installed and we came home from work to admire it, all we saw was a sea of pink.

Julian wanders in, absorbed in his headphones and his mini-disc player, and starts when he sees me.

"Oh, hi," he says.

My heart swells with love. He's fifteen or sixteen, gangly, his hair still very blond and straggling down to his shoulders, his face freshly-minted. That diffident slouch, the smiling eyes. He's dressed as he always was in a loose flannelette shirt and jeans, and I long to touch him, to feel the reality of that bony body.

"Hi," I say. "I'm your mum's Aunt Linda."

"Yeah? I didn't know she had an Aunt Linda."

"Neither did she, really. We've never met."

"I'm Julian. Where is Mum?" He holds out his hand and I shake it. I can't be dreaming this.

"She's gone to the shop," I say. "She won't be long."

He rummages in the cupboard, grabs a handful of biscuits and leaves again, not before giving me a conspiratorial wink.

A minute later she comes in clutching a carton of milk and a packet of sliced bread.

"Well!" she says.

"I met your son," I say. "He's gorgeous."

"Oh, right. He wasn't getting himself a snack, was he?"

"Not that I noticed." My instinct is more to protect him than be truthful to her. I can't be truthful to her, in any case.

"Will you have dinner with us?" she asks.

"I'd like that."

"It's a bit of a madhouse at this time of day. I'll get Richard to look after you while I get on with the cooking."

"I could help you." I really could. I know where everything is kept, and once I see what she's making I'll know exactly what to do.

"Thanks anyway," she says with a tight smile. "It's better if I just do it. The kids might help a bit later." I know better than to insist. She wants me out of her hair.

"Kids? You've got more than one?" I am longing to see Claire. Her presence pervades the house, but I still can't believe I'm actually going to see her.

"Last time I looked." She goes to the door and calls, "Richard!"

"I'm in here!"

We follow his voice into the living room where he's kneeling at the fireplace, his back to us, crumpling newspaper.

"This is my Aunt Linda," she tells him.

"Linda?" He turns his face up at me, so young and open that I catch my breath. There are a few lines around his eyes, but his hair is still thick and dark brown, brushed straight back and kept quite long, and some strange shift in perception lets me see his face and the older Richard's face merged together. He's wearing the grey jumper I knitted him when Claire was a baby, the elbows finally starting to unravel.

"Linda? The one who . . ."

"That's right. She's going to have dinner with us. Do you want to look after her? I'll just be in the kitchen."

"Thanks . . . um . . ." I turn to her, but she's gone.

Richard is staring at me.

"Wow," he says. "I can see a bit of a resemblance to Anne, but . . . wow. I reckon I'm looking at Stella when she's older. Almost."

He jumps up and comes towards me.

"Sorry, Linda. Have a seat." He gestures towards the couch. "I'll just get this fire going."

"That's nice," I say as the flames start to crackle and the warm smell of burning eucalyptus fills the room. I sit down on the old couch which is not so old now, hardly sagging at all. There's a newspaper next to me and I turn it slightly so that I can see the date. It's Wednesday 20 August 1997.

I knew it, I'd already worked it out, but it's still a shock to see it there in black and white.

"The wood's not great," says Richard. "I asked for box, but they brought stringybark. It's going to smoke a bit."

"That's no good." This happens pretty much every winter, I recall.

"I get better firewood when we go down to Mount Wallace to see Anne," he says. "I hired a trailer last winter, should have done it again this year."

I can tell he's watching me to see how I react to Anne's name. The image of her fills my mind, and I'm afraid there will be tears if I say anything.

"You are that Linda, I suppose? Anne's sister."

I nod.

"Sorry I'm being nosy," he says, relentless. "I suppose you realise that none of them know what became of you?"

I must have told Richard about Linda the first time we went to Mount Wallace together, back when Dad was still alive. Among the family photos on the crystal cabinet in the unused front room there was a prominent photograph, the last one taken before she disappeared.

Linda is posing for the camera in a full-skirted light-coloured dress that shows off her trim figure, her blonde hair pinned back at the sides and cascading over her shoulders in careful waves, a big smile revealing a gap between her two front teeth. Her mouth is dark with lipstick, but her eyes are clear and innocent. Nice girls didn't wear eye makeup in those days, Mum told me.

There is another photograph of my mother, Anne, at about the same age or a bit younger, wearing a drab long-waisted dress with her hair, also blonde, in a short bob. She's hugging a very small Linda, aged about two, who is scowling at something off to one side. Apart from their colouring the sisters are not very much alike, and I've always been told I look more like Linda. I've certainly got that accursed gap between my teeth.

The other siblings, my three uncles Jack, Mark and Frank, were all closer in age to Mum. No-one knows how or why Linda came along in 1933, eight years after Frank, and by all accounts she was always difficult. Mum recalled a baby who screamed day and night. The three brothers were moved from their big bedroom to an enclosed veranda on the far side of the house so they could get some sleep. As soon as she turned fourteen Mum was pressured into leaving school to help around the house, and she had to share the big room with the fretful baby.

"I used to put her in my bed with me," she told me. "No-one ever told me you shouldn't do that – no-one ever told me anything, now I come to think of it. I did wake up once to find she'd slipped right down under the covers, somewhere near my feet she was. She was sleeping so well I was tempted to leave her there."

"What about Grandma Dulcie?" I asked. "Why couldn't she look after the baby?"

"Good question. Your grandma took to spending most of the day in bed with all the blinds down. I imagine Linda came as an unpleasant shock, and she just didn't have the energy to do it all again; or maybe it was some sort of nervous breakdown, no-one ever talked about it."

When Linda was just three her father, my grandfather Herbert McCutcheon, died. He was only forty-seven. He had managed to avoid following his two brothers into early graves at Gallipoli and Villers-Bretonneux in the First World War, but he had left the best part of himself in the trenches.

Mum, the oldest child, managed to get a job in the local drapery store and her middle brother Mark was given permission to leave school just shy of his fourteenth birthday and start work at the sawmill. The eldest brother Jack had already run away from home. He was working as a roustabout somewhere in Queensland and learning to shear. The only one left at school was Frank, who was thought to be the brightest of the bunch, and Mum devoted herself to keeping him there.

Linda, given free run of the house while my grandmother wept in her bedroom, was smart and naughty. On more than one occasion the older siblings came home from work or school to find she had gone missing. They would spread out, shining torches into the growing darkness, calling and calling. Mum was the one who usually found her, under the house or up a tree.

Then the day came when no-one could find her. It was a hot, still Sunday morning in early January, 1950. She was sixteen, and the general assumption was that she had followed Jack's example and run away.

Richard used to speculate about where Linda might be and what she might have got up to. But when my mother was in the hospital, rapidly fading away, she started talking about her missing sister, and her yearning was palpable.

We threw ourselves into a determined effort to find Linda, advertising far and wide, and we even managed to get some radio time on the ABC, but it came to nothing. Richard was convinced that Linda must have seen the ads and hardened her heart, and he lost his sneaking regard for her.

"She's dead," Mum told me in one of her more lucid moments. "Something happened to her back then, I don't know what. She wouldn't have done this to me, you know?"

"I'm sure you're right, Mum," I said, gently holding her poor wrinkled hand. Her skin was as thin as tissue, so fragile I hardly dared touch her, afraid that part of her would come away.

"If she was alive she would have contacted me, sooner or later," Mum went on. "She wouldn't have left me fretting."

We didn't talk about it again, and I didn't remind her that Linda had packed a small bag and taken it with her, or that no body had ever been found.

Now, as far as the younger I – she – is concerned, Linda is sitting in her living room as large as life. The question is, will the younger Stella believe it or will she send this imposter packing?

I'm not too worried, because of course I know how Stella's mind works. She will be sceptical, but curious, and she will give me the benefit of the doubt while she searches around for some proof.

"It's a long story," I tell Richard. "I wanted to get in touch with Anne, but I just kept putting it off. How is she?"

"Oh, she's in pretty good shape. We can't get her out of Mount Wallace, she's involved in everything down there."

"She's not still in our old house, is she?" It's a genuine question, because I'm not sure when it was that Anne finally moved into a flat closer to the centre of town. It was a long time after Dad died, but I don't remember the year.

"No, not for a long time," says Richard. "She and George, Stella's dad, did move in for a while to look after your mum. Stella was there until she left school. But when Dulcie went they had to sell up and share out the money. You do realise Dulcie's not around anymore?"

"Well, she'd be over a hundred if she was," I murmur. "That would be something."

Jasper materialises in the room, jumps up on the couch beside me and sits with his tail neatly coiled around him, washing his face. I assume he's just been fed.

"Beautiful cat," I say, stroking his head. "Burmese?"

"Yeah. Bit of a one-woman puss, that one. He's been known to turn on people."

With that, Jasper steps delicately into my lap and curls up, purring. Richard laughs.

"I've never seen him do that with anyone except Stella," he says.

"Oh, I think they recognise a cat-lover," I say, scratching Jasper's ears.

Richard puts one last piece of wood on the fire and looks up, a slightly worried look.

"I suppose a share of that house would have been yours," he says.

"Dinner's ready." The clear voice comes floating in from the kitchen. My voice.

4

The kitchen table has been set, with a place for me on the end. The tablecloth, white with little red apples on it, is one I still have.

Stella and Claire are busy at the stove, wearing the aprons we bought at one of those school fetes. Under Claire's apron I see the brown skirt and pullover of her primary school uniform; this must be her last year there.

The aprons are fashioned identically, one red and one blue with broad straps that cross over at the back. Claire's sash is tied in a neat bow, Stella's hangs loose. I never realised how similar our bearing was, the slim straight backs. The hair colour is similar too, the blonde streaks in Claire's a little lighter. Claire's hair is also caught back at the nape of her neck, tied with a yellow ribbon.

As Richard and I enter the room Claire turns, her attention focused on the heavy casserole dish that she carries carefully to the table. My whole body constricts at the sight of her grave little face, and pain makes me catch my breath. No-one notices. Stella is watching Claire, a hand hovering protectively in case there's trouble with the dish, and Richard has gone to the door to call up the stairs.

"Julian! Didn't you hear your mother?"

"Claire," says Stella as we all sit down. "This is my Aunt Linda, your great-aunt."

"Aunt Linda?" says Claire, wide-eyed. "Aunt Linda, the one who . . ."

"The one who vanished," I tell her, smiling. "I've turned up."

Claire stares at the gap between my two front teeth, then her face splits into a grin, displaying the braces that the orthodontist promised would close her own gap. They didn't.

When I was a child I was fascinated by the story of Linda, lost at the magical age of sixteen, possibly sleeping somewhere in an enchanted castle, and I would pester my mother for stories about her. Claire, in turn, demanded to hear all the stories from me.

"Where have you been?" she asks, and jumps a little as Stella gives her foot a little warning nudge under the table.

"Here and there," I say. "It's okay . . ." Stella is frowning at Claire.

"It's not that interesting," I go on. "The last few years I've been in Perth."

"Are you . . . um . . . on your own?" asks Richard.

"Pretty much. I was married for a while, but it didn't work out."

"Children?" asks Stella. They are all burning with curiosity now.

"No, sadly." I haven't had much time to think about this, but I know I'd better keep Linda's life as simple as possible.

The food is served and attacked: a beef casserole that we had quite a lot in those days. I used to make a double batch when I had a quiet Sunday, and this lot has come out of the freezer and been heated in the oven, because I never liked or trusted the microwave. I still don't.

The food is not quite hot enough, but no-one says anything. Steamed vegetables are passed around to go with the meat. Julian has sidled into his chair next to Stella, and is wolfing his food the way he always did.

"Any sweets, Mum?" He raises his head for the first time, his mouth still full.

"Just fruit," says Stella. "There's no hurry."

"Gotta go out," Julian mumbles, carrying his plate to the sink.

"Out? Where are you going?"

"Just out. I'm meeting Natalie."

"Hmmm." I sense and share Stella's displeasure at the name. She shoots a look at Richard, who gives a little shake of the head as if trying to bring the room into focus.

"Not a good look, mate, on a weeknight," he says obligingly. "What about your homework?"

"It's all done." Oh no it's not, I think to myself. They're going to get a shock when they see his report this term.

As Julian leaves the room Stella sighs and gives me a wry look.

"I should be more tolerant," she says, "but he's got this girlfriend who's a real pain in the neck."

"How long have they been together?" I ask.

"Since Easter. Four or five months now."

Is that all? The pointless relationship with Natalie is going to continue for years. Poor Julian, wasting his time with this needy, whining girl. It would have been much better . . . *would* be much better . . . if he were to break it off now, before he builds up a substantial commitment to her. I wonder if I could say something to Stella or, better still, to him.

A little shock of anxiety hits me. Everyone knows that time travellers have certain obligations. If you go into the past you can observe as much as you like, but it's important not to change anything. Even a tiny, apparently insignificant change can set history shooting off in a different direction, resulting in all sorts of contradictions and paradoxes.

I look across at Claire, her clear grey eyes fixed on her plate as she chews thoughtfully, my dewy innocent child. Am I going to obey the rules and make sure I don't do anything to change the future? Hell, no.

5

Claire, I have calculated, will be turning twelve very soon. Four days after her sixteenth birthday I will be clutching her lifeless body in a stinking alley, howling at the sky as police and paramedics try to prise my hands off her.

People like to say that everything happens for a reason. To my mind that's pure nonsense, and it smacks of quasi-religious intelligent-designer-believing piety. But if it were true, if there could be some reason for my being inexplicably hurled backwards through time to this moment in our family's history, this possibly pivotal moment, then there's only one thing it could be: to save Claire.

With Julian gone the atmosphere at the table eases, and we drift into tricky waters.

"So," says Stella. "Perth? Are you in Sydney for a holiday?"

"Well, sort of." I glance at Claire and then back at Stella. "Things got a bit difficult over there. I don't think I'll be going back for a while."

"Right. And where are you staying?"

"Um – nowhere yet. After this I thought I might go back to Central and try one of those cheap places around there, just until I get myself sorted out."

"So you came in by train, did you?"

"That's right. Just from Melbourne, you know. Overnight."

"I suppose you left your luggage at Central?"

"Uh – yes." I've got about three hundred dollars in my purse, and surely I can manage on that for a couple of days. A couple of days may be all I need, anyway. Any minute now I might blink and find myself back in 2017, possibly sitting on the bus or standing in front of our building feeling slightly disorientated.

"There's lots to do in Sydney," says Richard brightly. "How long is it since you were here?"

"Well, never, really," I say. "I've been . . . Well, if I'd come to Sydney before I probably would have looked you up then."

"Anyway, it's nice that you came now," says Stella, reaching for my hand.

I smile at her without speaking, because tears have come to my eyes and I know she can see them. There's an uncomfortable pause.

"Would you like some coffee, Linda?" asks Stella, pulling herself together.

"Oh, uh – that would be lovely, but have you got decaffeinated?"

"Yes, that's what I drink," she says. "I find anything with caffeine keeps me awake at night."

"Me too," I say.

Richard gets up and puts the kettle on.

"Go and make yourself comfortable in the lounge, and we'll bring the coffee through in a minute," says Stella, and I obediently make myself scarce.

The other cat, Henrietta, is stretched out on the rug in front of the fire. She's not much more than a kitten, a dishevelled tortoiseshell.

"Hey, Henny," I murmur. She ignores me.

Claire comes gliding into the living room with a plate of biscuits. She puts it down on the coffee table and sidles up to me.

"Why did you run away?" she whispers.

Is this the moment, I wonder, my chance to utter the magic words, something that will echo in her memory and protect her in the dark days ahead? Something that will convince her that life is to be seized and grappled with, not squandered, never thrown away in a seeping alley?

"I was stupid," I whisper back. "I thought my family didn't love me enough, that they didn't care, but I was wrong. I should have thought of my family, Claire."

She frowns a little and slips out of the room as Stella comes in with a laden tray.

"Listen," says Stella as she pours and distributes the coffee. "We don't want you to go to some hotel. There's a spare room out the back, if you'd like to stay with us for a few days. It's a bit rough, but you might like it."

"I don't want to be any trouble," I demur.

"It's no trouble. Richard's just taking a radiator out there. It's a bit on the chilly side, but it will warm up."

I'm happy to stay in the outside room. We fixed it up as a little project one summer – maybe it was this last summer. The room must have once been an external kitchen or a sizable laundry, separated from the house by a small back verandah which we had partly enclosed.

We cleared out the junk, patched up the holes in the floor and painted the whole room white: floorboards, ceiling and rough-hewn lining boards. There was a boarded-up space where a window had once been, and Richard found a lovely old leadlight that just fitted. We put our old double bed out there with a quilt and lots of cushions, and I set up a small desk where I was going to do something creative, I wasn't sure what. I had a vision of my ideal life, where I would shut myself away from the family on a regular basis, and they would tiptoe around, fingers to their hushed lips. In reality I rarely went out there.

Richard comes in and picks up his mug.

"We can hop in the car, if you like, and get your stuff from Central," he says.

"Oh no, really," I protest. "It's very kind of you, but I can manage without my things for one night."

"Well, if you're sure."

"I might actually turn in soon," I tell them, gulping down my coffee. "It's been a long day."

We have to go through the motions of Stella taking me out to the back room and explaining where everything is. She insists on bringing me a nightdress of hers and a towel, then at last I'm alone. I really am exhausted, and don't trust myself any more to come up with plausible answers to all their questions.

The room is warm already, and I open the window a little way to try to drive off the faint smell of mould; then I sit down on the soft, slightly clammy bed and look around with some pleasure. The surfaces are clean and white and the faded colours of the patchwork quilt glow in the yellow light of the low-wattage bulb. The coloured panes of the window are dark now, but I can remember how the sun will bring them to life in the morning. Black-and-white photographs of the family are arranged on one wall and I'd like to examine them, but I already know them well. I scanned them all at some point and I look at them often on my iPad.

This thought reminds me of my phone, and I take it out of my bag. If this were an episode of *Dr Who* I could dial up Richard, even in another time, and weep out my story; but again there's no signal, and I don't expect one.

The phone battery is down to 65% and I'm not confident I'll be able to charge it, so I turn it off for the moment. I will go looking for a charger tomorrow, but I have a feeling I won't find one. I think USB cables were around in the old days, but the small connection we now use for phones might be a bit too recent.

In any case, I don't seriously expect to wake up in this room tomorrow. The only possible explanation for all this is that it is a dream after all, a particularly elaborate one. I will go to sleep, and when I wake up I will be either at home in my own bed, or still on the bus.

All the same, I decide not to take my clothes off, just on the off-chance that I really have turned into a time traveller. I don't want to find myself wandering through some unexpected landscape in the past or the future wearing just a flannelette nightie.

6

Consciousness comes back slowly, and I can feel a soft bed under me and a pillow that is not quite right. As my senses sharpen I'm also aware of a faint musty smell, and I open my eyes reluctantly.

I see white walls, the edge of a patchwork quilt, the leadlight window faintly illuminated in the grey light of a winter morning. I feel the slight pressure of a small cat curled into my side, and I know without looking that it's Henrietta.

It's hard to guess what time it is, and I forgot to reset my watch yesterday when I had the chance. As my senses sharpen I can hear sounds from the nearby kitchen, indicating that the family are up and getting ready for the day.

My door creaks and I quickly close my eyes. I feel a faint presence in the room and I know it's Claire, gazing at me. There is a soft plop as the cat jumps off the bed and goes to her. After a moment the door clicks shut, then I hear voices in the kitchen again. She is telling Stella that I'm still asleep, and they are deciding not to disturb me. I'm not sure if I'm actually remembering this, or if it's just because I know them so well and I know what they would be thinking and doing.

If a strange woman came to stay, a woman claiming to be Linda, surely I would remember it. I wonder if that's how it works. Yesterday – at least, yesterday in my time, in the twenty-first century – I didn't remember any such thing, because it hadn't happened. But that's me in there, Stella aged forty-something – forty-three, I think – and this is happening to me, to my family in my house. So I should remember it. And it's true, there's something niggling in my brain, a new memory that seems to have surfaced, of someone turning up unexpectedly and yes, staying in this room. But the thought is so hazy I could be just imagining it, and I have no sense of who this person was, how long she stayed or what happened.

What do I remember? Julian with Natalie, an annoying presence in the house, right into his early university days when he should have been out having fun. Our pussy-footed attempts to break them up. Julian telling me much later, one New Year's Eve after we had lost Claire, that Natalie had held him in a complicated web of emotional blackmail and that he had never really loved her. If only I had known.

Julian, my beautiful son who was so casual in his youth and now takes life so seriously. After Natalie he didn't attempt a relationship for a few years, throwing himself into work. Then the miracle happened, and he, the boy who always kept things to himself, told me about it the same day.

He was walking through the city on his lunch break, hurrying to get back to the office, when he passed a girl coming the other way. She had a thin, sharp face, brown hair in a long shining ponytail and the darkest eyes he had ever seen, and as they passed those dark eyes caught his and she flashed the briefest of smiles. He stopped and turned to watch her melting into the lunchtime crowd, wondering what it was about her that had struck him so. Perhaps it was the way her plain face had lit up and transformed into something beautiful when she smiled.

She turned a corner and he suddenly came to his senses, ran after her and asked her to come and have a coffee with him. She agreed, gravely, and they have been together ever since. Françoise. She had been in Sydney on a secondment from the Banque Nationale de Paris, where she worked, and was due to go home to France at the end of the week. He went after her and they lived in Paris, then Geneva; but they came back to settle in Sydney before their little daughters were born: Garance and Marie-Claire – Gigi and Mimi – three years old and full of mischief. I can't imagine life without them.

I thought the twins might help me to live with the pain of losing my own girl, my Claire. In some ways they did: I could tease out some of the love that had wound itself into a tight knot around my heart and lavish it on them. In the first, hardest months I would go to the little house early in the mornings and take the babies from Françoise so that she could sleep a little. I would wheel them around the park in the big French pram, and if one or other of them started to wail I would pick her up and gaze into those beautiful brown eyes and remember every second of the life of my precious Claire.

Every second, from the difficult birth and tears of joy, through the wonder of watching a little person evolve, to that terrible night in the alley after four endless days of searching for her. But before I had to relive that night the other twin would wake up and I could cradle them both, burying my face in their downy hair and breathing in that scent of sour milk, vomit and sweet baby.

But now I can see her again, every day while this lasts, and I have a chance to get her back. The thought makes my head swim. What I must remember now is her life from the ages of twelve to sixteen, so I can try to identify the moment when it started to go wrong for her. Then I have to find a way to warn Stella.

Time passes and I doze a little. Once all is silent in the house I get up and venture inside. Stella has left the breakfast things out and there's a note and a transport ticket for me on the kitchen table.

Welcome again, Linda, and here is a key for you. The blue card is a Travel Ten to use on the bus or ferry. Take the 433 from Gladstone Park to Central if you want to pick up your things. See you tonight. S xxx

Tiptoeing around, even though I know they're all gone for the day, I eat, shower and dress again in my clothes from yesterday. Catching the bus into the city seems as good an idea as any, and has the advantage that any nosy neighbours who happen to spot me will see me doing what Stella expects. I need to use my small amount of cash to good effect, and there should be some cheap shopping around Central and Chinatown.

7

As it turns out, it takes me most of the day to get the few things I need. I start with a plastic overnight bag from a two-dollar shop in George Street, but then walk all the way up to King Street without finding any of the ridiculously cheap Chinese clothes stores that I've been counting on. It seems they haven't opened yet, and clothes in the other down-market places are more expensive than in my day. All I manage to get is some underwear from Woolworths before I go searching through the suburbs for half-remembered charity shops.

Late in the day I find a hole-in-the-wall computer store and ask if they've got a USB cable with an end that will fit my phone. I don't know much about USB technology, but I feel that connecting my phone to a computer will either blow it up or charge it, and I might as well take the risk.

The young Chinese guy behind the counter is very interested in my phone, which I try to keep covered by my hand, only showing him the connection point.

"Is it camera?" he asks. "Very skinny. Where the battery go?"

"Oh . . . um . . . there's room inside."

I can tell he has spotted the Samsung brand name and he's not convinced by my story, but I snatch the phone away and put it in my bag. That would be all I'd need – for a bright young IT whiz to get a good look and consequently invent the smart phone about fifteen years too early. That would upset the world economy all right.

"No USB cable for that. Too small," he says, looking offended.

"Do they make them? Could I get one somewhere else?"

"No. No cable anywhere."

When I finally haul myself onto a bus home my money is almost exhausted and my overnight bag is less than half full with the new underwear, a toothbrush and a few basic cosmetics, a couple of jumpers smelling faintly of deodorant, some lumpy second-hand jeans and a few pairs of socks. I couldn't find any affordable shoes, so I'm going to look strange in socks and sandals, but at least they are teamed with a rather nice trench coat for which I paid too much. Perhaps this will be Linda's signature style, I think wryly. In any case, my feet will be warm and I'll look even less like Stella.

The bus lumbers out of the city and up onto the Anzac Bridge, still known as the new Glebe Island Bridge and not yet guarded by statues of an Australian soldier at one end, a Kiwi at the other.

I believe in science and logic. I don't believe in magic, religion or any other kind of mumbo-jumbo because it doesn't stand up to scrutiny. If Jesus turned a couple of loaves and a fish or two into a feast, where did the extra molecules come from to make that additional food? Were the fish real enough to have once been alive, to have had parents – in which case Jesus would have been manipulating the past – or did they come into existence already dead? And, with all those new molecules, the total mass of the Earth would have been marginally greater, so that must have had an effect on time and gravity. Does God not know about the law of conservation of matter, of which I think he's supposed to be the author?

If I were here as a result of a mad scientist bundling me into a time machine and dialling up 1997 I would be pretty surprised, but at least it would make sense. I might also have the comfort of knowing I could summon up the time machine again and take myself home. Or perhaps it would be a portal on a bus, like this bus, like the one I was on yesterday when it all started.

But what's actually happening doesn't make that kind of sense and it doesn't conform to any rules that I know of. All I can suppose is that it's happening entirely inside my head. If it is a dream, then sooner or later I'll wake up. If it's a cataclysmic event like a stroke or a psychotic episode there's no guarantee it will ever end. In either of those scenarios my actual body is somewhere other than what I am experiencing: lying in a bed, or maybe bound in a straitjacket in a padded cell, doctors probing me with lights to my eyeballs. It seems strange that I would feel so clear and rational if that's happening but after all, why not.

Perhaps the solipsists are right and my whole world, my whole life is an illusion. In that case there's no reason why I couldn't jump into another time continuum. There would be no physical laws to worry about, as I'd probably be just floating in an environment of sensory deprivation, and nothing around me would exist at all, except in my imagination.

However that may be, beguiled by the real-ness of what I am experiencing: the whiff of BO from that man holding onto the strap in the aisle; the kid behind me kicking the back of my seat as he whines, "But why, Grandma? Whyyyyyyyyy?"; the tinny strains of "Life on Mars" escaping from that girl's headphones – I can only go along with the experience as if it were real, and worry about the implications later.

In a dream, practical considerations evaporate, but I don't think that's going to happen here. So what, I wonder, will I do when my money runs out and I wear out my welcome in my old home? I can't present myself anywhere as Stella Lannigan, with her tax file number, her bank accounts, her healthcare, her credit cards. That identity is already taken. I can't use her qualifications and experience to get a job commensurate with her talents – and mine – even if anyone would consider a down-at-heel old bag-lady for such a thing. I could, I suppose, get hold of Linda's birth certificate and set up a detailed impersonation of her, but either she has no qualifications and no work history, or the real Linda is out there somewhere, ready to jump on me in indignation.

I get home before the others and hole up quietly in my room, but Stella ferrets me out.

"I've brought you some coat hangers," she says, entering after the briefest of knocks. "There are some hooks on the back of the door you can use for your clothes."

She takes in the overnight bag and the absence of anything much else. "Is that all you've got?"

"I had some trouble in Perth," I tell her, my eyes downcast. "There was a house . . . this bloke I was living with . . . I had to leave in a hurry." Her eyebrows are raised, but I know she's always imagined Linda leading a racy life, somewhere on the fringes, so she's not going to doubt my implied story.

"Okay. Well, if you need any help to get things sorted out . . ." Her voice trails off and she makes her escape. The offer is genuine, I know, but the last thing she needs in her life is more complications.

At dinner, I ask questions to encourage them all to talk about themselves. My memories of this time have inevitably blurred and lost detail, so I am overjoyed to hear exactly what subjects Julian is doing at school and the names of his teachers. I try to draw out Claire, but she seems overcome by shyness.

In the end Richard does most of the talking, eager to explain his job in the computer department of a big trading bank. "They've asked me to head a special project to prepare for the year 2000," he tells me. "It sounds good to me, and I think it'll be fairly long-term, because there'll probably be ongoing problems after the millennium bug hits."

"What's the millennium bug?" I ask, feigning innocence.

"Well," says Richard, "I don't know how much you know about computers?"

"A little bit."

"Yeah. Well, in the early days, when computer memory was really expensive, the software developers had to keep everything nice and concise. So in lots of instances, instead of putting in the date as, say, 01/02/1985, they'd just put 01/02/85. That saves two characters every time they use it."

"Why didn't they make it 1/2/85, then?"

"No, no, no, it has to be regular syntax. Forget the slashes, dates were in the format DDMMYY, okay? Anyway, the point is they weren't really thinking about what would happen when the date's 01/01/00, or anything after that. With only two digits for the year, the computer will assume that's 1900."

"So it will think that 01/01/00 is earlier than 31/12/99, not later?"

"That's exactly right, and everything will go haywire. Anyway, these old computer programs lasted a lot longer than people thought, and they're everywhere, especially in banks and government departments and other big organisations."

"Can they be replaced in time?"

"No. There are systems built on systems built on systems, and it's turning out to be a house of cards. So we're starting this big hunt and fix operation, finding all the two-digit-year dates and reprogramming those bits."

"It sounds hard."

"It's very hard, and a lot of the programming was done in languages that people don't learn any more, like Cobol and Fortran and other languages you haven't even heard of."

"Dad!" says Julian. "She hasn't heard of Cobol or Fortran either!"

"Yes I have," I say. "In the old days I worked in a few places where they had computers, and I do mean computers – the first one I saw took up a whole room. There were people lining up with boxes of punch cards to run their programs."

Stella's eyes light up. "Right! Some of the people I worked with in the early days used to tell those stories."

"Yeah," says Richard. "One of my first big responsibilities was to approve the purchase of a one-gigabyte hard drive. It costs about fifty thousand dollars. These days you can get a cheap PC with one gigabyte!"

I imagine showing them my sliver of a phone, with its 32-gigabyte capacity. They would think it was some sort of trick, and they'd start viewing me with suspicion.

"Do you work with computers too, Stella?" I ask innocently, to change the subject.

"Only incidentally. I'm a technical editor. People give me boring, badly written documents full of mistakes, and I fix them up."

"Really? That's a bit like what I've been doing," I tell her.

"Is that so?" She's sceptical.

"Well, at the place where I've been working in Perth, they have to prepare a lot of tenders, and they're always a mess," I say, thinking on my feet. "So I sort of put it all together and make sure it looks right."

I've had a bright idea. If this is one of her busy periods I might be able to do some work for her and earn some money. She does employ extra people at times – I remember a few lost souls who turned up from time to time and helped her out – and I wouldn't be out of place among that crew. First, though, I'll have to convince her that I can do it.

8

Once again I sleep longer and more deeply than I have done for years. Before my dream slips away I clutch at wisps of a balcony, a view of the sea and Richard saying something about a crocodile. White chairs and a glass-topped table.

I think the dream was about my life, my real life in the apartment with Richard, but I'm not entirely sure. Perhaps, I muse, that's all that other life is: just a recurring dream. Perhaps I really am Linda and this is how my crumbling brain is starting to deceive me. If that's true then I know nothing of life beyond 1997, and Claire is not going to die.

But if it's all real, and I have travelled back in time and I'm going to save Claire, what then, I wonder? Will I go back to my own time to find her grown up with a life, a career, maybe children? I imagine her and Julian living near each other, their families intermingled. Maybe Richard and I will have moved somewhere close to all of them, or maybe we will have bought that house on the Central Coast that we used to daydream about, a place where they can all come for weekends and holidays. Children playing on the beach.

I imagine the act, the moment when I do whatever it is I need to do to change Claire's fate. In that instant all my grief will dissolve, and my life in the twenty years after 1997 will reassemble into something different, something I can't predict.

I wonder how I will know it's done. Changing the past must surely change my memories of the past. Would some part of my mind remember the alternative too? I try to imagine what it would be like to remember that I once remembered something different.

If I can't rely on memory, I should try to find some way to tell myself that my mission is fulfilled and I can go home.

Home. I could go back to a life full of Claire, grown up now; to the sparkling future and the promise we saw in her. I could go home to find a plug has been pulled and all the grief that has blighted our lives for the past fifteen years has swirled away.

I need to know what I've achieved. So. When I – she – Stella set up this little room, she – I – had just read Doris Lessing's *The Golden Notebook* and found it deeply inspiring. From a beautiful little stationery shop in the city I bought a stack of slim notebooks, the ones from Florence with thick soft pages and marbled designs on the covers. They should be in the drawer of the old wooden desk under the window.

Rummaging in the drawer I find the five pristine notebooks in subtly different colours. I take the blue one and a pen from the earthenware mug on the table and get back into bed.

Right now I remember clearly everything that happened from this point in our lives – let's say the middle of 1997 – until the day I got onto the bus in 2017 to come home and found myself back here. I start to write.

Winter, 1997. I was overworked and doing long hours with the North and Dunworth job, the environmental report for Roads and Traffic and the ever-changing Railways contract...

I cross out "Railways contract" and substitute "Sydney Water". It's going to be important to remember correctly, because it might be the little details that change.

... Julian seemed to be cruising along but we found out later he was slacking at school. At the end of Term 3 his year advisor called us in for a talking-to. When he started Year 12 the next year he had improved but we still weren't happy about his relationship with Natalie. Richard was in one of his good periods, cheerful most

of the time, delighted to be in charge of the Year2K preparations. He thought there would be ongoing problems and he would have continuous work as one of the experts. Wonder what would have happened if he'd known it was going to be a non-event? Claire was in Year 6, not concerned about high school, still very close with Marika though some tensions were creeping in. If they had stayed friends things might have been different. We didn't expect her to get into a selective school and we had decided against Riverside Girls because Natalie was there and we thought she might be a bad influence.

I stop writing and glance over my work. Details notwithstanding, this is too long-winded. It will take days, if not weeks, to write down everything that happened in twenty years. Maybe I should just cover the last few months of 1997 with even more detail so I can easily see if anything changes. Or should I write about the things that happened later, the things I would like to change? I need to think carefully about this.

I'm in the kitchen making myself a plunger coffee, wishing they had bought the espresso machine now rather than ten years later, when Stella comes into the room.

"Sorry, didn't mean to give you a fright," she says.

I want to tell her she looks beautiful. She's wearing the expensive black suit, the one I agonised over for two years and finally managed to buy in a sale, with a pale blue silk top underneath. There are faint lines around her eyes but her skin is still clear and glowing. How did I go through all those years worrying that my looks didn't come up to some imagined standard? Such a waste.

"I thought you'd gone to work."

"I've got a couple of meetings in the city this morning, starting at ten, so I'm just going to go from here."

"So you're pretty busy?" I ask hopefully.

"Flat out." She grimaces. "It's one of those times I wish I was two people."

If ever there was an opening, this is it.

"I was wondering if I could help you," I say.

"Well ..." She's embarrassed, and I know what she's thinking. Bag lady.

"I know I'm not a young thing, and of course I'm a woman," I say, grinning. "But I've done your sort of work before, and my grammar and spelling are really good."

"Have you ... Well, you left school pretty young, didn't you?"

"School was a waste of time for me anyway, for all I learned there. But I did a few courses once I'd got sorted out," I tell her. "Besides, Anne drummed grammar into me at an early age."

She smiles. That was her experience too, of course. Mum's own schooling was cut short, but she was bright, and she was determined that Frank, then Linda would have the opportunities she had missed. Frank, a serious boy who was a boring man by the time I got to know him, paid her back by applying himself well and becoming the first person in our family to go to university. He did the circuit of country towns as a geography teacher and ended up with a bureaucratic job in the Education Department.

I – Stella – started out as a teacher too, with the unusual combination of Maths and English and a promise from the department that I would be placed in a prestigious selective girls' school to teach out my three-year bond. When, instead, I received a posting to a remote country high school, I asked Uncle Frank to intercede for me. All I got was a stiff lecture about nepotism. Hearing the news, Mum said, "I'm glad he used that word in such a wonderfully appropriate context."

She was pretty good, for an autodidact.

"Well, I'll bring some work home from the office later today and see how you go with it," says Stella now.

"That would be great," I say. "The truth is, I'm a bit short of cash, so if I can be of real use to you and earn a bit it would certainly help."

"Oh, you should have said!" She's reaching for her handbag, which is hanging on the back of a chair.

"No, no," I say. "I'm okay for the moment, and I'd rather pay my own way." She'll respect that.

"That reminds me," she says. "Mum's pretty keen to see you."

"Mum? Your mum, Anne?" For some reason I haven't thought about this.

"Yes, Anne. You don't mind that I told her, do you? That you're back?"

"No, no. Of course not." Mum. How old is she now? Richard said that first night that she's still active, involved in a lot of things.

Stella is still talking. "The thing is, I'd love to take you there, but I really am busy at the moment. I'll have to do some work this weekend, and there's the kids . . ."

"That's okay, I can go on the train."

Could I go to see Anne? I can lie to Stella, myself: in fact, it's remarkably easy. But lying to my mother feels different. Besides, she knew Linda.

"I think she's got a lot on today," says Stella. "Friday's her busy day; but maybe you could go tomorrow?"

"Sure. Tomorrow."

She leaves for her meetings and I wander around the house, a little dazed. After Mum died I was surprised at how much I missed her. In her last year or so, when her world narrowed as her strength and her mind started to wane, my life was a constant quest to find little things that would interest her, that we could talk about in my more and more frequent visits. After she was gone, those little things kept cropping up and falling on fallow ground, with no-one to tell them to.

She died on New Year's Day 2001, just before the whole world changed. She has less than four years left to live, and now I have a chance to see her again.

I spend the day alternately reading and walking around the neighbourhood, delighting in the things that have since vanished: that huge gum tree in the next street that will come down in a ferocious storm in 2015, smashing several front fences and Bob Riley's four-wheel drive; the rainbow-striped hippie house a couple of streets away, much loathed by the arbiters of good taste, which will eventually get a bland renovation in black and grey; the funny old charity shop next door to the hamburger joint, both to be replaced by smart cafés. I go into the Black Cat café, long gone by the time Richard and I moved to the apartment, and without thinking order a flat white. The bald man behind the counter – I should remember his name, but it has slipped away – hesitates for a fraction of a second, then brings me a weak black coffee with a dash of milk in it. I thank him wryly and hand over two dollars, reflecting that I had better ask for a latte next time.

Lying on my bed back at the house, I flip through a selection of books from the living-room shelves. I bitterly regret that I didn't put the book I've been reading, the last of the Neapolitan Quartet, in my bag when I went out to catch the bus three days ago . . . three days ago in 2017. I hope this doesn't mean I'll never know how the story ends.

After reading a couple of pages of *Cold Mountain* and realising that the film they made has soured it for me, I decide to go with *The God of Small Things*. I remember it as the best thing I read that year, and I don't remember much of what's in it apart from one devastating snippet. Something about two little girls. One loved. One loved a little less.

With one ear pricked up, listening for sounds from the house, I hear Claire come in with her friend, Marika. They were so close from about Year 2 onwards, and I never understood why they fell out with each other, nor can I remember when it happened. Curiosity gets the better of me, and I wander into the kitchen.

Claire is about average for her age in height, and skinny. Her fine bones never acquired much flesh. Marika is shorter and a little stocky, her skin olive and her hair dark-brown. They're wearing different school uniforms, and I remember that Marika switched to a private school in Year 5.

With Henrietta curling around their ankles, they are at the bench eating peanut butter sandwiches. When she sees me Marika nudges Claire.

"Hi," says Claire. "This is my friend Marika. Marika, this is my great-aunt."

"Great-aunt?" says Marika. "Wow!"

"You can call me Linda," I say. "What's the goss?"

They both fall into fits of giggles, which stop only when Marika takes a big bite of her sandwich.

"We're going to do some homework," says Claire. "We're both doing assignments on space travel."

"Sounds great," I say. "Well, let me know if you want any help."

"It's pretty easy, and we've got lots of books," says Claire. They pick up their schoolbags and head for the stairs.

Books, I think. That's nice. No internet. Of course the internet exists, but it hasn't taken over the world yet. As far as I can remember we were still using a dial-up modem, and Julian may have persuaded us by now to get a second phone line. He was as addicted to his bulletin boards as any Facebook or Snapchat user is addicted to their apps today.

Within a couple of minutes music is trickling through Claire's closed door, and I fancy I recognise the Spice Girls. I put the kettle on, make myself a cup of tea and sit at the kitchen table with it, smiling at the sound of thumps from above my head. There seems to be more dancing than homework going on.

A round-faced girl with wavy hair dyed a deep red and scraped back in a ponytail comes in and stops abruptly at the sight of me.

"Ouch," says Julian, bumping into her. "Move, Natalie. It's just my auntie."

"Hi, I'm Linda," I say, holding out my hand.

"Hi, I'm Natalie. Wow, are you staying here?" Her voice is breathy, her enthusiasm false, and I really can't stand her.

"Just for a few days. Are you at school with Julian? Your uniform looks different."

"I go to Riverside," she says. "It's all girls. Borrrrring." She makes a little face at Julian.

"Hey, maybe we can go and catch the movie after all," he says. "Auntie Linda, are you going to be hanging out here for a while?"

"Sure."

"It's just that . . . Mum likes me to be here with Claire until they get back from work, but, like, if you're going to stick around . . ."

"No probs," I say. "You two can . . . um . . . cruise."

"Oh, cool," he says. "I owe you. Can you tell Mum I'll be home about eleven?"

They go out and I hear her high-pitched laugh.

Why is it so hard to be natural with these kids, I wonder? If I can't relate to them as their mother then I'm just floundering. I suppose they see me as a cross between Auntie Mame and Mrs Doubtfire. It doesn't really matter, but I've got to gain Claire and Julian's confidence so I can give them some meaningful advice, and every time I see them both all I want to do is grab them and hug them.

Stella and Richard come in together, their mood mellow. I remember we sometimes met for a drink after work on Friday nights and ordered takeaway food on the way home.

"We've organised some pizza," Stella tells me. "Richard and Julian will go up and get it in a minute."

"Um . . . Julian's gone out. He'll be back at eleven. Claire's got a friend here."

She stumps crossly up the stairs and I hear a heated debate. Claire's voice rises above the others. "Please, Mum. Pleeeaaaasssssse."

Stella comes back.

"Claire and Marika are having pizza with us, then they might go to Marika's for the night. I've just got to go and call her mum."

"I'll help Richard get the pizza," I say.

"Don't worry, I can manage on my own." He disappears out the door and Stella is busy on the phone in the hall. I take myself into the living room and sit there feeling out of place as two delighted cats twine themselves together in my lap, purring loudly.

We eat pizza on the couch with the television going, and Richard pours cold white wine for the adults. The two girls whisper and giggle through the news, then run back upstairs to get Claire's pyjamas. A car beeps outside, there is a flurry of activity in the hall, then they are gone.

"Peace and quiet at last," says Stella, holding out her glass for more wine.

"Bliss," says Richard. He puts his big hand around Stella's to steady it as he pours the wine and they smile into each other's eyes. "Anything worth watching on TV tonight?"

"I don't know," says Stella. "I'm going to have a lovely long bath."

Her fingers trail across Richard's cheek as she departs, taking her wine. He gazes after her.

I know these signs. I can read their unspoken conversation. Our best lovemaking wasn't confined to bed with the lights out and everyone else tucked up. Whenever we got the chance we were spontaneous, playful – laughing and grappling on the couch, the stairs, the little patch of back lawn, the kitchen table and yes, the bath. But my presence is going to inhibit them.

"I'd better make a move myself," I say casually. "I thought I might take a bus to Glebe and catch a movie at the Valhalla."

"Oh!" Richard's eyes dart to the living room door as though a ghostly after-image of Stella lingers there. "What's on?"

"Um ... I'm not sure, but I overheard some people on the bus talking about it, and it sounded interesting." I stand up. "I'll just grab my coat and go."

"Right." He's already on his feet. "Enjoy."

I consider hiding out in my room, but it's risky. There's nothing for it but to catch the bus as I said, and in any case they'll ask about the movie, so I'd better know what it is. The trouble is I can't actually buy a ticket, because I don't know how much I'll need for the train fare tomorrow and I have to conserve what little money I have.

Wrapped in my trench coat at the bus stop I try to stop myself from imagining what they're up to. Was this one of the times we started in the bath and finished on the living-room rug, in front of the fire, knowing we wouldn't be disturbed? I remember the golden light, the flickering flames. Once, a spark shot out of the fire with a loud crack, singeing the rug a centimetre from my hip, and we laughed.

I try to stop imagining that I'm watching them, and I wonder idly how the morality of that would work out. It can't be wrong to watch yourself making love, like having a mirror on the ceiling; but it feels wrong and I recoil from the idea. Some people find the thought of being watched exciting, but for me sex doesn't really work as a spectator sport, and I'm usually repelled at the heavy-breathing simulations that crop up so often on the screen. The delight Richard and I still find together is felt, not seen, somewhere in that invisible space enclosed by our bodies. Besides, I worked hard to lose the inhibitions that I brought from a staid country upbringing and the merest hint that someone was looking on – or even, I have to say, imagining us in the act – would put me off completely.

It's cold and drizzling in Glebe and people are arriving at the cinema, so at least I've got the timing right. Back in these days I didn't get to the Valhalla much, with work and kids in the way, but I always loved it. It was an honest old suburban cinema, not an ornate picture palace like the few other survivors, and not really very comfortable, but it was steeped in atmosphere. The poor old place is already in its second life, if I remember correctly, and it's not going to last much longer.

I'm relieved to see that the film is *Three Colours: Red*, which I've seen enough times on SBS to be able to answer their questions. I'm a bit hazy about which of the three films it is, but I've see them all so it will be okay.

For as long as I dare I hang around in the warm and welcoming foyer, trying to imply with my body language that I am waiting for someone. Eventually, with everyone in and the film underway, I have to leave. To kill some more time I walk all the way home, the exercise warming me up, and let myself as quietly as I can into the darkened house.

9

Even at nine in the morning the house is quiet and the kitchen deserted, but the coffee pot is warm and the morning papers are not outside the door, so I know Stella and Richard are enjoying a leisurely Saturday morning in bed. We still do that when there's nothing much happening for the weekend, and an intense longing for Richard, the Richard who still puts his arms around my sagging body and tells me I'm more beautiful than ever, shoots through me like a stab of pain.

Stella has left me another note, this time with instructions on getting to Mount Wallace and finding Mum's place, as if I needed to be told. I have no excuse to put off the journey.

Luck is with me and I catch a train to Campbelltown within minutes of getting to Town Hall station, but I then have to twiddle my thumbs on a freezing platform for half an hour before I can pick up the connection to the Southern Highlands.

The train is deserted, so I sneak my phone out of my bag, turn it on and comfort myself by looking at a few photos: me and Richard in Vietnam last April; Julian in a Santa Claus hat laughing at the twins, who are ripping paper off their Christmas presents; the view from our balcony of a cruise ship coming around the point.

It occurs to me that if I change the future, some of these photos might be different. I've brought the blue notebook, just in case, so I flip to the back page and start writing a list.

Me and Richard in Vietnam
Christmas 2016: Julian and twins
View from balcony
Françoise at Koh Samui
Lunch with Lauren at Café Picardie

Scrolling through these photos is running the battery down, so after a dozen or so pictures I turn the phone off and put the notebook away.

We creep out of Campbelltown into dry, flat countryside, and the familiar bush scenery slips soothingly past the window. I keep my eyes open for the sign on the Menangle racetrack, where my grandparents and uncles used to go to the trots. The sign reads "Where Horses Fly", and it always conjures in my mind a vision of a smartly stepping trotter soaring towards the horizon with its sulky trailing behind, like Icarus with his chariot.

I rest my forehead on the glass, watching a succession of pretty little towns that can only be seen from the train. I still don't know where you find the sleepy roads that lead to them. Like European villages, the towns are dominated by church spires, most of them Catholic. Early in the history of European settlement canny leaders of the Catholic church came through all the newly-surveyed Australian country towns, grabbing the best and highest land for their churches and seminaries. Maybe a time traveller like me arrived at just the right time and advised them to get in quickly, ahead of the Anglicans, who had the same idea and can usually be found in the second-best position.

Not for the first time, I wonder why Richard and I opted to stay in the city. I know he sometimes shares my yearning for quiet country lanes, a view over a tranquil valley, the eucalyptus smell of bush litter crunching underfoot. On a winter day like this one, what could be better than coming in rosy-cheeked from a walk in the crystalline air and sinking into an armchair in front of a fragrant crackling fire, a basket of knitting or some other wonderful handicraft at your knee?

Growing up in Mount Wallace was irksome, and I couldn't wait to escape to the big city. We lived in a bland brick veneer house that was originally provided as part of Dad's job. The malt works closed down while I was in high school, and Dad moved on to become manager of the first big supermarket. He and Mum could have bought our house from the company, but they decided to move into the old family place with my grandmother, Dulcie, who was getting alarmingly frail. It was nicer there, and I was given the huge attic as my own personal space. I strewed rugs all over the wooden floor and lined the walls with the boys' beds, covered with old bedspreads and cushions. I could kneel on one of the beds and stick my head out the open skylight, gazing across the reserve to the wilder bush beyond, sloping up to the hill.

Grandma would have been about seventy-three when we moved in. Mum is older than that now, but she's like a spring chicken by comparison. And yet, and yet ... Mum is going to die at eighty-two, younger than her own mother. Does she wear herself out? Is there something I can do to give her a few more years?

I shiver a little with apprehension. Like Cassandra, I have the power of foresight. Will I, like Cassandra, be unable to do any good with it?

I take the notebook out again and write:

Mum will die on New Year's Day 2001. Can I do something now to help her live longer? Diet? Lifestyle? Health checks? If she survives it might make the difference re Claire.

*

The train pulls into Mount Wallace station with a long sigh. I get off with a handful of other people and, after a moment to get my bearings, head for the main street. The sky is a clear pale blue and there's an icy breeze blowing. I feel ridiculously self-conscious, as though one of the people with half-remembered faces is going to recognise me and call me out. Indeed, an old woman by the station entrance, dressed in shapeless layers, is looking at me a little too closely. I'm sure I've never seen her before.

It's lunchtime and the shopping centre is as crowded as it gets in this sleepy place. There are already a few quaint little antique shops and a handful of cafés, so I buy a takeaway coffee to fortify myself for the meeting ahead.

The town lies nestled in a cleft between two rocky bush-covered hills – we called them mountains, but the real mountains were beyond, to the west. The larger one was always referred to as the Big Mountain, and I used to go up there sometimes with my friends, but the dense bush scared me and I always feared I would get lost and wander there until I died.

A silly thought, I reflect now. All you'd have to do is keep going downhill.

The old house was a fair walk away up the other hill, predictably known as the Little Mountain. When I was small I assumed that the Little Mountain was called Mount Wallace, even though the Big Mountain at the other end of town was a more obvious candidate for that name. Instead there was no sign that either mountain had a name at all.

We did learn at primary school that there was a Mount Wallace in Antarctica, and as I grew older and desperate to get away to the city I thought that was quite apt.

Forsaking both mountains, Mum is now in a small block of flats much handier to the station and the shops. It only takes a few minutes to get there. Steeling myself, I drop my empty cup in a bin by the road, walk down the short drive and knock.

Anne Anderson, my mother, answers the door immediately. She's only a little stooped, her hair thick, iron grey and freshly waved, her eyes bright. She's wearing roomy brown terylene slacks and a long, loose multi-coloured shirt, and the moment I see her I burst into tears.

"There, there!" She takes my shoulders, propels me into her spotless lounge room and sits me down in the big soft armchair. "Stay there, dear, I'll get you some water."

I'm still struggling to pull myself together when she comes back with a glass of water and a box of tissues. She sits on the footstool opposite and pats my knee.

I blow my nose and sip some water.

"Well, you're not Linda, anyway," she says.

I shake my head, tears coming to my eyes again. I dab at them with a fresh tissue.

"Please don't throw me out," I say, when I'm able to speak. "I'm going to explain, and I'm not going to lie to you."

"That's nice. I've made some sandwiches for lunch. Are you hungry?"

I nod and follow her into the kitchen. The old scrubbed wooden table from the big house has long gone, replaced by an octagonal Laminex table of which she's very proud. She has laid it with one of Grandma's embroidered cloths and set out a couple of plates of sandwiches and her version of a salad – just lettuce, tomato and very thinly sliced onions. There's also some sliced cucumber floating in a bowl of vinegar, and I feel my tongue and palate shrivel at the memory of its acidity.

Anne hands me a plate and I put a couple of sandwiches on it. Curried egg, I note with nostalgic pleasure.

"You have to be family," she says, cocking her head to one side.

"Yes, I am family." I take a bite, savouring the soft white bread and the taste of her favourite curry powder. I haven't had food like this for aeons.

"You are about Linda's age, though I suppose you could be younger. The boys would hardly be old enough . . . I suppose there's Jack. He was only twelve when Linda was born, but if you're a few years younger than her I suppose he could have just . . ."

"Not Jack," I say.

"Well, not Dad," she says. "I mean, in any other family, you'd think . . . Well, it went on a lot, didn't it? Half-brothers and sisters turning up when no-one expects it. But Dad was Dad, with a big family already, and he wasn't at all well . . ."

"Anne," I say. "I can't explain this, and it's not going to make sense to you, but I'm your daughter. I'm Stella."

She looks at me with narrowed eyes.

"Are you trying to say I've gone senile, and I'm sort of living in the past? That it's later than I think and Stella's older now?"

"Not exactly."

"Because I'm not going to believe that," she says firmly. "There's nothing wrong with my brain."

"No, there's nothing wrong with your brain," I say. "I said I can't explain this because I can't. I don't know how it's happened or why it's happened, but I've come back from the future – from twenty years in the future."

There is a long pause.

"I think maybe I should get the doctor to you," she says carefully.

"I'm fine," I say. "There's nothing wrong with my brain either."

"Well, one of us is deluded, and I don't think it's me."

"Could we talk about something else for a minute?" I ask. "I have to say I'm really happy to see you."

"Well, that is nice, I suppose. Am I to take it that in 'the future' you haven't been seeing me? You did say twenty years, didn't you?"

"That's the sort of stuff I really shouldn't tell you."

"Never mind, dear," she laughs. "In twenty years' time I'd be nearly a hundred, and I'm not counting on living that long." She pauses.

"You know, you really do remind me of Stella."

"Am I what you imagine Stella to be like in twenty years? When she's sixty-three?"

"That's not something I've ever tried to imagine; but I do think about Linda and what she'd be like, and there is a resemblance all right."

"I'm sorry I'm not her."

"That's all right. I've always pictured her coming through that door, but I never believed it would happen."

There's a moment's silence, then Mum jumps up briskly.

"I'll make tea," she says. "Go back in the lounge room, it's warmer there."

I trail into the overheated room, looking through the sparkling glass doors of the crystal cabinet at her treasures, some of which I still have. There are crowds of photos on the mantelpiece and the low sideboard, showing Linda and the brothers at various ages, plus baby photos of me and my kids and one of my wedding photos.

There's a pile of Mum's magazines on the prized nest of tables: *Women's Weekly*, *Woman's Day* and *New Idea*. The cover of *Women's Weekly* shows Princess Diana, as it usually did in those days. She's on the deck of a yacht, wearing a bikini.

Mum's knitting bag is sitting on the floor next to her knitting chair, the one with arms at just the right height to support her elbows without impeding her work.

"What are you knitting?" I ask as she comes back into the room.

"Oh, just a hat for young Claire. Do you like the colours?"

"They're gorgeous." I finger the soft wool.

"I've just started it. I got it from the *Women's Weekly*."

"Do they still have knitting patterns?"

"Not really, but they had a feature on hand-knitting. Seems it's the latest craze."

She picks up the magazine and thumbs through it to find the page, with me looking over her shoulder.

"There, see? I don't need a pattern to make that."

I take the magazine from her hands and leaf back to the story on Princess Diana. Something in the pictures has caught my eye.

"Is this Dodi al Fayed?"

"Yes. I don't think much of him."

"She's not with him for long," I say, half to myself.

"No, it hasn't been long," she agrees, going out again. In a moment she's back with a plate of biscuits. I look up at her.

"I can prove I come from the future," I tell her.

10

"Princess Diana and Dodi Fayed will go to Paris soon," I say. We are both settled in armchairs with cups of tea. "I don't know when this is, but it's pretty soon. Wait!"

I get up, fetch my bag and pull my phone out.

"I'm going to record this, so you won't think you're misremembering it," I say, turning the phone on.

Mum looks curiously at my phone. "Is that a tape recorder? It's very thin. Where does the tape go?"

"Don't worry about that. It works." I stop the recording and play back the last few seconds:

"Is that a tape recorder? It's very thin. Where does the tape go?"

"Don't worry about that. It works."

She looks at me, wide-eyed, and I start again.

"In Paris, Diana and Dodi are pursued by photographers, which is happening all the time, and they're getting sick of it."

She nods and is about to speak, but I raise a hand to silence her.

"They go to the Ritz Hotel. It's night-time. I think Dodi's family owns the Ritz Hotel. They've bought Harrods, you know that, don't you?"

"That's right," she says. "You know, Stella's never been a Diana-watcher."

"Believe me, everyone in the world is going to know all this. So, they will leave the hotel and get into a car with Diana's bodyguard and a chauffeur called Henri Paul, who's drunk. And they're still chased by cars and motorbikes, into a tunnel."

"You're right about the photographers," says Mum, "but Diana would never get into a car with a drunk driver! Especially if she's got a bodyguard minding her."

"If I were making this up I'd try to make it more credible," I say. "But I'm not making it up. So listen, the car crashes in the tunnel. And Diana, Dodi and the driver are all killed."

"No!"

"I'm really sorry about this, but that's what is going to happen," I say. "Now, about a week later, there'll be a funeral. Stella is not a Diana-watcher, but she'll watch this. She'll watch it, you'll watch it, everyone you know will watch it."

The light winks on my phone, faithfully recording my words. I hope the battery holds out.

"People will pour into London for the funeral, and the streets will be packed. And the flowers! Mountains of them, piled up outside the palace – I can't remember which one.

"The funeral will be really sad, of course, and Elton John will sing a special version of 'Candle in the Wind'. Then they'll drive off through London and the whole route will be lined with people crying and throwing flowers on the hearse. Sometimes they have to stop and clear the flowers from the windscreen so the driver can see. And this will happen all the way to her family's home – what's it called? Apthorpe? Something like that.

"They'll bury her on an island in a lake out there, and they'll bring all the flowers from London, truckloads of them, and cover the island with them. And there she'll lie, under a blanket of flowers."

I stop the recording and turn off my phone.

"Althorp," says Mum. "That's very beautiful. It's like a fairy tale, isn't it?"

"It's going to happen," I say. "I don't know the date, but it can't be too far away. I know it's going to happen, because I saw it all twenty years ago."

"You really are a mystery woman, aren't you?" says Mum. "What should I call you?"

"I don't know. It would be less confusing for others if you call me Linda, I suppose. Do you mind?"

"We can go along with that for the moment. But look, Linda, if you really think Princess Diana is going to be killed in a car accident, you should warn her."

"Warn her?"

"Well, if you really believe that, you can't just let it happen, can you?"

"But you know, coming from the future, I'm not supposed to change anything."

"But this is Princess Diana!"

"Well, I can't exactly ring her up, or send her an email."

"A what?"

"It's . . . they don't let people like us communicate with someone like her."

"You could send a letter. Oh, I know she wouldn't get it herself, but she has people who deal with these things. You need to send her a letter." She gets up. "We'll write it now, I'll just get a pad."

I sense that if I keep arguing she'll doubt me even more, so I keep my mouth shut. At my dictation, she writes the letter in her beautiful Copperplate hand. We decide to keep it brief:

Dear Lady Diana

("We're not supposed to call her Princess Diana," says Mum.)

I can't tell you why I know this, but I am certain of it. If you get into a car driven by Henri Paul at the Ritz Hotel in Paris, the car will crash and you will be killed.

"Just sign it *A well-wisher*," I tell her. "When it happens, you don't want them coming round asking you questions."

Mum signs the letter and confidently addresses the envelope *The Princess of Wales, Kensington Palace, London, UK*.

"Have you written to her before?" I ask.

"Oh – maybe once or twice."

She also knows how much the postage will be, and we plaster the envelope with forty-five cent stamps and write AIR MAIL on it for good measure.

"You can post it at the station," she says.

"All right. I think I should be going now."

"Probably a good idea," she says, glancing at the clock. "There's a train in about forty minutes. I'll give you a lift."

"No, no, I can walk."

"It's fine," she says. "I have to pop out to the shops anyway."

"Thanks, then." I start to put my sandals back on, having removed them discreetly just after I arrived. Under my daughter-in-law Françoise's influence I don't feel comfortable wearing shoes inside anymore.

"Were you going to walk in those?" She's looking at my feet.

"Well, with one thing and another they're all I've got."

"Wait." She comes back a few minutes later with several boxes of shoes. "There might be something to suit you in there. I'm never going to wear them. You look like you're about the same size as me."

"Yes, I am." I sort through the shoes and take a pair of brown Hush Puppies. "These will be great, thank you."

"I've got a dress here, too. It looks ridiculous on me, but it might fit you."

She holds up a very fine greyish-blue woollen dress with a label dangling off it.

"I can't take that," I say.

"Take it, take it. Madge talked me into buying it last time we went to Sydney to see a show, but it's too small and too young for me. You don't know my friend Madge, of course."

"Madge, who says 'Toodle-pip, Annie' when she leaves?" I've always been able to do a fair imitation of Madge.

"Be careful, dear. You're going to frighten me."

We go outside, and I look at my watch.

"There's plenty of time," I say. "Would you mind awfully if we drive past the old house? Is it still the same as it was?" By the time she died the house had changed hands a couple of times, and the last owners renovated it beyond recognition.

"Yes, just getting shabbier every year. We can have a look."

In the little blue Datsun that she bought new twenty years before this, we proceed slowly up the hill. Mum sits bolt upright, gripping the wheel with both hands, her head swivelling in all directions. We always laughed at her, but she never had an accident.

The streets are familiar and not familiar. I haven't been here since Mum died, and my memories of the last few times I was here are swirling and fading into memories of the streets I walked as a girl. There were more unsealed roads then, puddles swarming with tadpoles, patches of grass studded with dandelions, which we would gather and make into long daisy-chains.

We take the road that was once the main street of the town, lined with shops. Most of them were closed and boarded up by the time I came along, and by now most of those buildings have been demolished and replaced with town houses and small blocks of flats. The shops that still operate are clustered around the station, just around the corner at the bottom of our hill.

Up near the lake, nestled under the bush that rises steeply to Little Mountain, our old house is just the way I remember it: a rambling, unpainted weatherboard place with bits tacked on here and there and dormer windows in unexpected locations. The trees have grown up so much you can hardly see the house from the still unpaved road.

Even before we moved in with Grandma Dulcie we would go here for lunch every Sunday, laden with bowls and packages because Grandma didn't cook anymore. I don't think she ever cooked much, and it's a mystery how her five children survived.

When I was older I would sometimes come on my own after school, trudging up the dusty road from the bus stop in my hot, prickly school uniform. I would make a cup of tea for Grandma and raid the biscuit tin, which Mum replenished every Sunday. Grandma, who must have been barely seventy at the time, was an ancient crone, tiny and stooped, always dressed in black. She didn't talk much and didn't eat much, but she slurped her tea with great enthusiasm, her false teeth clacking on the cup.

Sometimes, when I was very young, Uncle Jack would stay for a few days with Grandma, on a break from shearing, or en route from one shed to the next. Mum and Dad would take me up there after tea to face bear-hugs from Jack, who would be well in his cups; in fact I don't remember ever seeing him sober. Uncle Mark would be there too with his kids, whom I never saw much because they were at the Catholic school and because Mum and their mother didn't get on. We would eye each other warily and the eldest, Doreen, would pinch me whenever she got close enough.

Grandma always brightened up when Jack was around.

"Come on, son," she would say. "Give us a bit of 'The Man from Snowy River'."

Jack would oblige and recite the whole thing in ringing tones, with suitable declamatory gestures and tears long before the climax:

So he waited, sad and wistful – only Clancy stood his friend –
"I think we ought to let him come," he said.
"I warrant he'll be with us when he's wanted at the end;
For both his horse and he are mountain bred."

Most of my growing-up years were spent in the other house on the far side of town, but we referred to this place as home. All the same, Mum always knew she would have to sell it and share the money with "the boys".

"Funny old place," she says now. "A lot of memories there."

She turns the car and we drive down towards the station.

"I don't know what I'm going to say to Stella," says Mum, half to herself.

I've been worrying about this.

"Do you think you could do me a really big favour, and not tell her yet? That you know I'm not Linda?" I ask.

"You want me to lie to her?"

"Not exactly, but you could just say you're not sure who I am. Well, you're not, are you?"

"So you're not going to tell her what you told me?"

"She'll think it's too weird. And she won't feel comfortable having me in her house."

"Well, how long are you planning to stay there?"

"Not long, really, but I think I can help them get a few things sorted out. Just for a little while?"

"Hmmm. I could keep quiet for a few days, I suppose. Are you going to come back here again?"

"If you'll have me, maybe in a week or two?"

"All right," she says. "By then I'll have put my thinking cap on and worked out who you really are."

"That'll be a relief." I smile at her. When she stops outside the station I want to give her a hug, but it feels awkward.

"Off you go," she says briskly. "Don't forget to post that letter. The box is over there."

I linger outside until she's driven off, and I feel slightly guilty about it, but I don't mail the letter.

11

When I walk in, the kids are eating at the kitchen table and Stella is bustling around in a pretty wine-red dress that I remember with pleasure. Her hair is freshly washed and she's wearing make-up.

"Oh!" she says. "We weren't sure when you were coming back. We thought you might stay the night with Mum."

"Maybe next time," I say. "We need to get used to each other."

Richard comes into the kitchen, opens the fridge and gets out a bottle of white wine.

"Hi, Linda," he says. There's a slight coolness that I only detect because I know him so well. The other Stella detects it too, and she starts talking too much.

"We're going out for dinner, it's something we arranged ages ago. There's plenty to eat here – if you fancy the pie the kids are having, there's half of it left. I got it at this great place in the market this morning, you could cook up a few veggies to go with it if you like . . ."

"It's fine, I'm fine," I protest. "Don't worry about me, please."

The doorbell rings and Claire scrambles out of her chair and runs to answer it. She comes back a moment later with an impossibly youthful Lauren and Phil. I stare, goggle-eyed, especially at Lauren. She's so beautiful. And slim! Her hair is still a lustrous dark brown. When it goes grey – in her mid-fifties, if I recall – she'll start dyeing it blonde, and it won't suit her. She has that high-coloured, rosy Irish look which will coarsen when she's older, and when she puts on all that weight her face will change markedly, but I still love her at any age.

Phil also looks pretty svelte, his hair already greying but his face still narrow and alert. They said his early-onset dementia must have started when he was still in his forties, but there's no sign of it. He's joking with Claire and she's giggling delightedly.

"Linda," says Stella. "These are our friends Lauren and Phil."

"Pleased to meet you," I say, remembering in time not to lunge forward and kiss them both. In my time you're expected to kiss perfect strangers, but people were a little more circumspect back then.

"Stella was right," says Lauren, shaking my hand. "You two are awfully alike. How does it feel to see your younger self here?"

"Amazing," I say truthfully, "and she's looking particularly gorgeous tonight."

Stella laughs and ruffles Claire's hair, a sure sign that she's embarrassed. Claire dodges away, frowning.

"And how was Anne?" Naturally Lauren has been filled in on all the details.

"It was wonderful to see her. I didn't realise until then how much I'd missed her."

"Anne pretty much brought Linda up," Stella explains. "I suppose she's almost like a mother to you, Linda?"

"Exactly," I say. "She's in fine form, by the way. She seems twenty years younger than our mother was at that age . . . I mean . . . I mean when I left. When I left. Mum must have been fifty-something then, but she was already an old lady."

"Yes, poor old Dulcie," says Richard. "Anne, on the other hand, is going to be young and energetic until she's a hundred."

I wish.

Phil looks at his watch. "The table's booked for seven," he says, and there's a flurry of activity.

"I'm sure they could fit another person in," says Lauren. "Would you like to come with us, Linda?"

"No, no, thanks so much," I say. "I think I'll get an early night."

"Okay. But listen, we're having a party next Saturday night. It's our twentieth wedding anniversary. Why don't you come along?"

"Oh . . . um . . . thanks, I might."

They go, and I help myself to some pie while the kids scrape their plates and put them in the dishwasher.

"And what are your plans for the evening?" I ask them.

"We're just going to watch a video," Julian says. "It's *Indiana Jones and the Last Crusade*. Unless you want to watch something?"

"No, no. I might watch with you, if that's okay?"

"Yeah, sure."

"I'll finish off the kitchen, if you like, while you get the video set up," I offer.

Claire lingers for a moment as I start wiping down the benches.

"I wanted to get *The Princess Bride*." Her tone is aggrieved.

"Oh, I love that movie," I say. "Maybe you and I could watch it some night? Have you seen it before?"

"About ten times," says Julian, coming back to raid the fridge. "Do you want some ice cream, Aunt Linda?"

"Just Linda, please," I say. "No, thanks."

"Mum said not to eat the ice cream," says Claire.

"Just a little bit. She won't notice."

Between them they almost empty the ice cream carton, so I think Stella is going to notice. I finish the kitchen and join them in the living room. Claire has changed into her pyjamas and dragged her doona downstairs. We settle down while the cats wander among us, making their selections. Jasper favours my lap again and Henrietta claws her way under Claire's doona. The kids each have

THE LOST GIRLS

a couch and I insist that I'm comfortable in the armchair, though I would really like to snuggle up with Claire and the cat, the way we used to watch movies together.

Julian starts the video, and I am jolted at the poor quality of the fuzzy image on the small television screen. How quickly we have become used to high-definition television and big screens, which were an exorbitant luxury back in these days.

I forget about the shortcomings of the image as we all get caught up in the story – or at least Julian and I do. Claire falls asleep almost immediately, the little cat now nestled under her chin.

After about an hour Julian pauses the machine.

"Do you want a snack?" he asks me.

"Maybe just an apple. Do you think we should put Claire into bed?"

"Oh, I guess so. She always does this."

"I'll take her."

I draw Claire to her feet, bundle the doona under my arm and gently lead her up the stairs, knowing that if I do it right she won't really wake up and she won't remember tomorrow how she got to bed. She brushes her teeth in a sleepwalking trance, then I tuck her into bed in the chaotic room. Her eyes are closed, and I risk giving her a kiss on the forehead and murmuring "Good night, sweet girl."

Julian has put a substantial pile of cheese, nuts and even chocolate biscuits on the coffee table, and he is munching his way through the feast.

"Do you like the movie?" he asks, reaching for the remote control.

"It's not as good as *Raiders of the Lost Ark*," I say, "but it's up there."

"Yeah, I reckon it's the second-best one," he agrees. "It's a pity they won't be able to make any more."

"No? Why not?"

"Well, look at Harrison Ford."

"I don't know," I say. "I reckon he's got a few more turns left in him."

"You think he's the older woman's crumpet?" asks Julian cheekily.

"No, that'd be Sean Connery. Why do you think I like this movie so much?"

He presses play again, but almost immediately there's a light tap on the outside door. Julian freezes, the remote control still in his hand. Another tap.

"Ummmm – Aunt Linda, would you do me a big favour and . . . sort of . . . disappear for a minute?"

Disconcerted, I look around for an escape.

"Maybe the laundry?" he suggests, and I scuttle in there while he goes to open the door. I hear lowered voices, but the volume rises inexorably until I can make out Natalie's high-pitched tones.

Julian, his voice more controlled, speaks at length, then finally the door clicks shut and there's silence. I peep out, half-expecting to find that he has gone out with her, but he's standing in front of the TV, winding the tape back to the place we were up to.

"Sorry," he says, slightly flushed.

"Everything all right?"

"Sure, sure. Only . . . I said I couldn't go out, because I had to babysit Claire. So Natalie was trying to talk me into going to some party."

"Well, I am here, so I suppose you could have – "

"Yeah, but . . . Sometimes I just want some space, you know? But if she knew you were here she would have made a big deal out of it, because she'd see that I could have gone."

"I see."

"It's just simpler this way," he says, finding the place and starting the movie again.

We watch to the end without talking, and I must admit I get a bit dozy after a while. I wake up fully to the whirring sound of him rewinding the tape.

"I might just watch some music stuff after this," he says. "Do you mind?"

"Oh, I think I'll go to bed."

I get up and go to the door, then I turn. He's slumped on the couch, juggling the remote controls, with the pre-occupied look I sometimes see in my older Julian when he's wrestling with a problem.

"It's none of my business," I say, "but if you don't feel like doing something no-one's got a right to pressure you."

"Oh, it's okay."

"Is this relationship really important to you? Like, do you see yourself being with Natalie for a long time?"

"Not really," he says, looking slightly alarmed. "I'm not totally sure how we got into it at all, really. But she's sort of got a way of making me do things, and she gives me such a hard time if I won't."

"Well, maybe you should have a think about it, because the longer you stay with her the harder it will be to leave." And with that I withdraw to my cold little room, wondering if I've gone too far.

12

My run of sound sleeps seems to be over, and I toss and turn all night, worrying about Claire, then Julian, then Claire again. I fall into a half-sleep and dream that Anne comes swooping in to denounce me as an imposter, and my whole family are lined up in front of me looking outraged. Richard has become the older Richard and he's saying "How could you?" over and over.

In the middle of the night I sit up, wide awake, and climb out of bed to write in my notebook.

Julian stays with Natalie for at least four years. No other real relationship until Françoise. Have I done something to change that?

At one point I hear voices outside and I recognise Lauren's laugh. It feels very late, and they're all talking too loudly, but I drift back into sleep before I really register anything.

We had many of these dinners, with the freedom of late nights once our kids were too old for babysitters, and I don't remember which particular occasion this was. I do remember their twentieth wedding anniversary, though. It was one of the great parties, and I'm seriously tempted to take up Lauren's invitation.

In the morning, once more, everyone is sleeping in. The first one to appear is Claire, already dressed, bright-eyed and chatty.

"Did I miss the movie?" she asks. "I can't remember anything about it. Can we really get *The Princess Bride* one day?"

"Sure, I'd love to," I say. "Umm . . . I don't think there's any milk, so I'm just about to go and get some."

"Oh, great," she says. "I'm starving."

"Why don't you and I go out for breakfast?" I say suddenly. "I'd love some coffee, and I think they'd have raisin toast or something in that Black Cat café."

"Wow," she says. "That'd be so cool. They'll all be in bed for hours." She waves a hand in the general direction of the stairs. I feel a stab of worry about my finances, but I've got about thirty dollars left, so that should do it.

We walk up to the main street together, just as we did a thousand times: when she was a little creature stumping along, refusing to get into the stroller; when she was an earnest six-year-old clutching assorted objects for show and tell; the day before she started high school when we made a dummy run, catching the bus and working out where to get off, because she wanted to do it by herself on the first day; later, when she was a gorgeous lanky teenager as tall as me, increasingly distant but occasionally stunning me with a sudden confidence, an arm over my shoulder, a merry laugh.

When did she start to change? Why did I not notice?

At the café, we take a table towards the front where we can watch the street. I order coffee for me, hot chocolate for her and two serves of raisin toast.

"Thanks," she says. "This is yummy."

"So, we haven't had a chance to talk yet," I say. "What's happening in your world? How's school?"

"Grown-ups always ask that," she says. "School's just school. It's getting a bit hard, but I can do it all so far."

"You're going to high school next year, aren't you? Do you know where you'll be going?"

"Balmain High, I suppose. Mum made me do the test for selective schools, but I won't get in. Anyway, none of my friends will either."

"Are they all going to Balmain High?"

"I don't know yet. But my best friend Marika's already changed schools. She's at SCEGGS."

"Would you like to go to SCEGGS too?" Maybe I could persuade Stella and Richard. At that stage we were against private schools, but afterwards I regretted not sending Claire to one straight away.

"Not really. Marika's the only person I'd know there, and she's got a lot of new friends – music friends – and they don't like me."

"I'm sure they do."

"No." She shrugs. "It's okay, I don't really do music. I stopped practising on the piano and Mum sold it."

I feel a stab that should be guilt, but it feels more like anger towards Stella. There was a shining path for Claire to develop the talent in those slender fingers and get herself a pass into an august group – I remember how important groups were in her teens, and how you had to be accepted into one – and Stella, obtuse Stella, sold the piano?

"But you're still good friends with Marika?" I say, clutching at straws.

"Yeah, we're still friends, but sometimes she can be a bitch."

"Oh."

I still can't remember exactly, but I'm wondering if the falling-out with Marika happened around this time. Starting high school without a best friend was a hard time for Claire. Surely with Marika on her side she would not have taken the dark path she did.

"Everyone can be grumpy some of the time," I remind Claire. "Being friends with someone means you remember all the good stuff and don't worry too much about the bad. Right?"

"Right," she says, more polite than convinced.

THE LOST GIRLS

Back at the house, Claire goes straight upstairs. Stella is in the kitchen making toast and tea. Richard appears in running gear, kisses the top of her head and disappears.

"I hope you don't mind," I say. "I took Claire out for breakfast."

"No, that's nice," she says. "It's good for her to know she's got more family. She adores Mum – Anne – but, you know, Mount Wallace's a bit too far away."

"Well, it's lovely getting to know her, but of course I'll have to find a place of my own soon."

"No hurry," she says. "After I've had breakfast I'll show you the work I've brought home, if you like. We've got an old computer in the house. It's a bit crappy, but it's good enough for a bit of editing. Julian can set it up in your room."

"Sounds great," I say. "I haven't worked for a while, and I'd like to get stuck into something."

In fact I haven't worked for three years, and I hope my skills are not too rusty, and that I'll remember how to use the older operating system. Would it be Windows 95? God knows what version of Word went with that, but I suppose I'll remember when I see it.

"I've been wondering," says Stella. "How did you find me? How did you even know I existed?"

I'm not prepared for this, and for a moment I'm speechless.

"Oh, umm . . ."

"Sorry, you don't have to tell me if it's – "

"No, no, no, it's okay. But it was a bit underhand," I say, thinking fast. "I ran into someone from Mount Wallace, and I sort of . . . told her I was someone else."

"Who?"

"Who did I meet, or who did I say I was?" I'm playing for time.

"Well . . . both."

"Right. Well, I was on holiday – in Bali, actually, staying in a little *losmen* in Monkey Forest Road in Ubud, with . . . well, never mind who with. And I ran into this Australian woman about my age, and she said, you know, something like 'You look familiar, did we go to school together? I'm from Mount Wallace.' I realised who she was – Lorraine Delahunty, did you ever know her?"

Stella shakes her head, but of course she wouldn't expect to know everyone in Mount Wallace, especially in Linda's generation.

"I thought my secret was out, but she couldn't put a name to the face, so then I said, 'June McDonald, don't you remember? I was in the hockey team and you were the captain. Lorraine, isn't it?' Well, of course she didn't remember any June McDonald, because I made that up, but she was too polite to say. And then she actually said, 'I thought for a minute you were Linda McCutcheon, that girl who disappeared.'"

I laugh.

"God, the plot thickens!" says Stella.

"Anyway, we got talking about people, and she told me that Anne had had just one child, you, and that you were in Sydney and married to someone from the Lannigan family."

"Oh, right. That name. You know Richard's only about a third cousin of Sheila Lannigan? I haven't even met her." Sheila Lannigan was a minor celebrity back then, I recall, getting small parts in Hollywood films at a time when few Australians had a chance.

"Well, at least it gave me a name to look up in the phone book, and there you were."

"So you came looking for me? Why not Mum?"

I shrug. "There's a lot of emotion there. I wasn't sure I could handle it."

Stella goes a bit misty-eyed and gives me an awkward hug.

"Welcome back to the family, anyway," she says.

By the time Richard comes back from his run I'm safely out of the way, riffling through the printouts Stella has given me, making a few notes. She has promised that as soon as Julian gets up he'll organise the computer. The files are with the papers, saved on a chunky device that awakens a lost memory in my brain.

"Wow!" I say when Stella hands it to me. "A Zip disk!"

"They're perfect for this kind of work," she says. "You can put a hundred megabytes on one of these! Of course

Julian thinks I should get a Jaz drive because the disks can take a gigabyte, but honestly, who would ever want to store that much? And the drive costs over a thousand dollars."

"Right," I say. "Don't get a Jaz drive."

What a lot of technology we've chewed through! Diskettes, Zip disks, CDs, rewritable CDs, DVDs, thumb drives and external hard disks; and now we just store everything in the cloud which isn't a cloud at all, but a collection of shockingly enormous mainframes stored in underground bunkers all around the world.

Back then, I remember, I still favoured the humble floppy disk that you could whack into any computer, pull out and hand over to the next person. Sneakernet, we called it, because it forced you to get out of your chair and walk across the room. You might occasionally meet your colleagues face to face, maybe exchange a few words.

I park myself at the table in my room and spread out the printouts, but before looking at them I pull out the notebook and write:

She didn't buy the Jaz drive. But is that because I just told her not to? Is there an earlier version of my life in which I did buy it? Maybe I have to write down every detail before I have these conversations, or else how would I know?

As I flip through the job Stella has given me it stirs faint memories. This was a difficult and annoying project, but at the same time it was straightforward: just a matter of slogging through a lot of garbage and turning it into something meaningful. I did employ outsiders to help with work like this, and I don't remember that anyone ever did a particularly good job; but maybe I'm about to change that. If Stella is not impressed with my work I'll be wanting to know why.

13

The week passes remarkably quickly as I ease into a familiar routine of chaining myself to a desk and focussing on the document before me. It's strangely comforting, and my main worry is that I'll be suddenly whisked back to my own time – or worse, to some other time – and leave the job unfinished.

Stella is, of course, delighted with what I'm doing, and she visibly relaxes as the days pass. There is an unspoken agreement that I will be in the house in the late afternoon, when the kids come home from school, and as a result both Stella and Richard work later than usual.

I remember wishing I had a kind of fairy godmother who would materialise in my life and help me like this, but I don't have any real memory of it happening – just a few fleeting impressions of a shadowy figure who may or may not have been a distant relation, and who may or may not have stayed with us. It must be because I didn't stay long, so my anxiety on that front increases. Whatever I can achieve by being here, I'll have to achieve it soon.

I have reached a time in my life where I can't sleep much and I'm at my best in the mornings, so I turn on my computer early, sometimes before dawn, and focus on work until all the early morning noises from the house finish with a last slam of the door. Then I enjoy a leisurely breakfast and a read of the paper – naturally the prophetic articles are the most amusing, as they are invariably wrong – then work again until early afternoon.

Stella yearns to be the cosy, nurturing mother she remembers Anne to be, plying her children with wholesome home-made food. Her kitchen cupboards are full of baking ingredients quietly creeping towards their use-by dates – every few months she has a clean-out and starts again. I pull out the old exercise book of family recipes and make cookies, pikelets and cupcakes, to Claire and Julian's delight. Later in the week, after Stella hands over my first pay packet, I shop for other ingredients and start making some of our favourite family dinners, many of which were handed down by Anne.

"How come you make lasagne just the way I do?" asks Stella one night. "We never had that at home."

"Oh, um – I used the recipe on the packet," I point out. "Is that what you do?"

"I guess it is," she says. "Anyway, it's delicious."

Richard joins in the chorus of appreciation for my cooking, but I sense that he's not entirely happy, and his tension affects Stella. He tries to be sociable and manages quite well, but he has always liked his seclusion, and is only really comfortable when there is no-one apart from immediate family in the house. I stay out of his way as much as possible, but I know the problem is just the fact of my being there, even if he doesn't see me.

I take long breaks in the afternoons and walk, exploring the neighbourhood I know so well. Now and then I come upon a building that by my day has been completely transformed, and am reminded of what it looked like before. The tumbledown house with a huge garden down by the water is still a fairy tale cottage, and I remember Claire declaring on several occasions that she is going to live there when she's grown up. Fifteen years from now the house will be renovated and extended, sanitised, the garden replaced by some prissy formal shrubs. The last time it came to my attention it was on the market yet again, with a price tag of several million dollars.

A few blocks away there is an abandoned power station, its doors boarded up and most of its windows smashed. Several local teenagers, including Julian and his friends, have established hangouts in odd corners of the building, and they sneak in there to smoke cigarettes and dope, lounging on ruptured mattresses left over from council clean-ups, stuffed through the gaping window cavities in the dead of night. Of course Stella and Richard know nothing of this. It's something Julian ruefully confessed to me on his thirtieth birthday, after a good dinner and a few glasses of wine. I suppose that knowledge could have had me fretting every time he's out late, but it doesn't because I know nothing bad is going to happen to him.

By my day the old building is long gone, a row of elegant townhouses in its place. Every square inch of our inner suburb has been scrutinised and evaluated, and there are no more forgotten spaces, secluded niches or overgrown laneways.

One afternoon I encounter Mrs Grainger standing by her front gate, one hand on her letterbox and a far-away look in her eyes, as though she's forgotten what she came out for.

"Hello, Mrs Grainger," I say brightly.

"Eh? Hello, dear."

"My name's Linda," I say. "I'm just staying with Stella, up the road. She's my niece."

"Eh?" I wonder if she knows who Stella is.

"Stella and Richard? With the two kids?"

"Very nice boy," says Mrs Grainger. "I don't know about that young girl, though."

"Claire? What's wrong with her?"

"Her and her friend. Cheeky little things."

I'm so taken aback by that I forget about the questions I wanted to ask the old biddy, and when Claire comes home from school I tackle her about it.

"You know that funny old lady who lives at the end of the street, Mrs Grainger?" I say.

"She smells."

"Well, maybe she does a bit, but I don't think we should hold that against her, should we?"

"I dunno." She looks uneasy.

"You haven't said anything to insult her, have you?"

"Course not. Anyway, she's deaf."

"Maybe not as deaf as you think," I say.

The trouble is I'm so anxious not to say or do anything that might upset Claire and turn her prematurely against the world that I can't say anything of any depth to her.

Maybe I should be taking a different approach. I know Claire is close to her grandmother, Anne, though they don't see enough of each other. There has been talk, however, of Claire going to spend some time at Mount Wallace in the next school holidays, and I am doing my best to encourage that. I'm convinced Anne is a good influence, and I hope I can somehow nurture that relationship.

I can't warn Anne about Claire's dark days to come, because to everyone's shock Anne will sicken and die a few months before Claire starts to go off the rails. It must have been one of the factors in Claire's change, but she would never talk about it. It seems to me that if Anne could stay healthy and not die so soon, maybe she could help Claire in a more meaningful way. I've got to go back there and see if I can encourage Anne to improve her lifestyle.

Maybe my task is to stay around for the next four or five years and influence Claire myself. The thought is alarming, but I'll do it if I have to.

Sometimes my yearning for Richard, my older Richard, is unbearable, especially when faint hostility from younger Richard is wafting in my direction. I catch myself thinking about my Richard, waiting fruitlessly for me in our apartment, frantic with worry; but that's not necessarily how it will be. I could be transported back to the precise time when I left, with no-one any the wiser.

But on the other hand, I might not go back at all. Richard and Julian will search endlessly, unable to accept that I have simply vanished; then they will have to live with the agony of not knowing. It would be even worse than Linda's disappearance. At least in her case the evidence suggests that she ran away and chose to cut herself off from her family. They know I would never do that.

No. If I can't go back I will have to somehow survive in this time, in the morass of lies I have created, with no identity. I will have to survive for twenty years, until I am an old woman, older than Anne was when she died. On the appointed day – what was it? Yes, 7 November 2017 – on that day, late in the afternoon, I will take the bus to our apartment building and ring the bell, which will be back in its proper place. I will tell Richard, who will not recognise me, what has happened to his wife, and of course he will throw me out.

But wait: Richard will recognise me as Linda, who by then will have been living alongside the family for twenty years, and he will think I have finally gone completely insane.

But wait again: why don't I go there on the morning of 7 November and catch Stella, me, on the way out? Why don't I persuade her to stay at home, in fact to avoid the city for as long as possible? Because on that morning, she, I, must have stumbled into a crack, a rent in time, one of those wormholes they have started to talk about. She, I, was literally in the wrong place at the wrong time and if she, I, were to stay at home on that day none of this would happen.

And meanwhile I will have saved Claire. That part will not be undone. Before I go to Stella's apartment that morning I will go to Claire's house, a pretty little cottage she has found somewhere nearby where she will be living with ... let's see ... a lovely young husband, three cats, a chubby little baby with whom she exchanges coos and smiles all day long. I will insist that Claire, with her baby, come with me on my mission to warn Stella, and I will put my arms around her and the baby while I tell my tale, and Stella will agree not to go out, just to humour me, her dotty Aunt Linda, and I won't let go of Claire until I'm sure she is not going to vanish from my arms.

My longing is so strong I can see Claire, a mature young woman, and I can see her brown-eyed baby, and the images are so clear and detailed they must be memories, not my imagination, and that must mean it does happen, I do save Claire.

14

In the rational light of morning I know that I have changed nothing yet. If I had saved Claire I would not have this image of her, the unthinkable image I quickly put out of my mind: her white face, the blood mixed with vomit, the unseeing eyes.

In my notebook, I write: *I blame Abigail.*

I drop the pen as though it were burning my fingers. Just writing that name makes me clench my fists, a bitter taste rising from my throat.

Abigail. Small, slim, pretty little face with undersized features, lustrous long dark hair. Sharp teeth, or am I adding a layer to my memory of her? Claire was in Year 10, well into first term, when we made the agonising decision that she should change schools. The suggestion had come up at the end of the previous year, after the shock of her mediocre report and below-average results. Our bright girl was fading before our eyes, and nobody could account for it. Every teacher's comments told the same story: work not handed in, tests not studied for, lack of participation in class. When I asked Claire about it she wouldn't meet my eye.

"I don't like school."

"Why? What's wrong with it?"

"It sucks."

"But tell me why?"

Before I could really process Claire's predicament, in the middle of the usual pre-Christmas flurry, Mum called to say that she couldn't come to Sydney for the party we always held on the Sunday before Christmas. The plan was for Mum to stay with us through Christmas Day and the New Year, as she usually did.

"Can't come?" I babbled into the phone. "But Mum, the trains will be awful on Christmas Day, especially if you're not feeling well."

"You'll have more fun without me there, dear. I just don't feel up to it this year. The journey, you know? I think I might just skip Christmas."

I dropped all my plans, rushed to Mount Wallace and carted her to the hospital. She died two weeks later, on New Year's Day. Claire took it worse than anyone. She cried for days and wouldn't talk to anyone at the funeral. When I put my arms around her she was stiff and unresponsive.

I was consumed with guilt. Work had been going well and I had even been travelling a bit, leaving the family to look after themselves. Richard had weathered the non-event of the Year 2000 bug and got himself into another demanding project at the bank, managing investment in the new Euros. There was talk of us going to Geneva for a while. Julian was about to start his third year at university, doing well and still living at home, so we thought he and Claire could look after each other.

There was no Aunt Linda around to help, I'm sure of that.

15

Try as I might, I can't detect any dark shadows beneath Claire's sunny exterior. If cracks were visible in her demeanour I might have something to work with, but she seems perfectly happy, open and candid.

Julian, on the other hand, is brooding and taciturn. On Friday night Stella and Richard make a big effort for the kids, buying fish and chips and producing a new special edition video set of all three *Star Wars* movies. We vote on which one to watch first, and *The Empire Strikes Back* wins resoundingly. While Julian is setting up the tape I help Stella tidy up the remnants of the meal.

"I could break out the ice cream," she says thoughtfully. "Would that be trying too hard?"

"What's the occasion?"

"Nothing, really. We're just trying to cheer up Julian. He's broken up with his girlfriend, which to be honest is a great relief, but he's a bit down."

Gears shift and mesh inside my brain. There's something about that statement that seems momentous, but I can't quite remember why. Maybe it's the timing. Of course Julian broke up with Natalie, she was just one of a series of short-lived relationships with rather silly girls, but I think she was the first. Natalie. I barely remember her. I think I said something about her to Julian, and it must have sunk in – but that can't have caused the breakup, because I remember that it happened anyway.

Still, there's something about the whole thing that makes me uneasy, and I have a strange urge to tell Julian he should give Natalie another chance.

My sweet boy. I glance at him affectionately while we all settle down in front of the TV. Why is he so bad at relationships? Even now, in his thirties, he can't seem to make up his mind what he wants, or stick with any girlfriend for more than a few months.

Claire manages to stay awake until the arrival of our heroes on the Cloud Planet, then she disappears into her doona. At the end of the movie Stella gently leads her up the stairs, and I make my excuses and go to bed, leaving Richard and Julian to watch a late-night replay of an AFL game.

It still seems prudent to stay out of the family's way on Saturday, so I get up before them, buy myself some breakfast and a couple of coffees at the nearest café and flick through the weekend papers. The real estate section is enormous, and I search through the apartments to let. There is a modest studio in a run-down building I'm familiar with, but they don't seem to have open inspections. You're supposed to call the estate agent, but instead I finish my coffee and hurry to their office. A handful of other hopefuls are already waiting, and after a few minutes an extremely young agent in a too-big suit emerges and takes us down the road to the building.

The flat is small, seedy and smelly, and I immediately corner him and demand details.

"You can fill in an application now if you like," he says, waving a wad of papers. "We'll need some ID, a couple of references from other places you've rented, and four weeks' rent in advance. You'd need to give me a holding deposit, too." He glances at the young couple who are going through the kitchen cupboards and muttering to each other with expressions of distaste. The two other singles have both taken one look and left.

I promise to think about it and get back to him, but the problems seem insurmountable, starting with the question of ID.

On the way up to the main street I dump the forms in a bin, then catch the bus to Leichhardt and walk along Parramatta Road, looking for the old Stanmore Twin cinemas. I know the cinemas were closed and the building torn down around the turn of the millennium if not earlier, so it's a pleasant relief to find it all still there, very run-down but still functioning, as is the indestructible milk bar next door. I join a very small crowd to take in a session of *Fargo*, the original movie, which is just as enjoyable the tenth time around, or however many times I've seen it.

Afterwards I walk into the city. I was planning a nostalgic trip to the wonderful old Grace Brothers Broadway store, but it's already closed, the vast buildings a construction site. I keep walking through the Chinese quarter – which doesn't seem to have changed – to the central Grace Brothers, the epicentre of city shops, where I buy a pair of plain black shoes to wear with the dress Anne has given me, and with that action make up my vacillating mind to go to Lauren and Phil's party.

The old Soup Plus is still there in its George Street basement, with its big black cauldrons of steaming soup at the front counter and dimly-lit rows of wobbling communal tables. I treat myself to a late lunch of vegetable broth with a chunk of brown bread. By then the rest of my ambitions for the day are looking too ambitious, so I catch the bus home, sneak into my little room when no-one is looking and pull out my notebook.

Have decided to go to Lauren and Phil's party, which I remember as being a highlight. Hence keeping out of Stella and Richard's way. We had one of those days that sparkle like a diamond in the memory. Lunch in that café that was just down on the waterfront for a couple of years. Fresh cool breeze. Watched the eighteen-footers racing, then home the long way round through all the parks, chattering families picnicking.

I look out the window at the day which is just as I remember it, washed with pale sunshine.

. . . Our bed was bathed in light and we spent a warm afternoon there. Both kids out . . . in fact they didn't come home at all. Julian was off somewhere with his mates and Claire was at Marika's. Walked together to the party, our arms entwined. Were we ever that happy again?

I'll have to keep myself well out of that pleasant scene, I reflect. I'll make some excuse to go to the party a little later, by myself. Contented, I curl up for a long nap, warmed by two cats snuggling on either side of me.

When I emerge it's already dark, and the atmosphere in the kitchen is even darker. Julian is at the stove, morosely stirring something in a pot. Should Julian even be here? It feels wrong.

There are raised voices from upstairs, which Julian studiously ignores, then Stella comes in, pulling on her coat.

"Oh, hi Linda," she says abstractedly, her face unhappy. "I'm off to the party now, just going to help Lauren sort out some of the food."

"Okay. Have a good time."

"Lauren's very keen for you to come. Richard will be leaving around seven, so he can bring you if you like?"

"Sure. I'll get ready."

There's a feeling of dread inside me, and I can't quite process it. It's not unusual for Richard to get into one of his grumpy moods at the most inconvenient time, but I thought I remembered this as a happy day.

"Is Claire here?" I ask.

"She's staying the night with Marika," says Stella. "I'll see you at the party." And she's gone.

I retreat back to my room and read the account I've just written of today. It seemed such a clear memory when I was writing it, but now I'm not so sure. There are still some stray wisps of us at the party, lit up with happiness, our arms entwined, staying on as the hours flew past and finally drinking tea over a post-party debrief with the equally euphoric Lauren and Phil after everyone had left; but I don't know how that is going to happen. I'm not sure if I can trust my memories anymore.

16

Richard appears promptly in the kitchen and he has made an effort to dress well, as I have. Anne's soft blue dress fits me beautifully, draping over and flattering my reasonably well-preserved body. I've brushed my hair well and put on some lipstick. Looking in the mirror in my room I smile, imagining how my Richard would respond to my appearance, whistling, putting an arm around my waist and probably making some lascivious remark or other.

This Richard looks without seeing me. He's polite, but his mood is black: there are a thousand tiny signs that tell me this.

What have they quarrelled about? My memory doesn't supply an answer, but now I recall my feeling of apprehension when I arrived at the party without him, fearful that he would not show up at all, that I would spend the whole night fielding questions.

The most likely thing is that they've argued about me, because I've overstayed my welcome.

"I had a look at some flats today," I tell Richard as we walk through the dark streets.

"So you're not going back to Perth?"

"Well – um – no, not for a while. So I'm going to need my own place here."

He's not going to disagree with that.

"See anything good?"

"Oh – some possibilities."

I can't say Richard cheers up, but his mood is no worse when we arrive. Stella comes over and puts her arms around him. Lauren is with her, luscious in a voluptuous floor-length red velvet dress. I remember that dress all right, and how dull I felt next to my glowing friend; but Stella looks beautiful in a knee-length silk tunic in rich, subtle colours over narrow black velvet pants.

"Linda!" says Lauren. "I'm so glad you could come. Let me introduce you to a few people."

I can appreciate the effort she has made to prepare the shabby old house, which is usually a chaotic mess. The door to their study off the entrance hall is firmly shut, and I remember that all the clutter has been shoved in there. The remaining rooms are tidy, with soft lighting, batiks and Indian bedspreads draped over the armchairs and couches, and jars of flowers on every flat surface. Lauren steers me around the living room, favouring the older guests: her parents, the elderly couple who live next door, an aunt or two. I'm much more interested in her generation, the people I knew well, many of whom have either drifted away or died in the last twenty years.

Richard has separated himself from Stella and wandered into the dining room, where he is soon deep in conversation with a clutch of men. I recognise Jim, a workmate of Phil's, Larry and Geoff, a sweet couple from further down the street and a grim-faced older man whose name I can't remember. Stella circulates with a tray of savoury tarts, her smile a little too bright.

I hover by the kitchen door, a glass of punch in my hand. It's refreshing, and I take several gulps before I remember to be wary of it. A whole bottle of vodka was slurped into the punchbowl at some point, I recall, and a lot of people were staggering about later in the evening.

Phil squeezes past me on his way through.

"I don't think we've met," he says pleasantly. "My name's Phil."

So his memory is starting to fracture.

"I'm Linda," I say. "Stella's aunt."

"Oh. Nice to meet you." He passes on, unflurried.

More people arrive and the volume rises. Stella, drinking too much of that punch, is visibly relaxing and starting to enjoy herself, talking and laughing a lot. I observe her having a long conversation with a very good-looking dark-haired man, who seems to find everything she says intensely amusing. Looking again, I realise who he is: Marko Stiptic, the husband of Rose, who is related in some way to Phil – possibly a cousin. I nose around and locate Rose, pale in a frumpy floral dress, holed up in the kitchen with a couple of other women. One of them is washing glasses while another dries with a sodden tea towel, and they are talking about childcare.

"Family day care's the way to go," says one. "My carer is marvellous – the sort of granny my mum should have been, if she'd ever get off her arse."

"Pretty hard to organise with three kids," says the drier-up. "We had to sack our nanny because she wouldn't put in the hours, but I think we've found a good *au pair*."

"I'm glad ours are both at school now," puts in Rose. "Our last nanny was a real troublemaker."

Her washing-up friend gives a little wry smile, which is lost on the other woman, but not on me. Marko, dashing and charming, ran some sort of business from an office at the back of their house, so he would be around a lot during the day. I can imagine what sort of trouble there was with the nanny. Sometime soon he and Rose will have a spectacular break-up, when she discovers a string of affairs he's had, culminating with a pregnant sixteen-year-old girl, the daughter of one of his clients.

Back in the living room, I find Richard has drawn Stella to one side and they are having an intense whispered conversation.

"It's still early," I hear her say. "We can't just . . ."

He whispers some more and I can't catch a word. She glances in my direction, and I quickly turn away.

A minute later the front door slams and I know it's Richard. Stella, her head high and her eyes defiant, is circulating again, talking and laughing. This is not right, but the cogs in my memory won't shift fast enough for me to know how the evening will end.

Lauren, smiling, appears with a tray of champagne and, ignoring my protests, hands me a glass.

"I've hardly spoken to you yet!" she says. "How are you liking Sydney?"

"Oh, it's . . . um . . ."

"Lauren!" Her sister Fiona is beckoning from across the room.

"Sorry, Linda. Have you met Judith? She's Phil's boss, sort of. Linda's just arrived from Perth, Jude." And she parks me with an older couple who are chatting with Imelda and Reg, a rather opinionated pair of Lauren's oldest friends.

"Perth? I just got back from there," says Judith. "Where in Perth do you live?"

"Oh . . . Fremantle." Put on the spot, it's the only area I can think of.

"Oh, gorgeous," says Judith. "Well, I thought I was going to be stuck over there. Some idiot checked in and didn't turn up for the flight, and of course we couldn't leave until their luggage was off-loaded."

"All this security is such a pain, isn't it?" says Imelda. "Coming back from LA last month it took ages just getting through those X-ray machines and what-not they have there. What on earth do they think we're trying to smuggle onto the plane?"

"A bomb?" I suggest.

"Yeah, right," says Reg. "No-one's going to have a bomb on a plane they're actually on, are they? They don't want to blow themselves up."

"Well, they might have weapons," says Judith's husband, whose name I can't recall. "Planes have been hijacked."

"Those days are gone," says Reg. "The hijackers never get what they're demanding, do they? I reckon they've pretty much given up."

I sidle away to another group, who are debating whether the saintliness of President Clinton is genuine or just media spin. "Honestly," says one of them, "they're like the royals in Victorian times. They can play up as much as they like, and the press won't touch it. Look at the way the Kennedys carried on."

"Okay," says another, "but Clinton's smarter than that. He knows that everything he does is going to be scrutinised."

"So," I say mischievously, "what about Monica Lewinsky?"

"Who?"

"Oh, just something I heard. Do you think there'll be another Democrat president after Clinton?"

"Definitely," says a man with glasses. Is it Peter, a workmate of Lauren's, or that journalist who lived in their street? "Yeah, the presidency will stay Democrat now until they're mad enough to nominate a woman, or maybe a black man."

"Heaven forbid." I drift on, tuning into one conversation after another. I've never realised it before, but people nearly always talk about the future, speculating on what they think is going to happen.

"We're heading for another major crash." "These dotcoms can't last." "The millennium's going to be a disaster." "It won't be long before they forget about all this security and things get back to normal." "She's going to do brilliantly in the HSC." "Hillary would be a much better president than Bill, but she'll never get the chance." "John Howard won't last more than one term." "Video tape is dead. Soon we'll all have DVD recorders."

I can't enter into any of these conversations, and I can't look at half the people in the room without seeing the heartbreaks and complications that lie ahead of them. Slipping away seems to be the best idea, and I look around for Stella to tell her I'm going.

A small blonde woman buttonholes me. "Hello!" she says. "Linda, isn't it? Lauren says you come from Mount Wallace. So do I!"

I size her up, trying to hide my alarm. She's not much older than the other Stella – several years younger than me, surely.

"Ummm – I haven't lived there since about 1950," I say. "I don't suppose you were even born then?"

"Well, just," she says. "I was still a baby when we left. That was in 1950, too. But we used to go back and stay with my grandparents, right up until I was in my teens. I'm Stephanie Carey, by the way. My dad owned the furniture shop. Do you remember that?"

"Oh yes, of course." A furniture shop? There wasn't one when I was growing up, the town in slow decline. Did Mum ever mention it?

"I know where your house was," she's saying. "Mum used to tell me about the girl who disappeared from there. I never thought I'd meet her! Mum said you used to work right next door to Dad's shop."

"Oh!" I say weakly. "Yes, that's right. That furniture shop! That was your dad – Mr Carey? So . . . how are your parents these days?"

"Mum died, a few years ago," she says. "Dad's still okay physically but his mind's gone, you know? He's in a nursing home."

"I'm sorry to hear that."

"He's okay sometimes. He rambles on, and sometimes it makes sense, in a way. But he thinks I'm Mum half the time."

A woman about her age grabs her arm.

"Steph! I haven't seen you for ages!"

I mumble an excuse and retreat. Stella is nowhere to be found. Marko is nowhere to be found either.

In a little isolated thread of memory I recall again that surge of attraction. She doesn't really know him.

He exudes the air of a man of mystery, the hint of a tragedy somewhere in his past, and he's been looking at her with open admiration. Richard has been prickly all week, he's spoiled this party she was so looking forward to, and she's feeling angry and reckless.

I start a discreet search, but I'm not fast enough to avoid being trapped in a corner when someone taps on a tinkling glass, and my heart sinks when I realise that I have to live through Reg's long, boring speech for a second time.

Surely Richard and I watched this together, arm in arm, giving each other surreptitious nudges and struggling to repress giggles like a couple of naughty school-children.

But we didn't. Through a sea of heads I can just glimpse Stella and Marko, side by side near the back door, straight-faced. I lose sight of them before we are mercifully released, and I push my way towards where they were standing.

They're not in the room. They're not on the semi-enclosed back verandah, where people are huddled together against the evening chill and the air is blue with cigarette smoke.

I'm about to go back in, then I hear her laugh. They're in the garden, half obscured by the lemon tree, pretending to look at Phil's ferns and orchids hanging from a frame on the shed wall. They are slowly moving away, through hanging tendrils, into the dark.

She's going to do something very stupid, or she's going to hate me.

"Stella!" I step onto the path and wave. She jerks her head up.

"Sorry, I just wanted to tell you. I'm feeling a bit off, and I think I'll go."

"Off?" She moves towards me. "What's wrong?"

"Oh, nothing. Just a bit shaky, and . . . well, nauseous." She'll think I've drunk too much. "I might have a bit of a migraine coming on. I'll be okay – I know the way home, I'll just take myself off and go to bed."

She'll never let me go alone with a story like that.

"You can't walk home," says Marko, putting a kindly hand on my arm. "Come on, I'll drive you."

"Yes, we'll take you." Stella puts an arm around my other shoulder and exchanges a look with Marko.

This is not going to plan. I'm giving them the biggest chance they could get to slip away together.

"Sorry, no," I manage. "Sorry, when I'm like this I really can't face getting in a car. The lurching, you know? It's not far, I'm really happy to walk."

"I'll go with you," says Stella. She knows when she's beaten.

Richard appears at the living-room door when he hears us come in. The TV is on and *The Shawshank Redemption* is playing.

"Why are you watching that?" Stella demands.

He shrugs. "Happy ending?"

"Excuse me," I murmur, moving towards the haven of my room, but I glance back in time to see Stella put her arms around him as he pulls the door shut.

17

In the morning I go for a long walk, seeking a cheap, shoddy block of flats that I remember from the old days. The flats were really just bed-sitters and the rents must surely be low.

I remember roughly where the building was, and I also seem to remember that it had a hand-written sign giving the phone number of the letting agent. Maybe they won't be so fussy about references and ID.

After a few false starts I find the place. It's not so bad. The sun is shining on its dusty windows, and the jasmine winding over its permanently-open gate is in flower, sweetening the air.

I write down the details, then buy a takeaway coffee and find the sunniest, most sheltered bench in the park. My plan is to stay out all morning but the sunshine is offset by a biting wind that cuts through all my layers of clothing, and eventually I admit defeat, pick up a sandwich for lunch and smuggle it into my room, where I lose myself in an old copy of *Jane Eyre*, faintly redolent of mould, that Stella keeps on her one-of-these-days bookshelf.

Stella had so many ideas and plans. Work was relatively satisfying, she loved her children and was prepared to devote herself to their care, but the day was coming when she would have time to finally be herself. That's the way I thought of it: the day when I would be free to do something creative and fulfilling. On three occasions I enrolled in an art course. One was watercolours, which I thought would be manageable. One was even botanical drawing – I loved the idea of the discipline, the careful observation and painstaking meticulousness of it. But something always came up and I never attended a single class.

Later I decided that writing was to be my calling. All that knowledge of grammar and precise expression had to have some application more interesting than business documents. I collected old books, the classics that I was supposed to have read at school and university and had really just skimmed through, and I kept them in the outside room, my studio as I thought of it. Reading them was going to be my preparation, my private training program.

I even bought an expensive hardback set of *Remembrance of Things Past*, the Moncrieff translation, twelve books altogether – some of the seven titles were too long for a single volume. When I take the first one, *Swann's*

Way, down from the shelf I find little black specks on the title page. Maybe I'll start it after *Jane Eyre* and try to get past the first thirty pages this time. Surely something happens eventually?

One weekend, despite being overwhelmingly busy at work, I took Mum to an exhibition of patchwork quilts at Darling Harbour and we walked along the waterfront afterwards, still dazzled by the glowing colours and exquisite hand-stitching.

"My grandmother made patchwork quilts," said Anne. "I remember watching her working on a great big frame when I was a little girl. Grandma Dulcie must have given them all away when she died."

"That's what I'm going to do," I said. "Make them, I mean."

Maybe I would have done that, if things had turned out differently.

At lunchtime I eat my sandwich, then venture into the kitchen to make a cup of tea. The kettle is already singing and Stella is sitting at the kitchen table with her arms around Claire.

Claire raises a stricken face to me. "Princess Diana's dead!" she wails.

Over her head, Stella gives me a rueful look.

"That's awful," I say. "What happened?"

In the hall the phone is ringing insistently.

18

Anne is babbling, barely coherent. I make a placating gesture to Stella, who gives a little nod and returns to Claire, then I turn towards the wall and hunch over the phone.

"It can't be true," Anne is saying. "Is it a trick? Did someone tell you they were going to do this?"

"No, it's nothing like that. You'll see. Just watch what happens in the next few days."

"What about our letter?" asks Anne. "Do you think she would have got it? Why didn't she take any notice?"

"They probably get letters like that all the time."

"If only we could have done something," says Anne. "But I still can't take it in. She had a bodyguard. None of it makes sense."

"I know, I know."

"When are you coming down again? We have to talk about this."

"In a few days," I say. "I'll come for the funeral. It'll all be on television, and we'll watch it together."

Richard is already in the living room with the television going, and we slowly converge there. All normal programs have been suspended, and all the channels are struggling to produce a narrative from the scant amount of information they have.

Even Julian comes in.

"Everyone's talking about it on both my bulletin boards. We knew before it was on the news," he says proudly.

I think cable television might have just come in, but we don't have it and no-one we know has it; so there's no CNN, no BBC, no Sky News. Some of the commercial channels have feeds from these services, but there's still nothing new to report, and I remember that there will now be a long dead period while Europe sleeps.

"Enough," says Richard after a while. "I know it's terrible and all that, but she's just one person. How many more people have died all over the world while we've been sitting here?"

"Yes, come on," says Stella. "We'll be seeing it all on the news tonight." She makes a move to turn the TV off.

"Leave it on!" cries Claire, still tearful. She and I stay in the room while the others wander away. I don't want to see any more of the coverage, but I do want to watch her.

Did this remote event have a bigger impact on her than we all thought?

After a while she moves over to the couch where I'm sitting and snuggles up to me.

"What happened when you ran away?" she whispers.

"Sorry, what?" I have to pick up the remote control and turn the volume down while she repeats the question.

"Well, it was a bit scary," I say, glad of the chance to distract her with a story. "It was the middle of the night, you know. Everyone was in bed." I know that's true, having grilled Anne many times when I was about this age.

"Did you run into the bush?"

"The bush up behind the house?"

"Yes." She shivers. "I always thought you ran away into the bush, up the Little Mountain."

"No, no, that would be too spooky. No, I thought a lot about how I could get away, far away. I didn't want to get lost in the bush."

I shiver in turn. For some irrational reason I too have pictured Linda's bones up there somewhere, in the dark tangle of dense rising bushland behind the old house. I used to go fearfully searching sometimes, and once I actually found a skull, pretty obviously not human, and ran shrieking and stumbling back to Grandma Dulcie.

"So where did you go?"

How do you lie to your child? She looks at me with trusting eyes and I want to tell the story, the ideas I have pieced together over the years, the explanation that makes sense to me. The one with the happy ending because after all, here sits Linda.

"Well, I had all the money I'd been saving up, though it wasn't really much, and I thought about catching the train. There was one due at five-thirty in the morning, a train to Sydney, but it would have been a long, cold wait and I was worried that someone would see me. You know, someone from the town who knew me."

"Why didn't you stay at home, in bed, until it was time for the train?"

"I'd already tried that once, but I went to sleep and missed it. I couldn't set my alarm, you see, because the house had pretty thin walls and it would have woken everybody else. So I stayed awake until I started to worry that I was going to drop off, then I left."

"But you didn't go into the bush?"

"No, I walked down the road. Down the middle of the road, actually. There was no-one around. It was nice, in a way."

"I'd still be scared."

"I was, a bit. There was no moon and it was dark except for the tiniest reflection of starlight on the road. There was no-one in the street, but I could see a few cars and trucks on the main road, all on their way to somewhere.

"My idea was to go to Sydney, of course. Well, it was the only city I knew about, really. So I started walking in that direction. I wanted to get out of the town as fast as

I could. It didn't take long, but I was still so worried that I hid whenever I saw a car coming from the town, in case it was someone who knew me.

"Then I thought it would be better to try to get a lift from someone on the other side of the road, someone coming from outside Mount Wallace, just passing through. So I crossed over, and next time I saw a car coming from the Sydney direction I stuck out my thumb. I'd read about hitch-hiking in books."

"Isn't it dangerous to hitch-hike?"

"Yes, it is, and you must promise me you'll never do it."

"Okay."

"Right. Well, that car and the next few ignored me, but then a truck stopped. I got in, and the driver said something like, I've got a long way to go and I need someone to keep me awake; so I said okay, I can do that. And I really did feel wide awake by then."

"Couldn't he listen to music or something to stay awake?"

"They didn't have things like Walkmans in those days. They didn't even have radios in their cars and trucks. Well, the first thing he asked was where I was going, and I had no idea. So I asked where he was going, and he said Cooma, in the Snowy Mountains."

"That's where people go skiing, isn't it?"

"Yes, somewhere near there. I'd never heard of Cooma, but I loved the idea of the Snowy Mountains, so I said that was where I was going too.

"The driver said his name was Sergei, and I said I was Matilda. It sounded like a silly name, but it was all I could think of just in that moment. Maybe I was thinking of 'Waltzing Matilda'.

"It was a long way, much longer than I had imagined. Everything went slower then, and the roads weren't that great. I told him stories, every story I could think of, and then I made up a few. I said I had run away from an orphanage in Brisbane and I'd been hitch-hiking south for weeks. I'm sure he didn't believe me, but I don't think he cared.

"We stopped for breakfast in a picnic area somewhere past Canberra, one of those places where you just pull off the road. He gave me one of his sandwiches, and I had a bit of coffee out of his thermos. I'd never tasted coffee before. Then he said he needed to lie down on the front seat and sleep for a couple of hours and that I could sleep in the back.

"When I woke up we were on the move again and the road was rough. I crawled into the cabin, and the driver said we'd be at Cooma soon, and did I want to be dropped off there, or go through to the village with him? I liked the idea of a village in the Snowy Mountains – I thought it would be like Switzerland, the way I imagined Switzerland – so I said I'd go there."

"And was it like Switzerland?"

"Not a bit. It was the roughest, most beautiful Australian bush, with gum trees up to the sky, some of which they were cutting down."

"Why?"

"Have you heard of the Snowy Mountains Scheme?"

"No."

"They don't teach you anything at school, do they? It was an enormous project they were doing in the Snowy Mountains. They built huge dams and used the flowing water to make electricity, hydro-electricity. There were thousands of people working there from countries all over the world. Something like thirty different languages."

"So did you stick around?"

"Yes. I started teaching all the immigrant kids how to speak English. The towns where we lived were more like camping grounds, with lots of tents – freezing in the winter – and no-one cared about your qualifications or your real name or anything like that."

"And did you keep calling yourself Matilda?"

"Yes. Matilda Dreadnought."

She laughs, but I sense that she's a little disappointed with my story. She expected something more glamorous.

To keep her interested, I say: "Of course, that was only until I met the count."

"The count?"

Stella puts her head around the door.

"Claire, it's time to go to the Robinsons'," she says.

"I'll tell you the rest later," I promise Claire, as she reluctantly gets up to leave. "There's lots more."

19

Stella offers me some more work, which is a relief because I'm going to need more money. There was a job I remember I really hated at the time, an environmental impact statement in support of a new rail link in the south-west. I suspected there was something slightly dodgy about it, but couldn't find anything concrete. So that's the job I get.

I still think I was right, but a couple of years after this the plans were shelved, so I can work on the document with a clear conscience and save Stella a bit of angst.

I'll do this job for her as quickly as I can and get some money, then I'll have to leave. My presence here is changing things, I can feel it, and I can't predict what the long-term effect will be. My once-clear memories of the next twenty years are fainter, and I don't know what to believe any more.

The next evening we gather in front of the TV to watch news broadcasts that are dominated by the death of Princess Diana. World leaders are falling over each other to express their sympathy.

"This is too much," says Stella. "She was just one person."

"The funeral's going to be on live TV all around the world," says Julian. "Like, in real-time. They've got a complete link-up with all the satellites that are up there. I've heard it's going to be watched by more than a billion people."

"Well, I don't think I'm going to be one of them," says Stella. "I don't fancy getting caught up in all that mass hysteria."

"You've got to watch it," I protest, slightly alarmed. I'm not sure if I would remember very much about this event if I hadn't watched the funeral. I don't know if I would have had enough to tell Anne, to convince her of who I am.

"This is going to be a piece of history," I go on. "It's one of the great events, like the Kennedy assassination or the moon landing, but Julian's right: this time we get to see it as it happens."

"Hmmm. Maybe."

I'm still feeling uneasy about what happened on Saturday night. I can remember it all clearly now, from the younger Stella's point of view as well as my own, and I'm sure it's a memory I have turned over in my mind in the intervening years, wondering about the cracks in Richard's and my seemingly idyllic relationship. I remember the anxiety, the frustration, my bitterness and anger towards him and . . . I realise now . . . my anger at the unwanted guest in our back room, the catalyst for his bad mood.

So why did I write something so different from the truth? Back in my room I open my notebook and read the last entry:

Have decided to go to Lauren and Phil's party, which I remember as being a highlight. Hence keeping out of Stella and Richard's way. It was one of those days that sparkle like a diamond in the memory. Lunch in that café that was just down on the waterfront for a couple of years. Fresh cool breeze. Watched the eighteen-footers racing, then home the long way round through all the parks . . .

As I read through the account nothing rises in my memory. It could be that I was remembering some other time, one of our many lovely days, and got it confused with the day of that particular party, but if that's so I should be able to place that memory now, and I can't.

My recollection of the day of the party is clear and painful enough now, starting with a pointless quarrel over who should do the Saturday shopping, through Richard telling me I was too soft on Julian, to the usual bitter standoff about the housework. I don't remember the unwelcome guest being mentioned, but I have a strong feeling she was the elephant in the room.

If such a guest has actually changed our history, even without intending to, this is how it might feel. The things that would have happened otherwise might disappear without a trace. The new things that do happen slide in to take their place. But I am here now as a sort of overseer. Wouldn't I remember that I once remembered something different?

I think back to other events in our lives in the intervening twenty years, the ones I can remember clearly. My next birthday, for example, when Richard sprang a surprise trip to Bali on me, and the kids helped by packing my bag with the most unlikely stuff and nothing I would have chosen myself to take. The thought still makes me laugh, but am I remembering the event, or remembering my memory of it? It's only a few months after this time. What if we don't resolve our differences, and the trip doesn't happen? When would I stop remembering it?

I write in the notebook:

For my forty-fourth birthday, 12 April 1998, Richard will secretly buy tickets and take me to Bali. Kids will pack a bag of silly stuff e.g. high heels and my red dressing gown. I will cry, but with happiness, when I see it.

Flipping back through the notebook, I come across another entry:

Julian stays with Natalie for at least four years. No other real relationship until Françoise. Have I done something to change that?

Yes, I have done something to change that, I realise with a little thrill of fear. I remember having that thought when I saw Natalie in the house. I remember saying something to Julian, that night we watched the Indiana Jones movie, giving him a way out. It felt like the right thing to do, and it still does.

But who is Françoise?

I skip through the notebook, but there is nothing to enlighten me. On the back page, though, I find my list of photographs, and one of the items is *Françoise at Koh Samui*. Maybe I'll recognise her when I see the picture, I muse; maybe it will all come back.

The phone's battery is even lower, and I'm going to need it when I watch the funeral with Mum. I skim through as fast as I can and find a picture of me and Richard in Vietnam, but nothing that looks like Koh Samui, and no sign of a stray young woman who could be Françoise.

I turn the phone off and look at the list again. *Christmas 2016: Julian and twins.* I don't think that image was there either. That's just last Christmas. What twins, I wonder?

I can't think of any twins who might have spent Christmas with us.

Stella corners me in the kitchen early in the week. She's spending the day working from home – which I know also means she's catching up with the washing and putting something in the slow cooker for dinner – and everyone else is out.

"So, the Snowy Mountains Scheme?" she says.

"I might have embroidered my story a bit," I say sheepishly. "I got myself into some situations back then that I don't care to remember, let alone tell an innocent little girl."

"Okay, but you'll have to come clean with her eventually, when she's old enough."

"I will. But in the meantime I've got to work on the next chapter: my brush with royalty."

She rolls her eyes. All her life – all my life – I've made up stories about what happened to Linda. The Snowy Mountains one is pretty recent: only a few weeks before all this happened I read an article about the scheme and realised that it was just getting started when Linda left. There must have been people working there who wanted to disappear from their normal lives.

I have also speculated that Linda went to Coober Pedy, Darwin, Broome, Alice Springs and even London. During the Vietnam War I pictured her running some tumbledown boarding house in Saigon, and when we went to Greece I wondered if I would run into her on one of the islands; but the Snowy Mountains have the advantage of being closer than all of them.

In the early days it wouldn't have mattered much if Linda had kept her own name. It wasn't easy to trace people before records were digitised and centralised. But I confess that I have idly Googled her occasionally, and the only thing that has ever come up, courtesy of Trove, was a brief advertisement that appeared in the *Sydney Morning Herald* a few times, in 1950 and again on a couple of subsequent anniversaries, pleading for information on her disappearance. If there is a Linda McCutcheon in the world she's not on Facebook, LinkedIn, Instagram or any other social media. If she changed her name back then, which is quite possible, or married at some point in the interim, then there's no way of finding her, even in my time.

But I can still wonder.

In my free time I have been trying to keep up my notebook of memories, still not sure what I should include, and I try hard to remember accurately. I start to write, as best I can remember, an account of Claire's friendship with Abigail, the bane of my life.

Abigail. If I could obliterate her from Claire's life then surely everything will turn out differently. This strong sense of purpose I have must mean something. I know it doesn't make sense, but I have a goal in being here, and

I have to achieve it quickly then leave this family to live their proper lives.

Their proper lives. The lives they were meant to live, I mean, including Claire.

After Mum died on New Year's Day, 2001, Claire was quieter than usual. I was too distracted by my own grief to notice. She stayed in her room a lot, reading. Just before Easter she told me that she was unhappy at school, that she had drifted away from the little group of girls she had been a part of, and that she felt excluded. Sensing a wounded bird, the boys in her class had taken to teasing her cruelly.

At the end of the previous year she had been adamant that she wanted to stay where she was. Now, she couldn't wait to leave. She didn't want to go to SCEGGS, where her former friend Marika was excelling, so we found a smaller, more nurturing private school on the Inner West train line. St Monica's, it was called, but it was not an overtly religious school. She went off in her brand-new uniform on a warm, windy Monday, the first of the fallen leaves scurrying around her shiny black shoes.

I came home that night, my heart in my mouth, to find her radiant.

"It's great," she said. "You need to see the library, you wouldn't believe how much stuff they've got there. We had art today in the best art room you can imagine,

but all my friends say I should drop Japanese and do French instead. They all do French."

"You've made friends already?"

"Yes, especially Abigail. You'll love her, Mum. She's really pretty and you know what? She thinks the same way I do about every single thing."

It wasn't long before I met Abigail, who started coming home with Claire after school and hanging around for hours. Most weeknights she ate dinner with us; she and Claire would exchange a brief look then take their plates and disappear to Claire's room. No adult ever came to pick Abigail up. In the middle of the evening she would take herself off into the darkness of the night, insisting that she would be fine on the bus.

Abigail, it seemed, was an orphan, an attribute that only added to her allure. Her single mother had been killed in a car accident a few years earlier, and Abigail's aunt had moved into the house to become her guardian, bringing a husband and two little boys.

"The boys are horrible and the auntie's like a wicked stepmother," Claire told me. "She's only there for the money. She hates Abby."

"What money?"

"I don't know, but it's a posh house and Abby's going to inherit it and lots of cash when she's older. And every birthday she gets a thousand dollars, just to go on with, but her auntie's trying to get it all away from her."

Abigail was friendly, even gushing to me, but I sensed damage under the surface. Her story, which I had no reason to doubt, nevertheless made me uneasy. Julian, who was in third year at university but still living at home, openly disliked her and made uncomplimentary remarks when Claire was not around. To my mind, however, she was not unlike his own succession of empty-headed girlfriends.

The first time Claire asked if she could spend a night at Abby's I insisted on getting the aunt's phone number.

"Oh, that's fine," said the aunt breezily on the phone. Her name was Donna and she sounded very young. "I don't worry about Abbs, just as long as she lets me know where she is."

"Is Abby all right? It must have been very disturbing for her, losing her mother."

"Yeah, it was pretty bad and the accident was horrific, of course. Freakish, they said. But Abbs seems to have bounced back all right."

"Are you . . . was Abby's mother your sister?"

"Well, sort of . . . well, more of a cousin. A second-cousin, if you sort it all out. Abby's father is kind of related to me too. He wanted to move in here with her but we put a stop to it, thank Christ."

I didn't much like the sound of that, but Claire was happier than she had been for a long time, and even seemed to be doing better at school. Some months into their friendship, she asked if she could spend the June long weekend with Abby, and we agreed.

When I dropped Claire off at the house – which was rather large, one of those beautiful inner-west Victorian houses that have seen better days – Abby came running out to meet us, and I felt my stomach clench into a knot of worry. She was wearing the briefest of mini-skirts with an ample display of bare midriff, and her face was garish with makeup.

"I'll just have a word with Donna, then I'll be on my way," I said stiffly.

"Oh, they've all gone to the shops. I don't think they'll be back for at least an hour."

Claire gave me one of her looks, and I had no choice but to leave.

I found out later that Donna and her family had gone away for the weekend, leaving Abby on her own. There were a lot of things that I found out later.

With Stella working at home I am eager to get out of her way. I slip out of the house in the middle of the day and take a couple of buses to the suburb where Abigail lived.

An image of the house is ingrained in my memory, but I've got the name of the street wrong. After a few false trails I find the place, looking exactly as I remember it. I hang around for a while but there's clearly nobody at home.

St Monica's, the school where Claire and Abby met, only takes girls from Year 7 upwards so Abigail, who was the same age as Claire, would not be there yet. She must be at one of the local primary schools. I wander the streets until I find one and loiter outside for a while. It's the middle of the afternoon, though, and the kids are all in their classrooms.

The next day I come back earlier. By the time I am within two blocks of the school I know my timing is right: shouts and shrieks tell me that it's lunchtime. I hover outside the fence for a while, staring intently whenever I see a knot of older girls walking around together. The vast majority are Anglo-Saxon in appearance, mostly blonde; but there are plenty of brunettes, like Abigail, and almost any one of them could be her.

That night I quiz Julian on his plans for the next day, and extract a promise that he'll come straight home after school to be with Claire. So on Thursday I make my excursion late enough to be outside the school gate when the bell rings. It really is a bell, and the sound takes me back to my own schooldays.

I feel too conspicuous to stand with the little knot of mothers who are chatting by the gate, so I retreat to a corner and wait. A group of girls who seem to be the right age come my way, strolling along the street in the general direction of Abigail's house. Any one of them could be her, but my money is on the smallest. That sharp little face could easily grow into Abigail's. I follow them at a discreet distance as they gradually peel off in different directions, but by the time we get to Abigail's street the only one left is the blonde, who's medium height and a bit chubby. I follow her, heart in mouth, until she passes the house and continues on.

When I get home, late, raised voices are emanating from Claire's room. A door slams and Marika comes down the stairs, brushes past me without a word and stumps outside.

I go upstairs, knock on Claire's door which is still shut, and interpret an inarticulate grunt from within as an invitation to enter. She's sitting on her bed, looking miserable. Papers covered in handwriting are strewn across the floor.

"Hi," I say.

"Hi."

"Is everything all right?"

"Yes."

"You weren't fighting with Marika, were you?"

"No."

"Well, that's good, because friends are important."

Later, I tell Stella that I'll be going to Mount Wallace again tomorrow.

"Do you think you could take Claire?" she asks. "She's a bit mopey because she and Marika were going to do something together on Saturday, but now Marika's going to some birthday party or other. They go to different schools, and Marika's got a whole lot of friends Claire doesn't know."

"Sure, it would be great, if she wants to come," I say. This doesn't feel right, because Princess Diana's funeral is on Saturday, and Stella and Claire are supposed to watch it together, snuggled on the couch with the cats. I think that's why I remember it so vividly. I was not particularly moved by the event, but it seems to me it was one of the last times Claire was a little girl, seeking comfort in my arms.

In the event, Claire doesn't want to come, and she can't be persuaded.

20

When my train pulls into Mount Wallace there is a lovely evening chill in the air, the sky a delicate duck-egg blue, the mountain outlined with a brilliant halo from the sinking sun. Anne is waiting in front of the station in her little car.

"This is nice," I say, getting in. "But I could have walked."

"I know, dear, but I was just waiting at home anyway."

She glances at me often on the short drive to her flat.

"I don't know what to make of all this," she says as we get out. "You told me a lot of things last time, and I've started wondering if I remember it right, or if it's – what do you call it? – déjà vu. You know, I just think I'm remembering it."

"You can hear the recording again when you're ready."

She has been busy cooking for me, and I eat with pleasure. No gourmet alternatives will ever taste as welcome to me as her thin chicken soup and vegetable-laden beef casserole.

We balance the plates on our knees and watch the early news while we eat. The leading story, as it has been every night this week, concerns the preparations for Diana's funeral, and the breaking news of Mother Teresa's death is pushed into second place.

"Now there was a saint," I say. "They should have put that story first."

"You're probably right, at that. Will she be made a saint some day?"

"Oh, you believe me now, do you?"

"Well, let's say, for argument's sake ... I suppose there'd be a lot you could tell me, about the future."

"There is, but I won't. With Mother Teresa, though ... I'm not entirely sure because I don't keep up with such things but yes, I think they do make her a saint."

"That's good."

I get my phone out of my bag and bring up the recording app. "You have a listen to this while I do the dishes."

When I return to the living room she's staring into space. I take the phone back, wincing a little when I see how low the battery is, and turn it off.

"Has it happened just the way I said so far?" I ask. She nods.

"There'll be a lot more in the funeral tomorrow, and I could have got some of the details wrong. It goes on for a long time."

"I still think this must be all inside my head," says Anne. "When people get senile they forget where they are, don't they? They start talking about things that happened in the past as though it was yesterday. Maybe we're both in the future, do you know what I mean?"

"Does it feel unreal to you? Does your brain feel foggy, or sort of disconnected, as though you were in a dream?"

"No, I feel perfectly normal."

"Exactly. And another thing I can tell you, though maybe I shouldn't, is that you're never going to get dementia. That's what we call senility in my day. So you needn't worry about your brain."

"All right, so you are from the future. How did you get here?"

"I don't know, Mum. It just happened."

"It feels strange, you calling me Mum. I don't know if I can call you Stella. I've still got Stella."

"Let's stick with Anne and Linda then."

She smiles at me. "You're looking pretty good, dear, if you really are Stella in twenty years' time. You always were a lovely girl."

"Thanks, Mum. I mean Anne."

"So are you going to tell me which numbers are going to come up in Lotto on Monday?"

"Well, I wish I knew, but unfortunately I didn't come prepared."

"I'll just put my usual numbers in, then."

"You do that."

I could tell her, I suppose, that her usual numbers are never going to come up; but I have a feeling that this is the kind of apparently innocuous information that I really should keep to myself. If I tell her that, she'll stop buying a ticket with those numbers every week for the rest of her life. She might select some other numbers. She might actually win, and that could have an unpredictable effect on all our lives.

"What I really want to know is whether we're ever going to find Linda," she says.

I'm not prepared for that question, and I have to think for a while.

"Even if she hasn't turned up by 2017, that doesn't mean she'll never turn up," I say.

"In 2017, she'd be . . . what . . . eighty something?"

"I do understand," I say. "It would be nice to know what happened to her."

"I've always looked in antique shops, you know, for her bracelet," says Anne.

I remember, then, that she could never pass an antique shop, or a junk shop or a pawnbroker without going in.

"What bracelet's that?"

"Her charm bracelet. I always thought that if I found it in a shop somewhere, that would mean she was dead. She loved that bracelet. She would never have parted with it while she was alive."

"Have you told me about the bracelet before?"

"I must have, at some stage. Look, she's wearing it in this." She gets up and takes one of the familiar photos of Linda from her side table. There is indeed something on Linda's wrist, but the image is not clear.

"Would you know it if you saw it?"

"Of course. Young girls used to love charm bracelets, didn't they? You had one yourself."

I remember mine, a little guiltily. Mum gave it to me when I was about ten and I acquired three or four charms at various times, but I wasn't really interested, and it took me months to realise that I'd lost it.

"We gave it to Linda on my wedding day," says Anne. "You gave the bridesmaids a gift, that was the tradition. It was gold, and we started her off with four gold charms. There was a shoe, a house, a little dog and . . . what was the other one? A rose. She was thrilled to bits. And she saved up money and bought more charms, funny little things that she liked: a four-leaf clover, a tiny house, a fish, a little teapot. But she couldn't afford the gold ones, so she bought silver. Normally, you see, it would be all gold or all silver."

"So that made it a bit different?"

"Yes, and there was one little turquoise bird someone gave her. I'd know that bracelet anywhere."

My mind flicks back to my time. I could search on Google Images.

"I can't tell you anything about Linda," I say.

"I suppose that means you don't know what happened to her." She sighs.

"Well if you think about it, I probably wouldn't turn up pretending to be her if I knew she was out there somewhere."

"Hmmm."

"Actually, that reminds me," I say. "Have you got Linda's birth certificate?"

"Why?"

"I don't know how you'll feel about this, but I need to survive in this time, your time, and I've got nothing. I mean, no ID, no qualifications, no history. I can't even get a flat without ID. With her birth certificate I can get a passport, a driver's licence – things like that."

"But the real Linda might already have those things."

"Then we'll know, won't we? We'll find her."

"All right." She goes to get the precious certificate, and I stow it in my bag.

"That Iris Woodridge wants to see you," says Anne suddenly.

"Who?"

"She lives in one of those dark little houses by the station. They've always lived there, the Woodridges."

"Would I know her? I mean me, Stella."

"Probably not. Awful fat slummocky thing. She never married, never had kids, nor did that brother of hers."

"So she wants to see Linda?"

"Yes, she must have spotted you that first time you came. She rang me, right out of the blue. Is Linda back? she says. I told her you were living in Sydney. So she rang me again, a couple of days ago, and asked if she could see you next time you're here."

"And she was a friend of Linda's?"

"No, that's the thing. She was quite a few years older. More Frank's age. Her brother was younger, but he was a creep. Linda hated him, all the girls did."

"Do you think she'd know I'm not Linda?"

"She wouldn't know the time of day, that one. Just ignore it. You don't have to talk to the likes of her."

We watch TV for a while, each lost in our thoughts, then Mum gets up and goes to the kitchen. A few minutes later she comes back bearing a tray with two cups of weak tea and two slices of cake. She does this every night, but she only makes the cake if there's a visitor. Otherwise she has a Marie biscuit. I wonder if you can still get Marie biscuits in my time? I haven't seen one for a while. Maybe I should advise her to stock up.

"You know, I might disappear at any time," I tell her as we sip our tea.

"Really? Just like that?"

"I imagine so. I mean, I'm sort of counting on going back to my own time, sooner or later. So when that happens, I'll just vanish. Every night when I go to sleep I wonder if I'll wake up in my own bed, back in the future."

"Good heavens."

"I'm just warning you. You might find my bed empty in the morning."

"Would I remember that you've been here?"

"I don't see why not. This is real, so there's no reason for you to forget."

She puts her cup down.

"Do you think that's what happened to Linda? She didn't just vanish, she went to another time?"

"Oh, God," I say. The cake suddenly tastes dry in my mouth.

"When I was a little girl, maybe five or six, I had a dream," says Mum. "I dreamt I was playing in the back yard and a beautiful lady was there. She was wearing a white dress and she had long fair hair, and I assumed she was a princess."

"Go on."

"She took me by the hand and we went for a walk. I don't know where we went, but there was bush all around. The whole time she was talking to me, sort of telling me to be always good, and kind, and saying I was going to be happy. I can't remember much of what she said."

"Did you only have the dream once?"

"Yes, but what if it wasn't a dream?"

"Well, I can't say it's impossible," I say. "But if that was Linda, I wonder where she went after that. She didn't go back to her own time, did she?"

"She could have gone anywhere, past or future," says Mum.

"I hope not. I've got to go back to my own time. My whole life is there. Richard..." My voice breaks and I feel tears in my eyes.

"It's all right, dear. I'm sure you'll be all right." She pats my knee. "You can always stay here with me, you know. You won't need ID and all that other nonsense if you just stay here."

"Thanks."

I wash the cups for her and we both go to bed early. She has put flannelette sheets on the single bed in the narrow spare room and turned on the electric blanket, and it's really too warm. Some of my favourite childhood books are arranged on the shelf that serves as a bedhead, and I browse through them for a while, listening to the faint buzz of her radio through the wall. She'll be up and down all night, listening to the radio and eating apples. The thought is comforting. I sleep soundly and am quite glad to wake up and find myself still there in the morning.

21

When I get up I vacuum Mum's flat, wipe the grime off the kitchen cupboards – her eyesight is not so good – and do her washing. This is what I always did when I visited her in the later years.

"I'll do the cooking tonight," I tell her. "I'll walk down to the shops a bit later and buy some stuff."

"No fancy food, dear. Some of that fancy food gives me heartburn."

"Don't worry. I'll make something you like."

The shopping centre is busy, for Mount Wallace, and I keep an uneasy eye out for the woman I saw on my first day, or anyone else answering Mum's description of Iris Woodridge. Most of the faces I see are young, and I don't recognise anyone. I buy myself a coffee and lurk in a corner of the café for a while.

Mum and I have a quiet lunch, reading the Saturday papers, which I find fascinating. I marvel at everything from house prices, to television programs, to political analyses. Once again I contemplate staying in this quaint, innocent world for another twenty years, and quail at the thought. From here on it's going to be one long process of material acquisition, spiritual impoverishment and international disasters. I don't know if I can bear to witness all that again.

In the afternoon Mum goes into her room for what she calls a lie-down and she's soon snoring. I set off for a long walk. My feet draw me up the long hill to the old house, and I stand looking up at the attic windows. Linda had the attic room before I did, and I imagine her pale face gazing back at me.

I do a circuit of the town, skirting the area in the middle which is off-limits, like a castle keep. All you can see through the fence is trees and grass, but somewhere in there is Wattletree House, the girls' boarding school that we always understood was not for the likes of us.

When I went to university I met a few girls who had gone to Wattletree House, and when they talked about their schooldays it was as though they'd grown up on the other side of the world. They were allowed out sometimes – we did see them occasionally, strolling along the main street arm-in-arm in their long school coats – but the Mount Wallace these girls saw was not the town I knew. Nevertheless, I did fantasise at one point about sending Claire there, just to get her away from the evils of the city. Maybe I can broach the idea with Stella.

I walk back and start preparing Mum's favourite meat loaf and an assortment of vegetables.

"It's starting," says Mum, and I join her on the couch. We watch in silence as the male members of the royal family, joined by Diana's brother, walk solemnly along the road. Mum wipes at a tear when she sees the flower-covered coffin and the camera zooms in on the simple wreath labelled "Mummy".

We listen to the interminable speeches.

"Who's that?" whispers Mum.

"Tony Blair, he's the Prime Minister. He's only been in for a few months."

"Who's that?"

"Charles Spencer, the brother. Listen, he's going to shake them up a bit."

"Is that Elton John?"

And so on. I come and go, tending to our dinner, and eventually we eat, still watching.

"This is very nice, Stella," says Mum, her eyes never leaving the screen.

She called me Stella.

As before, I find the most moving part of the funeral is afterwards, when the car crawls through the streets of London and distraught onlookers shower it with flowers. Even when they reach the countryside the road is lined with people, and more flowers rain down from the overhead bridges.

Mum looks at me and her eyes are bright with tears. I move closer and put my arm around her.

"I felt like I knew her," she says. "I wrote her a letter once, and she answered. It really was from her, she signed it."

She puts her head on my shoulder and her emotion, the grief of the crowd and the innocence of the day all descend on me and I weep with her. We weep for Diana, for Linda, for Claire, even for myself. We weep together for all the lost girls.

In the morning Mum suggests we go for a drive to Bowral.

"The tulip festival isn't on for another week or so, but a lot of the tulips will be out, and there are some lovely gardens in any case," she says.

We drive the short distance sedately in her little car, and get there so early most of the shops are still closed. The place is already a tourist mecca, dotted with craft shops, galleries and quaint little cafés. Fortunately, Mum's favourite is already open and serving coffee and fresh scones still warm from the oven, so we settle in. The scones are large and fluffy, and Mum covers hers with lashings of strawberry jam and whipped cream.

"After this we'll have a quick look through the antique shops, then go and see some gardens," Mum proposes.

"How often do you come here?"

"Oh, every few months. They don't have a big turnover – the second-hand shops, that is."

"People are asking me what happened the night Linda left," I say, sipping my coffee. "I don't have many details, though you must have told me at some stage. What can you remember?"

"Well, of course, I'd left home by then. It was 1950, January 1950. Your father and I had been married for about three years, and we were renting the sleepout at the back of the Morrisons'. If we'd gone straight into our own house I would have tried to get Linda to come and live with us, because I was worried about leaving her with Mum."

"Do you think she would have accepted?"

"Maybe. She was getting resentful and rather difficult, but I think it was partly because she felt sort of abandoned. I don't think she ever forgave me for getting married."

"She'd had plenty of time to get used to the idea, hadn't she?"

"Certainly. I was twenty-seven and your father was nearly thirty when we got married. We'd been engaged for six years, but the war got in the way. I didn't want to wait, but he was always so cautious, George was, and a bit on the glum side. He was worried I'd end up a widow. As it was, he didn't really see active service at all. They were always being sent somewhere after the event. Anyway, finally we tied the knot and I moved out of home, but I always encouraged Linda to come and see us whenever she felt like it."

"She was sixteen, wasn't she, when she went?"

"Yes, just. Her birthday was in October and she disappeared in summer, not long after Christmas. I've forgotten the exact date, but it was early January. She'd left school a year before that. You were allowed to leave at fourteen in those days and she wanted to, but I'd persuaded her to put in another year. She was bright, she could have made something of herself.

"Mr Carey who owned the furniture shop in the main street, he asked her to come and work for him. It would have been a good job in the office, not just behind the counter. But she chose to go and work at the grocer's next door, don't ask me why. It didn't even pay as much."

"Was this Mr Carey sweet on her, do you think?"

"Lord no, dear, Gil Carey was a respectable married man, older than me. They had a baby about that time, a little girl."

"Gil Carey. I met his daughter! She's a friend of Phil and Lauren, you remember them?"

"Fancy that! I never knew the girl. She was still just a wee thing when they left. Did she tell you how her parents are?"

"Her mother's dead and her father's in a home. She said his mind has gone – I suppose she means he's got dementia."

"That's sad," says Anne. "Mind you, he was a bit of a drinker and they say that affects the brain."

"So," I prompt her. "About Linda?"

"Yes. Well, that last day, a Saturday it was, Linda came and had tea with us. She was in a good mood, really quite sparkly, which was a bit unusual for her at that time, but I didn't think anything of it. Your father went to bed early – he'd been playing golf, and he used to get very tired. We didn't know then that he had a bad heart.

"Anyway, Linda and I had a cup of tea and a piece of cake and a lovely chat – I can't remember what about, just little things I suppose. Then she said she had to go."

"Home?"

"I suppose, but I did get a faint impression that she was going somewhere else – you know, meeting someone – I didn't ask, because she'd been hanging around a bit with some local kids who I thought were trouble. I couldn't stop her, and if I'd mentioned it we would have had an argument, and I didn't want that. We were having such a nice time together that day."

"Did you feel bad about that, afterwards?"

"Not really. I've always been glad that we parted on good terms.

The waitress is passing and Anne beckons her over and, before I can protest, orders another round of scones.

"Anyway," she continues, "when she disappeared, Grandma Dulcie and your father decided to get the police involved, and they questioned those friends of hers. It turned out the boys were away that weekend – they'd gone kangaroo shooting up near Fitzroy Falls – and the girls she was friendly with hadn't seen her."

"Who were these friends of hers?"

"Oh, a bunch of good-for-nothings. Not a brain between the lot of them."

She stops and looks around uneasily.

"I suppose I should watch my tongue a bit. You never know who's listening."

The waitress comes back with more scones, threading her way through the now-crowded tables. Anne takes the plate from her with a smile.

"Thank you, dear." She starts spreading a thick layer of cream on a scone while I look on with some consternation.

"Do you really want to eat that?" I can't help saying.

"Yes," she says firmly. "I really do. Now, where was I?"

"Um . . . Linda's friends?"

"Yes, well, there was Barry McMahon, and the two Stewart boys, cousins they were, and sometimes Robbie Riley was with them. And the girls were Pam Riley and . . . what was her name . . . Dawn something. Her family was only in the town for a couple of years."

"Are you sure the girls were telling the truth, when they said they hadn't seen her?"

"Yes. The two of them were together at the lake that night. It was a warm night. I got to know Pam a bit in recent years, through the bowling club, and she mentioned it to me a couple of times. Like, she was sorry she hadn't seen Linda to talk her out of running away."

"So if Linda was going to meet someone, who could it have been? Some stranger who persuaded her to go off with him?"

"If there was a stranger in town people would have known. It's a smallish place now, but it was really small then. Pam did tell me years later that she thought Linda had a boyfriend. If it was true she kept it very quiet. Pam thought it might be the Baker-Green boy. That was another family who didn't stay in the district long. There were just a couple of things Linda had let slip. But Pam didn't mention it to the police, because she wasn't sure, and she knew that if it was true Linda wanted it kept secret."

"This Baker-Green boy didn't disappear at the same time, then?"

"Heavens, no. I believe he went on to become a doctor – well, that's what his mother always said he was going to do, and she was the sort of woman you don't say no to. They moved back to Sydney just after all this, anyway."

"What was his first name?"

"Let's see ... I think it was Paul. Anyway, when Linda left my place – as I said, it was fairly early – she took some food with her, some leftovers for Mum, and she did take that home. Mum was already in bed, so she didn't see Linda. She came home and went out again, and apparently took a few clothes and her overnight bag, and all her savings, which she kept in the bottom of her wardrobe; and no-one saw her."

"Would she have had much money?"

"A bit. She'd been working for a year, in the grocer's. She gave Mum most of what she earned and she'd bought clothes and make up, that sort of thing. But she could have saved enough to catch a train somewhere, and maybe to keep herself for a little while."

"Did the police question Paul Baker-Green?"

"They did not, because they didn't know about him."

We've long finished our coffee and she has polished off the rest of the scones. The proprietor is looking meaningfully in our direction. I realise there are people hanging around waiting for a table, so we get up to leave.

"What was Linda wearing that night?" I ask as we head out into the sunny street.

"A white dress." She looks at me with a rueful smile. "Her good white dress, and she had her hair out. She looked like an angel."

"Or like the lady in your dream?"

"Just like her. If I remember rightly."

22

We trawl through the antique and curiosity shops, but I feel Mum's heart is not in it. She's done this many times before. I browse alongside her, and in one shop buy a pretty blue and purple paisley scarf. There are other opportunities to expand my sparse wardrobe, but I'm enjoying the unencumbered feeling of owning very little.

In the last shop Mum buys a heavy silver watch-chain, the sort girls often wore as a necklace in the nineties, and probably still do.

"This has been here for months," she murmurs. "They haven't really got anything new."

The shop assistant gift-wraps it for her and when we get outside she hands me the small parcel.

"This is for Claire. It's her birthday on Tuesday, and I'm not going to get that hat finished in time. Could you . . .?"

"Of course, she'll love it," I say. "I'll have a look for the bracelet in Sydney. If I see anything that could be it, I'll take a photo." I put a hand on my bag where my phone is nestled, wondering how much longer the battery will last.

We start driving around the streets, looking at the lovely old houses with their vast gardens, and I suggest we park somewhere and walk a bit.

"It's a bit hilly," Mum objects.

"All the better. We could do with some exercise after all those scones."

"I suppose so." She stops the car and we get out.

"My old legs can't take much," she warns.

"You shouldn't give up on yourself, Anne. You should go easy on the jam and cream, too."

"Now, dear." She stops in the middle of the footpath. "I'm not going to ask you how much longer I'm going to live, because I really don't want to know. All I want is to enjoy the life I have left. Why should I endure years of misery just so I can get to some magic number?"

"Sorry." I take her arm and gently lead her along the street. I'll have to try some other way to get her to live longer, but I can't be sure it's the right thing to do. If she survives a year longer and we lose Claire anyway it will break her heart.

It's not long before Mum has forgotten our conversation and is proposing that we go to a little pub in another of the Southern Highlands towns for lunch.

"They do a lovely Sunday roast," she says as we get into the car. "You don't have to get back yet, do you?"

"No, I'm staying away. It's Father's Day today, and I'd rather leave them to it. I feel a bit in the way."

"Don't you think you should tell them who you are now? I'll back you up."

"They'll think I'm a lunatic."

"You convinced me. Isn't there some other momentous thing you can tell them about?"

"There'll be plenty of momentous things in the next twenty years, but I don't know of another one that's happening soon. They're not going to wait another four years until . . . well, until there's an event I could describe in detail."

"But I can tell them how you told me about Diana's death, and you've got your recording on that contraption."

"They'll just think I've pulled the wool over your eyes, and that will make it even worse. It's better if I go on being Linda for as long as I can."

"All right, dear, but remember: if it gets too hard you can always come and stay with me."

Richard and the other Stella would probably like that, but I have to be back there to work on Claire.

Nostalgia is a funny thing. When I was the other Stella's age I was always looking for excuses not to come to Mount Wallace, not to spend any more time than I had to in Mum's warm, familiar, old-fashioned apartment. Now her offer is tempting, redolent of comfort, sound sleep, a trouble-free life. I find myself planning to ask her for all the details of our family history – she has told me before, but I wasn't really listening. Maybe I'll get a little cassette recorder and get her to dictate her life story and I'll get it digitised when I'm back in my own time.

"I'd better not spend too long here," I say. "I'm working for Stella at the moment, and I need to keep doing that and save up some money."

"Come back and see me again soon, won't you? Bring your other self so I can see the two of you together."

"I'll try."

I try to time my journey so that I'll get back to the family house after dinner, but when I open the door I'm greeted by pleasant cooking aromas. As I stand irresolute, my hand on the doorknob, Richard comes up behind me. He's wearing running gear.

"Bloody dog shit," he says. "Would you mind grabbing me an old knife from the kitchen?"

I comply and watch him scraping the sole of his shoe.

"One day they'll make dog owners walk around behind their dogs with a plastic bag and scoop up their shit," I say.

He laughs. "People will stop having dogs if they do that."

He wipes off the knife in a garden bed and we go inside.

"Happy Father's Day," I say.

"Thanks. They made me have breakfast in bed." He makes a wry face. "Stella's cooking up some sort of feast for dinner. Are you hungry?"

"Oh, I don't think I – "

"Come on, there'll be lots of food, and the kids will behave better if you're here."

I'm disarmed by his good mood, and I realise it's quite unusual for these times. There seems to be no trauma in Richard's background to account for his dark view of the world, but it's entrenched in his character. To my relief, he has improved as old age approaches. Either that or I've grown used to it.

Stella is happy, too, and over dinner she asks me for details of my time with Anne, laughing at my description of the food, the trip to Bowral to admire gardens, the scones.

"And you watched the big funeral together?"

"Of course."

"Did she cry?"

"We both did."

Claire asks, "Are they going to have a funeral like that for Mother Teresa?"

"I don't think they'll ever have another funeral like that," I say.

23

On Monday morning I make my long-delayed phone call to the estate agency. A bored young woman tells me there are no vacancies in the cheap block of flats, and they don't manage any other buildings like that.

"If there was a flat and I applied for it, what information would I need?"

She goes away, leaving me dangling for a long time. The phone is attached to the wall, so I'm stuck in the hallway. There isn't even a speaker option on the phone. With my free hand I flick through the tattered phone book.

It turns out there are three Baker-Greens in Greater Sydney, none with the initial P, but there is a Dr LP Baker-Green in Crows Nest. I write down the phone numbers and addresses of all the Baker-Greens. Even Crows Nest is a bit out of the way, but I suppose I could get a ferry to McMahons Point, and it's not too far to walk from there. The other Baker-Greens are in distant parts.

Finally the voice returns.

"We'd want ID, like driver's licence or passport, bank account details and two references."

"Oh. Okay. Well, can you please call me if something comes up?"

She takes down the number, or seems to. I sit for a while on the hard-backed chair in the hall, thinking gloomy thoughts.

There's no street directory in the house. It's probably in the car, which is parked in the street. I could get the spare key out of the drawer and have a look, but I'm worried that someone from the family will see me being over-familiar with their possessions. I walk down to the newsagent's, leaf through the street directories on their shelves and draw a rough map of the Crows Nest street. While I'm at it I examine the suburb where Abigail lives, looking for primary schools. There are two more possibilities, one just as close to her house as the school I found last week.

Back in my room I try to work, but I can't focus on anything except a debilitating inner debate, like those tedious dreams that go on and on and are never resolved. Should I set out for Crows Nest, or for Abigail's suburb?

Eventually my Abigail obsession wins, but by the time I find one of the newly-discovered schools it's well past home time. There are a few stragglers still leaving the school grounds, the girls wearing a neat uniform of navy skirt and jumper with a red stripe around the neck. I walk the streets for a while looking for other girls in the same uniform, but there's no-one worth following.

Guilty at the thought of Claire coming home to an empty house, I spend more of my dwindling money on a taxi home. Julian is in the kitchen eating a towering sandwich.

"Hi Auntie," he says. "Can I get you something to eat?"

"No, I'm fine thanks." It does occur to me that I've forgotten to have lunch and my stomach is feeling painfully empty.

"Is Claire here?" I ask.

"She's got choir, I think. Mum's picking her up."

I'd forgotten about choir – one of many interests that didn't last long.

"Actually, I will have a sandwich, thanks," I say. "But about a tenth the size of yours."

I watch with contentment while he makes it.

"How are things?" I ask him casually.

"Good."

"Is . . . um . . . are you and Natalie getting back together?"

"No!" He looks shocked. "She hates me now."

The break-up must be a good thing for him, I think uneasily. Now he can grow up a bit and form a relationship with a smarter, nicer girl. Someone he's got more in common with. Someone, I think guiltily, whom I would like.

But all I remember is a string of unsatisfying relationships and my Julian, back in my present, living alone in that little apartment he bought before the prices went crazy.

He, the older Julian, told me a while ago that he believes in love at first sight and that it happened to him once, but he let her slip away. It was soon after he'd started his first job in the city, up in the financial district. One lunchtime, on his way back to the office, he passed a dark-eyed girl coming the other way, and their eyes met for an instant. Julian stopped dead, wondering what it was about her that had struck him so. Perhaps it was the way her plain face seemed on the verge of transforming into something of dazzling beauty.

The girl passed on, her brown pony-tail swinging gently. Julian half-turned, thinking he should run after her; but he was in yet another disastrous relationship with a girl who seethed with jealousy, and it seemed insane to add another complication to his life.

At the lift, about to go up to his office, he berated himself for his stupidity, ran back to where he had seen the girl and searched for the next half-hour. He searched again at lunchtime the next day, and the next, and ever since then he's been on the lookout for her. But she'd vanished.

I take my sandwich with me and walk back up to the shopping centre, quietly munching.

In the bookshop I find the very first Harry Potter book. For some reason Harry Potter wasn't on our radar until the second one appeared, and I always wished Claire had started reading them when she was that little bit younger, so she could have grown up with Harry, so to speak.

I buy the book, a silly birthday card and some pretty wrapping paper and ribbon, then wander back just in time to put the dinner on. Claire and Stella come in at the last minute, laden with groceries.

"I'll make dinner tomorrow night," Stella tells me. "It's Claire's birthday, and we like to do something a bit special on the day. I assume you can join us?"

I'm torn, because I would love to see Claire's face once more at her twelfth birthday dinner, enveloped in the love of her family. But this is the sort of event I have to withdraw from, because my presence could make some tiny difference that would grow into something disastrous.

"That's very kind," I say, "but I've made an arrangement for tomorrow night. An old . . ." I can't say an old school friend, she'll want to know who it is, she'll ask Anne, I can envisage complications. "Someone I worked with for a while, in . . . Adelaide. I ran into her by chance in the city. It's just drinks, but we might go for a meal later on."

"Okay. Right. Well, have a good time."

24

The next day I work until mid-afternoon. I leave my offering and Anne's on the kitchen table, then make my way to the city, where I scour a few shops for Linda's bracelet. When I've had enough of that I take a train to St Leonards and walk back along the highway to the Crows Nest shopping centre.

My vague plan is to get something to eat, but all the lunch places have closed and I can't find anything else that's quick and easy. I peer through the dusty glass of a jeweller's shop at a small display of "estate jewellery" – their term for second-hand items. There are no charm bracelets.

Consulting my rough sketch map, I cross the road and turn right. Dr LP Baker-Green lives in a pleasant double-fronted Victorian house behind a high brick fence in a wide street dotted with gnarled deciduous trees, their bare branches silhouetted against the pale blue sky.

I hover on the pretty tiled front verandah, considering and discarding things I might say to Dr LP Baker-Green. A phone call might have been better, but here I am.

Doorbell. Silence. Footsteps.

The door is flung open and a tall, good-looking man in neat clothes and tartan slippers is standing there. He's my age, grey-haired and slightly stooped, wearing glasses, and his friendly face falls apart when he sees me.

"Linda!" he says, his voice hoarse. He grabs me in a bear-hug, pulls me inside and reaches out a foot to push the door shut.

He puts his head back to look at my face, which is probably as shocked as his, then embraces me again.

"Oh, Linda." There's a crack in his voice and he's about to kiss me. For a moment I want to go with it. He feels warm and comforting, and I realise now how much I've missed physical contact.

"I'm not Linda," I manage to say.

We are motionless for a moment, his arms still around me, his face showing bewilderment.

"Please, can I come in?"

I follow him to the kitchen, where something is boiling on the stove and he rushes to attend to it.

"I'm sorry," he says. "It's just . . . You're just the image of someone I . . . It was a long time ago, but I thought I'd know her anywhere."

The kitchen is large, old-fashioned and cosy. There's a pine table with some chairs in the middle of the room. I pull out a chair and sit down.

"I know who you're talking about," I say. "That's why I'm here. I'm related to Linda – sort of a second cousin. My name's . . . um . . . Matilda. So you're Paul?"

"Yes. Well, it's Lancelot, Lancelot Paul, but I've always been called Paul."

"And you lived in Mount Wallace for a while?"

"Yes. Listen, do you know where Linda is?"

"No, that's why I'm here. The family gave up looking for her a long time ago, but her sister Anne never got over it. I just thought I'd try to find out what I could."

"Are you from Mount Wallace?"

"Originally, but I left there when I was really young. I haven't had anything to do with the family for most of my life, but I've just recently been back there, spending a bit of time with Anne."

"I never met Anne," he says. "Linda adored her."

"Yes. Anne more or less brought her up."

"So I gathered."

"You and Linda were close, then?" I ask.

"You could say that." He goes to the fridge and gets out an unopened bottle of white wine.

"I have a personal rule that I don't drink alone," he says. "Will you give me an excuse to open this?"

"Oh, why not."

He fetches a corkscrew and two very fine glasses, sits down opposite me and pours wine.

"This is good," I say, taking a sip, then another.

"Please." He reaches over to refill my glass. The wine is going straight to my head.

"I shouldn't." I hold up a slightly shaking hand. "Not wise on an empty stomach."

"I can fix that!" He throws open the fridge and pulls out cheese, pâté and some little tomatoes, then adds a packet of dry biscuits from the cupboard.

"Matilda," he muses as I tuck in. "Did you spend much time with Linda when you were young?"

I shake my head, my mouth full.

"I'd love to have seen you together," he says. "You must have been like twins."

"Where did you fit in?" I ask. "Did you know her at school?"

"Not really. I did see her there, when we first arrived in Mount Wallace, but then she left school. A few months later I discovered her working at the grocery shop in the main street, and I used to find excuses to go there. Really, right from the first time I saw her I was smitten."

"Did she feel the same way?"

"I really think she did."

"Why was it a secret?"

He sighs.

"You didn't know my mother."

He gets up and rummages through an overhead cupboard for some sort of seasoning, which he seizes and sprinkles on the bubbling mixture in his saucepan, wrinkling his brows as he takes out a spoonful and tastes it.

I can't help noticing that the cupboard is scrupulously tidy, with several jars labelled in neat handwriting and all facing outwards.

It seems to me that men living on their own are inclined to be either superlatively organised or extremely muddled. I brood a little on the fact that Richard would definitely fall into the latter category. If I really don't come back it won't be long before our apartment descends into chaos.

"My mother," says Paul, sitting down again with one eye on the stove, "was what you'd call upwardly mobile. Her family had been some sort of squattocracy a couple of generations earlier, but they'd slipped a few rungs down the social ladder, and she was determined to get back up there. Dad wasn't that interested. He was happy to be a country solicitor with a nice easy-going lifestyle, but she wanted to get back up to Sydney with a more prestigious job for him; and she'd decided I was going to be a doctor. Not just any old doctor, though. I had to be a brain surgeon or something like that."

"But you had other ideas?"

"I didn't much care at the time what I was going to be, and I wasn't particularly rebellious by nature. She had a strong personality and my dad and I had always gone along with her. But when I met Linda I realised that I could have a whole life of my own which was nothing to do with my mother."

"She didn't approve of Linda?"

"I didn't test those waters. I knew she would have been horrified. She was trying to match me up with a girl at Wattletree House, you know that private girls' school in Mount Wallace? But apart from that, she wanted to stand over me and make sure I was studying as hard as I could. I was about to start my last year of high school and she was obsessed with my results. Having a girlfriend who worked in a grocer's shop was definitely not part of the plan."

"Wasn't that a bit hard on Linda?"

"Yes, but she had a great sense of adventure, and she liked the idea of a secret romance. She didn't want her family and friends to know about us either – she used to complain that everybody was sticking their noses in, and not letting her live her own life."

"Even Anne?"

"Especially Anne," he says. "Her mother didn't supervise her at all, and we both used to sneak out at night and meet in various places. That winter the station master used to let us sit in the waiting room late at night, and he'd make sure we had a pile of wood to keep the fire going."

"At the railway station?"

"Yes, remember those old waiting rooms on the platform that used to have a roaring open fire? Of course there were no trains going through at night and it was locked up, but he told Linda where to find the spare key. Lovely old bloke, Stan. He was obsessed with gum trees, he could name every eucalypt on the east coast and identify anything if you brought him some leaves and a couple of gumnuts."

"I've never heard of him." I smile and accept some more wine.

Jumping up again, he gives his pot another stir, then has a peep inside a steaming rice cooker on the kitchen bench.

"Listen," he says, "I've got quite a nice concoction going on the stove here. I suppose it's a sort of curry. Anyway, I'm cooking some rice to go with it and I've got plenty of that."

"It smells delicious," I admit.

"Won't you stay and have some with me? Food tastes better in company, don't you think?"

"All right, you've persuaded me."

I'm about to settle back in my chair, but he throws a tea towel over his shoulder, leans over and gently takes my arm.

"In that case, let me escort Madame to the dining room," he says.

Laughing, I follow him to an enclosed back verandah overlooking a small but exquisite garden.

The verandah is entirely walled with louvre windows, half of which are open, and the night air is chilly but exhilarating. Subtly positioned lights play on an eclectic mixture of native and exotic trees and shrubs. I recognise grevilleas, a native frangipani just coming into flower, tree ferns and a barely-contained jasmine whose perfume is overwhelming.

He flicks an imaginary speck of dust off a small round table and motions me to sit, then closes the windows and ducks back into the kitchen. Before I can offer to help he has produced mats, bowls and forks, then he somehow finds room for the rice cooker and the steaming pot of curry on the table.

"Oh, one more thing." He darts out again, then reappears with a thick, soft plaid blanket, which he drapes around my shoulders. It warms me instantly.

"Bon appétit," he says, passing the rice.

"So where is Mrs Doctor Paul?" I ask, helping myself.

"Long gone. I mean hey, she's still alive, but she's Mrs Someone Else now. The truth is, I never got over Linda."

"Really?"

"That's such an important time of your life, when you're young and impressionable, and the whole world is new and fresh and . . . I suppose you feel it's yours. You feel invincible."

"You do."

"And Linda and I were feeling that together."

"And then she vanished?"

"Then she vanished."

I came here ready to investigate the idea that Paul Baker-Green murdered Linda way back then and found a way of hiding her body. I was thinking I might confront him with that accusation; but it's manifestly absurd.

"What happened?" I ask.

"It was summer," he says, then chews for a while, gazing into space. "Yeah, one of those hot, endless summers, when the air smells of dust and the night seems to be holding its breath, and the bush is crackling all around. You know?"

"I know."

"We were seeing each other nearly every night. Sometimes it was really late by the time our families went to bed and we could slip out, but we couldn't get enough of each other. We'd go to the station, or up by the lake, or into the bush up behind her place. The locals called it the Little Mountain, but it was just a hill. Still, there was a rocky spot way up there where you could see out, right across the town and down the valley. When the sun was about to come up there'd be a pink glow right across the horizon, and one night we saw the full moon rise, a brilliant white light over the trees and then it suddenly popped up."

He gives me a sidelong look.

"On that Friday night, the last night before she left, we lost our virginity up on the Little Mountain. Oh, I know that's usually a fumbling affair that you'd rather forget about, but for us it was magical. We'd talked about it and planned it, and she'd brought a blanket from home and I'd brought some food, sort of like a celebration, and we'd fallen asleep afterwards and stayed nearly all night. I only just got home in time, and that gave me a bit of a fright.

"She had to go to her sister's the next night, and we agreed not to meet. I think we both wanted some breathing space, because we felt something momentous had happened in our lives. You know how it is when you're sixteen."

"Of course."

"She was working in the shop the next morning – remember how shops used to be open just until twelve on Saturdays? I was supposed to stay away, but I couldn't. Sometimes she'd be there on her own and we could slip out the back together – it had a little backyard with a few pot plants and a bench to sit on. You'd hear the bell tinkle if anyone came into the shop.

"But of course it was Saturday morning and they were busy, all working. But she must have known I'd come in, because when I bought something, a bag of biscuits or some such thing, she slipped a note into my hand. She loved doing stuff like that, but it worried me a bit. One of her friends was in the shop – Pam, I think her name was – and I'm sure she saw."

"She did guess something, and years later she told Anne," I say. "That's how I found out about you."

"Ah. I must say I wondered why no-one ever asked me any questions at the time; but that comes later.

"Anyway, the note said something like 'School 10 pm.' That meant we were to meet in the shelter shed of the Catholic school near her place. I remember feeling a bit disappointed. The school wasn't the most secluded of places, so it looked like she might not be planning a repetition of the night before. That's what was uppermost in my mind. You know, romantic teenage girls don't really understand how teenage boys tick, and vice versa."

I think about my teenage boy, Julian, and that girl, Natalie. I'm glad she's out of the picture.

"So we met," he says. "She was excited, starry-eyed, and after we'd kissed and carried on for a bit she said, 'We belong to each other now, don't we?' I agreed, and I meant it. But then she said we had to run away together, then and there. I realised she had a small bag with her and she was dressed for travelling in some kind of suit. You know, girls and young women dressed for the occasion in those days. She probably had a hat and gloves in her bag."

"So she wasn't wearing a white dress?"

"That lovely dress of hers? She would have had it with her. She said she had everything she needed in her bag. Her idea was that I would go home and sneak out some stuff of my own, and we'd wait for the early morning train to Sydney."

"In the waiting room at the station?"

"Exactly. I was tempted, I was longing to be with her, but I knew straight away that my mother would track me down and there'd be hell to pay. Even now I'm sure that's true. She would have found me and she would have separated us.

"So I told Linda we couldn't do it. I pointed out that in one more year I'd be leaving Mount Wallace and going to university. She could come to Sydney then and we'd be together, and no-one could stop us.

"Well, she got hysterical. I sort of knew she would. You couldn't tell Linda she had to wait for a year, and I couldn't make her see how it was for me. I was thinking about how I had to get my School Certificate and make something of myself. I had visions of her and me in a little house in the suburbs with lots of kids swarming around, you know?"

"I can see it," I say sadly.

"I did end up with two sons, both of them probably as boring as I am," he says.

"You're not particularly boring."

"Thanks."

"This is lovely food," I say. "You're a good cook."

He smiles at me over his glass.

"So, there must be a Mr Matilda?" he says.

"Yes, but he's far, far away. Possibly unreachable."

"Unreachable? Any kids?"

"A boy and a girl. So, tell me how the night ended."

"Not well. She seemed to realise, quite suddenly, that no amount of pleading would make me change my mind, so she jumped up and said she was going on her own. Well, now it was my turn to plead with her, but she was adamant. In the end she grabbed her bag and stormed off.

"I waited for a while, thinking she might relent and come back, then I set off for home. I had to go the same way as her, and I thought I might catch up with her on the road to the station, but I didn't see her. At the station

I peeped into the waiting room, but it was all locked up, empty and dark.

"By then I was sure she'd been bluffing. I assumed she'd gone home, and I started thinking about when we'd see each other again.

"You've got to understand, I was quite sure she hadn't gone. The next two nights I stayed close to my bedroom window, because if we didn't have an arrangement she used to throw little stones up there to get my attention. I knew she wasn't working on Sunday or Monday. On Tuesday I went to the grocer's shop, but she wasn't there and I was too shy, or maybe too cautious, to ask after her. It wasn't until the next day that I found out she'd really left. People had started talking about it; and I couldn't believe it.

"Then I thought she'd be back soon. But time passed, and . . . nothing."

"Would she have caught the train after all, do you think?"

"I don't know how else she could have got out of town. Maybe she waited somewhere else because she was avoiding me."

"Might she have hitch-hiked?"

He laughs. "There would have been more hiking than hitching. The roads were pretty dead at night in those days. It did occur to me she might have somehow got to Bowral, where no-one knew her. She could have got on a train that passed through Bowral about one in the morning, going south. She could even have stolen a bike and ridden there, something like that."

"Pretty intrepid."

"Well, that was Linda."

I finish my dinner and look up. "I should go."

"Let me drive you home." He starts to get up.

"After all that wine? I don't think so." I grab my coat and bag before he can argue, and make for the door.

"Well, can we see each other again? What's your phone number?"

That's a problem. I can't have him calling our house and asking for Matilda, and I can't change my mind and tell him I'm Linda after all.

"I'm a bit hard to reach at the moment," I say. "But we could meet somewhere?"

"Yes, let's. Tell you what, there's a really lovely concert on at the Opera House on Thursday. It starts at seven. Will you come with me?"

"Okay. Yes. The concert hall in the Opera House?"

"Yes, why don't you meet me in the forecourt at six forty-five? We can stroll in together."

"All right." I slip out into the chill of the night and make my way home, feeling better than I've felt for a long time. Whether that's because of him or the wine I couldn't say.

25

I feel I've been falling down on my job as general cook and after-school minder, so I go grocery shopping in the morning and spend the middle part of the day cooking.

Julian comes home at about one and finds me busy in the kitchen, pots bubbling on all the gas burners.

"Have you had lunch?" I ask him.

"If you mean have I eaten my measly sandwiches, yes I have. If you mean am I replete, then the answer's no."

"I've just made these Cornish pasties. I was going to freeze them, but you can have one now."

"Or two?"

"Or two."

He dumps his bag on the table and sits down.

"No school this afternoon?" I ask.

"Sport," he says. "It's tennis, or tenpin bowling, or slipping through the cracks."

"Which would be your specialty."

"Exactly."

Despite the banter he's morose as he chews the buttery pastry.

"I thought some nice food might cheer you up," I say.

"Oh, I don't need cheering. I think I might go emo."

"Emo?"

"Yeah, you know. Skinny black jeans and chains and piercings, and a white face with a tragic expression."

"How do you get the white face?"

"Not sure. But lots of people on my bulletin boards are doing it, especially the girls."

"Lots of look-alike photos?"

"You can't put photos on a bulletin board!"

"No, of course not. Sorry, just had a senior moment there."

"A senior moment?" He chuckles. "I wish I'd said that."

"You will."

"Anyway, emo. I'm going to start listening to music that no-one understands."

My cooking calls to me and I do a round of stirring, scraping and chopping.

"Do you know anyone called Françoise?" I ask him.

"No. Any more of those pastry things?"

"My God!" I say, handing him a third pastry. "How's school? HSC is coming up next year, isn't it? Have you started doing the preliminary stuff yet?"

"Uh – yeah, a bit."

"Are you working hard?"

"Sure." He looks alarmed.

I lean over and brandish a wooden spoon at him.

"I'm psychic," I tell him. "My ghostly contact says you're not working very hard at all. He tells me you're going to have a bit of trouble next year if you don't get stuck in pretty soon."

"Has Mum been sounding off about me?"

"She hasn't said a word. Oh, and I don't mean anything by the wooden spoon." I shove it into a pot and start stirring.

"Well, I've got a bit of homework, as it happens," he says faintly. "I might make a start on it."

"Good idea." I wish I could have taken out my phone and got a photo of his face. The older Julian would have found that amusing.

At dinner, talk turns to the old engineering works around the corner. In the last couple of days a notice has appeared on the wall, the first sign that someone wants to develop the building.

"It's a pretty ugly building," says Stella. "Do you think they'll pull it down?"

"That would be a pity," says Richard. "It's got that great industrial look, don't you think? And it's part of our history."

"It could be nice, I suppose. They'll probably get rid of those outbuildings and put gardens at the back, wouldn't you think? Then if they make apartments in the main building they'd have a great view. You'd be able to see the water, too."

"It might be worth putting a holding deposit down," says Richard. "You can get a bargain with some of these places if you're quick enough."

"What's a holding deposit?" asks Claire, her mouth full.

"We'd give them a bit of money now, so that when they've built the apartments we can buy one at a good price," explains Stella.

"You'd buy an apartment? To live in?" asks Julian.

"Yes, in our old age."

"And Julian and I could live here!" says Claire. "You can have the downstairs, Jules, and I'll have the upstairs with all the bedrooms, because I'm going to have lots of babies and you probably won't have any."

"No, we're going to sell this house eventually," says Richard. "We'll need the money when we retire."

"You can't sell this house!" Claire is appalled. "This is where we live!"

"It's okay, chicken." Stella puts an arm around her shoulder and kisses the top of her head. "It won't be for a long time yet."

Later, Claire and I do the washing-up. It's supposed to be Claire and Julian, but he gently melts away. I'm not sure why I'm so much softer on him than I was in our original mother-son phase, but I suppose it's because I'm not so worried about building his character. His character is going to turn out fine.

"They won't really sell the house, will they?" asks Claire, stacking plates in the dishwasher.

"I couldn't tell you that."

"Would you want to live in that old factory?"

"They could make it quite nice. But there won't be a garden out the back, they'll build townhouses. It's all about the money."

"Townhouses might be all right."

"Sure, but it's a pity. Underneath all that crappy stuff at the back, those tin sheds and storerooms, there are two little sandstone cottages, completely hidden."

"Cottages?"

"Yes, beautiful little places a hundred and fifty years old, possibly the oldest buildings in the suburb; but no-one knows they're there, and when the developers find out they're going to quietly demolish them before anyone sees."

"How do you know?"

"Oh, someone told me. Some old lady."

I've done it again. I shouldn't have said anything. But she'll forget about this, surely.

"Now," I say brightly. "I suppose you want to hear about the count?"

"Yes, please."

"Okay." I finish wiping the bench, cut two small slices of the orange cake I made today and sit down at the table. "The count. Of course, I didn't know he was any such thing when I met him. He was with a group of young men who'd come from Transylvania, you know?"

She looks unsure.

Wait a minute – is Transylvania real or fictitious? Where's Google when you need it?

"It's near Romania. They used to have royalty there, with kings and queens and castles; but after the Second World War they got caught up in the Soviet Union, so they were behind the Iron Curtain. It was hard for anyone to get out, to come here or anywhere else, but a few made it. This group, the ones I met, went overland, around the Black Sea, through Georgia and across the Hindu Kush, through blizzards and avalanches, then down into the tea plantations of India."

I loved the movie where they did that – I can't remember the name of it.

"Anyway, they were a lovely group of boys not much older than me, working on the Snowy Mountains project and staying in big old army huts in the village where I was. I started teaching them English after work.

"The count was just called Alexander, and it turned out that he had been living in London for five years and could speak perfectly good English, but teamed up with these other boys, because he was hiding out, and they were protecting him."

"Why?"

"People were trying to assassinate him," I whisper. "Back then the Transylvanian aristocrats thought they could get back home and start living in their palaces and be royals again, but they had enemies who wanted to wipe them all out. The enemies had assassins searching all over the world. Alexander thought that they'd probably sent some to Australia, to have a look to see who was here.

"Anyway, Alexander came along to my English lessons because he didn't want to draw attention to the fact that he could already speak English, you see?"

She nods, her eyes wide.

"Right from the start I thought he was absolutely gorgeous, so I used to wear my best white dress that I'd brought with me when I ran away, and wear my hair up in a victory roll. I had long hair then."

"What's a victory roll?"

"You sort of curl it up and back. It was very fashionable in the 1940s.

"I could tell Alexander liked me. He used to make jokes in the class, pretending he didn't know much English, and getting things wrong. Only the jokes were so funny and clever that I soon guessed that he knew exactly what he was saying.

"One day I made him stay back after the class. I said, sort of with sign language, that his English was so bad I was going to give him some extra homework so he could catch up. He came over to my desk, grinning like mad, and I said, 'My friend, it's a pity you don't understand anything I say because you are my favourite student and if you knew the words to ask me out I would certainly say yes.' I was cheeky in those days."

She laughs.

"So he immediately asked me out, speaking perfect English with a sort of upper-class English accent, and we started spending all our free time together."

"Oh!" she says. "Is a count sort of like a prince?"

"Absolutely," I say. "It was beautiful. We were smitten. We used to go into the bush, further up the mountain to a rocky place in a sort of clearing, where you could look out and see for miles and miles. Sometimes we'd stay there all night and watch the sun rise over the valley.

"But then, a couple of months later, he got a letter from his mother. She was living in exile in Paris, and she said it was safe there and he should come."

"Paris!"

"But the trouble was, his mother was a real snob. The family had slipped down the social ladder a bit, because Transylvanian royals weren't really royal anymore, but she was determined to get back up there, and the best way was for him to marry a princess. Not a big top-drawer one, though I believe Princess Margaret was available at the time. More like a Dutch or Norwegian or even a Spanish princess. There were a few of them around."

"But he wanted to marry you?"

"Yes. Well, we weren't really thinking of marriage yet, but he wanted to be with me.

"So we caught the train to Melbourne and he went aboard the ship, because she'd sent him a ticket for a first-class cabin, and I stowed away and went to Paris with him."

"Wow!"

"Claire," says Stella, coming in. "Don't you want to watch *Blue Heelers* with us?"

"Oh!" She's torn.

"It's okay, I'll tell you the rest later – about how I got to Hollywood."

I watch her go, wondering if I'm taking the wrong tack here. I want to plant the idea in her head that she should hunger for a life that's exciting, full of wondrous experiences: a world that's worth living for. But I have to be careful not to make Linda too reckless, and I shouldn't glamorise the fact that she ran away.

Stella won't approve of me making up these fantasies for Claire's benefit, but Stella doesn't know that I need a channel for telling Claire the things she needs to hear.

On reflection, though, perhaps I shouldn't have told her about the stone cottages. I wanted to present her with that image, and I've always thought it was sad that no-one knew. The developers did the deed late one night, and Richard and I slept soundly through it. All we ever saw was a pile of broken sandstone.

I felt bad when I found out, we both did. But it was already done and it would have cost us a significant amount of money to back out of the development, so we decided to let it go.

But the more I talk to Claire the more I'm breaking the rules of time travel, and I can't guess what the consequences will be. What if she runs away from home altogether because she admires Linda? Even innocuous things that I might say without thinking could have some future effect that I can't even imagine.

26

All day Thursday I find myself thinking about going to the concert with Paul, even though a big part of me says I should stand him up and put him out of my mind.

Perhaps I made a mistake by telling him straight away that I'm not Linda. I was so eager to get his story it didn't occur to me to resort to subterfuge, although that seems to come naturally these days. If I had let him believe I was Linda there might have been a possible safe haven for me in his pleasant house, drinking wine and eating good food.

Thinking along these lines gives me a pang of longing for Richard, for the comfort of his arms around me, and tears come to my eyes. All this is eating away at the edges of my identity, so that I still wake up sometimes wondering if I really do know who I am.

Perversely, though, I feel I can relax and be myself with Paul, even though my real self is something I can't reveal to him.

Besides, I manage to spend a whole day without fretting about Abigail or wanting to rush out and look for her.

In the late afternoon, with Claire and Julian safely in the house and their parents not yet home, I change into my nice blue dress and good shoes, throw on my trench coat and look in the mirror. With my hair brushed and good clothes on I look younger, a bit too much like Stella, I think.

I catch the bus to the city and wander through the bookshops, browsing. I spend too long at Dymocks and have to hurry through the lower levels of the Queen Victoria Building to Town Hall station, thinking that the quickest way to the Opera House will be to catch a train to Circular Quay.

A young girl carrying a violin case is walking ahead of me, and when she gets to the barriers she stops and turns around, scanning the faces of people approaching the station. I stop too and stand mute, staring at her. She is wearing the navy and red uniform of the latest school I've been watching, her hair in two long brown plaits tied with red ribbons. Her small face, slightly squinting now as she cranes her neck, is unmistakable. This is Abigail.

I step back into one of the passageways that turn off in different directions from the station, but not so far that I can't see her anymore. She stands on the spot for a while, looking around and jiggling a little, then she moves away to look at the array of train information on the wall. Then, appearing to come to a decision, she slips a ticket into the barrier and moves quickly through and out of sight.

Cursing myself for my lack of foresight, I rush to the barrier and peer through at the people milling about in the station forecourt. She's nowhere to be seen. I hurry to the nearest ticket machine and buy a ticket that will get me into the station, but there are at least two train lines that she could take to get home, if that's where she's going, and they go from different platforms. I gamble on the furthest one and jump on the long escalator that goes down into the depths of the station. There is an open area halfway down where you can see the other platform from the escalator, but you can't get off. And there she is, making her way along to the far end where it's not quite so crowded.

By the time I get back there, sprinting the wrong way up the escalator, pushing people aside, the platform is almost empty and the red tail-lights of her train are winking as it disappears into the tunnel.

The next train is in five minutes and I stand on the platform, unable to make up my mind. I think I know which station would be hers. I think I know which way she would go from there. Maybe I could catch up with her, but then what?

Now that I know what she looks like, I can watch for her here at this time of day. She had a violin case. Does that mean music lessons? Rehearsals? I don't recall that Abigail played a musical instrument, but it may be that she strayed from that path.

"*I stopped practising on the piano and Mum sold it.*"

When she walked along the platform to the other end she was dangerously close to the edge. She should know that you have to keep inside the yellow line. I would never let Claire do what she just did, on a crowded platform with the train about to come gliding in, unwary people turning suddenly with their elbows and briefcases sticking out.

I see, as though from a great height, our lives laid out on a chessboard. The pieces are already in place for a checkmate, many moves in the future. Abigail is one of those pieces, a pawn sitting snug in her row with the other pawns. Although she hasn't moved yet she will play a vital part in the endgame. I could reach out now and remove her from the board.

Paul must still be waiting for me at the Opera House. My family are at home, expecting me, or the person they think is me. My mother, even now, is probably planning my next visit, smiling to herself as she makes my bed in the guest room and plumps my pillow.

I have done this the wrong way. I should have stayed anonymous, stayed invisible, kept to the shadows. If, at the right moment, I could step swiftly forward on this platform, place my hands firmly against that slight back, my resolve uncompromised, it shouldn't even matter if someone sees me, if they shout and scream and lay hands on me and drag me to the police station. I am no-one.

They don't have DNA testing yet, do they? They can't connect me with Stella. Maybe it's not too late.

If no-one sees me do it they'll have no reason to suspect me, but I'd have to go away somewhere, disappear before they look at the CCTV. Do they have CCTV yet? Maybe I'll be spirited straight back to my own time, my mission accomplished. I'll wake up at home in my own bed and the phone will be ringing. It will be Claire.

"Mum, can you come over? The baby's had colic all night and I haven't had a shower for three days."

"Of course, my darling, of course. I'll be there right away."

I am resolved. My days here are numbered, and I know what I have to do before I disappear. If fate doesn't take me back to my own time when the deed is done I'll just get on a train and go somewhere, far away, and take my chances.

I wish I could find Paul and give him some excuse for standing him up, but I can't see him while this blackness is in my heart. I have to make a clean break and let him forget about me.

I take the bus home, let myself in quietly without seeing anybody, and take out my notebook.

I am going to kill Abigail. If I am caught I will have no excuse to offer. I will be viewed as a horror, an abomination. I will have no excuse because once it's done even I won't know why. Let it be said here. If I don't kill Abigail, Claire will die.

27

I spend most of Friday in Abigail's area, watching the school whenever the children are outside. In my time these actions would arouse enormous suspicions, and although no-one seems to look twice at me I'm wary.

I don't see Abigail at lunchtime, but after school my vigilance is rewarded when she comes trailing out through the school gate with a tall blonde girl and two boys.

I follow them at a distance as the girls chatter and shriek and the boys try ineffectually to impress them. I know from my experience of kids that they are all about the same age, but in terms of maturity the girls seem to be five years older. The blonde is skinny, but she already has noticeable breasts. They sashay down the street, tossing their long hair behind their shoulders. I note that Abby has taken out her regulation plaits and brushed her hair, which falls in luxuriant kinky waves down her back.

The boys talk loudly to each other, giving the girls sidelong glances. They have a soccer ball which they pass between them, and one of them likes to show off by chasing it onto the road, dodging cars. More than once a driver toots him and both boys chortle with glee and shove each other.

I am sure this is Abby, but I'd like to see her open the gate of her own house, just to remove any possible doubt. Frustratingly, the two girls turn a corner in the wrong direction, waving goodbye to the two boys, and a little later they disappear into a lovely old apartment building. This must be where the blonde girl lives.

I wait outside for a few minutes. No-one goes in and no-one comes out, and after a while I give up and grope my way back to the station.

If I really had to travel back through our history I wish I'd come to another period, the time when Claire met Abigail, or possibly just before. Abigail was a sly, scheming little thing, and my hatred for her oozes to the surface like sump oil on dirty water whenever I think of her. I could drop my hand onto that older Abigail's shoulder, wait for her to turn her pretty head, then smash her in the face with a cricket bat, a lump of wood, her own violin. I could push her off a bridge or into the path of a speeding car or into an inferno and calmly walk away, serene in the knowledge that I did it for my child.

Maybe not an inferno.

But this Abigail is an innocent girl, young for her age, laughing breathlessly at her bolder friend's jokes. Her school uniform is too big for her. The hem has been taken up, badly, and is already unravelling on one side. Halfway home she buried her nose in the fragrance of an extravagant display of jasmine on someone's front fence, and after, there were stray jasmine flowers clinging to her shoulders.

It might be harder, but that doesn't make it any more wrong.

What if I had come back to the time when Abigail was a baby? I could have waited outside her house until the young mother came out wheeling a pram, then I could have dashed forward, grabbed the sleeping infant and dashed her to the ground.

These thoughts fill me with horror, but I need to steel myself. I have to go as far as it takes to save my child.

It's not so hard to sacrifice your own life for someone you love. If one of you must live and the other must die, I think I would prefer not to be the survivor, living on with guilt, pain and loss. Better to make the grand gesture and be remembered with love and gratitude.

A much greater sacrifice is to do wrong for the one you love. To commit a hideous act that has everyone, even the loved one, reeling in horror and disgust. If I do this for Claire no-one will ever know my justification, because she will never meet Abigail and set herself on that path to destruction.

I won't know either. I will recognise only that I'm a child killer, a monster who has done this deed to an innocent girl for no reason that I can imagine. I'll have to remember to read my notebook, to read the whole story of Abigail – when I finish writing it down – so that at least I will understand.

However it plays out, the act that I am contemplating is the ultimate sacrifice. No forgiveness, no redemption for me, but if I am strong enough to do the deed then maybe my girl will live.

28

Back in my room after dinner I take out the notebook to write some more, to compose my justification for what I am planning to do, but I'm overcome with weariness and slip into bed instead.

Even so, I can't get to sleep as memories swirl through my mind.

Claire was happy for a while in her new school with her new friends, especially Abigail – possibly, I think now, only Abigail. Abigail had seen something in our girl, some hidden wound that made her easy to single out and prey upon, something we, in our obtuseness, had not noticed.

They began spending more time together, especially at weekends. On weekdays it eased off, and I found out later that Abby's counsellor had told her family, her aunt Donna in particular, that Abby needed to catch up with her schoolwork. I hadn't known until then that Abby had been seeing a counsellor since her mother died.

Somehow they managed to convince Abby, and in her slippery way she had made a show of pulling herself together. She must have been bright, because Claire reported that she had started topping the class in various subjects.

It was good for Claire, too. Under Abby's influence she also was applying herself. She especially loved French and seemed to have a facility for it. I felt guilty that I had never seen this in her before, and I enrolled her in an expensive Alliance Française course that took her to the city a couple of nights a week after school.

But that July Abby turned sixteen. This was some sort of milestone in her inheritance plan, and she seems to have received a lot of money, several thousand dollars. She had a big birthday party at her house, which involved Claire being absent from home for a whole weekend. When we got her back on the Sunday night she was exhausted, drawn and bad-tempered.

Abby announced that she was going to Bali with Donna's family in the second week of the school holidays as a special birthday treat, and at the last moment she invited Claire to go too.

Claire was wildly excited and I couldn't think of a good enough excuse to keep her from going. I tried calling Abby's house to talk to Donna about it. I wanted her to place some quite reasonable restrictions on the two girls;

but no-one picked up the phone and the messages I left on their answering machine seemed to fall on deaf ears.

The day before they were due to leave Abby came around to supervise Claire's packing.

"You don't need to bring much," I heard her say. "We'll buy it all when we get there."

"Abby," I said, entering Claire's room with barely a knock. "Could you ask Donna to give me a call? I'd like to talk to her before you all go."

"Oh, didn't you know?" she said innocently. "Donna and the boys are already over there, in Kuta. They went a couple of days ago."

"Have you been at home on your own?"

"No, my dad's there. He's going to house-sit."

A few days before Claire was due to leave, I got home from work to find her in the kitchen.

"Oh, Abby's dad rang," she said. "He heard you wanted to talk to him."

I tried to call him back, but as usual, there was no answer.

We took them to the airport and saw them off, but I had a knot of anxiety in my stomach for the whole week. In those days when people went away they dropped out of sight.

I did call the hotel a few days later, desperate for reassurance. After a long wait Claire came to the phone.

"It's fabulous here, Mum. I'm having a great time," she said.

"You girls are not going out at night on your own, are you?"

"Don't be silly, Mum. We're fine. We're just swimming and shopping and eating."

"Is Donna around? I'd like to have a quick word."

There was another long pause, then she finally came back on the line. "They're on a bike ride. They'll be gone all day. I'll tell her you called."

On the night they were due to fly home, at about the time their plane was due to leave, the phone rang.

"Mum, I'm really, really sorry to leave this so late, but can I stay a few more days?"

"What are you talking about? You've got school on Monday."

"Just a few days, Mum. We can change our tickets and they won't charge any more. It's so great here."

The line wasn't good, but her voice sounded too high-pitched, and was it slightly slurred?

"Claire, where are you? Are you at the airport?"

"Sorry, Mum, I can't talk now. This is a crap phone. Look, I'll see you on Thursday morning."

"Claire, no. Claire, listen to me –" But she was gone.

I called Alliance Française to tell them that Claire wouldn't be there for the first week of the new term. For some reason they put me onto her teacher, who asked in a charming French accent how things were with Claire.

"A beautiful girl and very quick to learn," she said. "She has a lovely accent, *très jolie*. But she is not coming to class."

"What do you mean, she's not coming?"

"She came in the first week, the Monday and Thursday, then never again."

I kept calling and calling Abby's house. At last, on the Wednesday, a male voice answered.

"I'm sorry to disturb you, but are you Abigail's father?"

"I sure am."

"I'm Claire's mother, Stella. Her friend Claire?"

"Hiya Stella. Is Abby okay?"

"That's what I wanted to ask you. Have you been in contact with her?"

"Me? No. Abby's at your place, right?"

Through my rising hysteria, in a dialogue at ridiculous cross-purposes, we ascertained that Donna and her family had gone to Queensland for the school holidays and were staying an extra week, that Abby's father was indeed house-sitting, that Abby had told him that she was going to stay with us, that Abby's father didn't even know that the school holidays had ended, and that the two girls were indeed in Bali on their own.

My first instinct was to get the Balinese police involved, but I thought better of it. Whatever the girls were up to over there, bringing them to the attention of the local police could have been disastrous.

On the Thursday morning, my heart in my mouth, I stood in the arrivals hall watching the stream of people returning from Bali, all the young women with plaits and beads in their hair, all the men blue with cold in shorts and thongs. Claire, Abby and a third girl I'd never seen before came out with the stragglers, tanned, plaited and waving gaily.

I couldn't speak. The three girls got into the back seat together, whispering, and after a few minutes they seemed to doze. I said nothing all the way to Abby's place, where I dropped her, the mystery girl and their numerous bags. I didn't speak until we were a few streets from our house, when I suddenly pulled over to the kerb and stopped.

"Where do I start?" I said with artificial calm, looking up at Claire's frightened eyes in the rear vision mirror.

"Don't start," she muttered.

"I know you were there without Donna. Why did you lie to me?"

"Fuck, Mum!" she snorted. "Would you have let me go if I'd told you?"

"Don't you fucking swear at me! Out! Get out of the car!"

She got out grumbling under her breath and went to the back of the car. I threw open my door and leaned out.

"No, I'm taking your stuff," I yelled. "You walk home, and you have a think while you're walking, then you come and tell me what you've been doing and why."

Then I drove off and left her standing there.

29

I'm tempted to go back to Abigail's suburb over the weekend and keep stalking her, but I imagine a protective phalanx of family, some of whom might notice me. I know that Donna wouldn't recognise me because she hasn't met me yet, but the thought of seeing her makes me shrivel inside.

As usual I try to stay out of my family's way, but Claire seeks me out in my little room. She knocks tentatively and sidles in, picking up Henrietta, who has jumped off the bed to wind herself around Claire's legs, purring.

"This place is nice," she says, sitting down in a patch of sunlight on the bed and looking around. "So that's where all the photos are!"

She jumps up to examine the pictures on the wall one by one, explaining to me who is in each one and where it was taken while I feign surprised interest.

"You must have some great photos," she says, returning to the bed. "All the places you've been."

"I haven't got any with me," I say, thinking nevertheless about all the images stored in my phone. "You know, we had funny old cameras in those days with films that only had eight shots. They were expensive to buy and expensive to develop, so you never took a lot of pictures."

"But what was it like?" she says. "Being in Paris."

"Ah, Paris." I stop as if trying to remember. What was Paris like in 1951 or thereabouts, I wonder. There must have been elegant women with little hats and big, full skirts. The men would be in pinstriped suits with nipped-in waists, or was that another time? There would have been beautiful long, shiny cars with square bonnets and running boards, Daimlers and Citroëns and Jaguars. Those street artists must have been on the Left Bank for at least that long, and the Shakespeare and Company bookshop, where impoverished literati get to sleep in beds between the shelves in return for a day's work, would have been pretty new.

"We rented a garret on the Left Bank and I stayed there," I said. "Do you know what a garret is?"

"No."

"It's a tiny attic room, right at the top of one of those old buildings with high, steep roofs and no lifts. Our building was a wonderful place, where all the other people were artists. From my little window I could see the spires of

Notre Dame and past that the river and the Louvre, and even a glimpse of the Eiffel Tower.

"So, I lived there and Alexander had to stay with his mother, the countess, in the Hotel de Crillon, which was on the other side of the river. That was an unbelievably fancy place, with huge rooms and every surface decorated and servants everywhere looking down their noses at you. Of course he got away whenever he could to spend time with me, but it was harder and harder. The countess kept dragging him off to operas and salons and all the other places where princesses might be found.

"I spent my free time exploring Paris, and it was just gorgeous. Promise me you'll go there as soon as you're old enough. There's a beautiful old department store called Samaritaine in the Rue Rivoli, on the edge of the river. You can go up onto the roof and there's a café up there, quite cheap, where you can have lunch and look out over Paris. The name, *Samaritaine*, is spelt out in huge letters, taller than a person, on the edge of the roof, and you can look through them. Promise me you'll go there while you're still young, because it won't be there forever."

"I promise and I'll stay in a garret and take lots of beautiful photos and give you copies."

"Fabulous," I say. "So anyway, one day, when we'd been in Paris about six weeks, there was a hammering on the door and it was the landlady. She was waving her arms and jabbering at me, and I had no idea what it was about. I'd been trying to learn French but I still didn't know much, which is why I hadn't been able to find work. Eventually a lovely Polish sculptor from the room next to mine stuck his head out the door. He knew about ten languages and he explained to me that she was asking for the rent. It seemed that Alexander had paid for the first week when we arrived, but he hadn't paid any more since then.

"Well, I had a little bit of money left so I gave her that, but I was still a week short. When Alexander arrived a bit later I spoke to him about it, though I was terribly embarrassed at having to ask.

"He was just as embarrassed as me. He told me he had spent all his savings too, everything he'd earned on the Snowy River, and his mother didn't have any money. Not a *sou*, he said. She hadn't paid her hotel bill, not for a single night, and countess or not they were going to kick her out any day, and he didn't know where they might go."

I'm trying to think on my feet, not sure whether I'm making this up, or recalling some story or other that I've read, or a movie I've seen. I hope I'm not about to find myself expiring in my garret like Camille.

"So he went back to see if he could find something to sell – I'm afraid I think his idea was to pinch a bit of his mother's jewellery, something she wouldn't miss – and I sat in my room crying. The next thing there was a knock on the door and it was the Polish sculptor, asking if everything was all right.

"I told him the whole story and he was so helpful. He rounded up some artist friends and they let me model for them. The pay was pretty low, but it was something. The sculptor asked me to cook dinner for him every night after that, and in return I got to eat."

"What did you wear?"

"Pardon?"

"When you were modelling for the artists. What sort of clothes did you wear?"

"Oh!" I don't think she knows about artists' models, and this is not the time to tell her. "Oh, drapey things, you know, like a Grecian statue. And sometimes they would dress me up as a princess, or an angel – that sort of thing."

She looks pleased.

"It was a battle to make ends meet," I say. "But it was such an exciting place to be, especially when my French started to improve. I would meet all the artists in bars and cafés at night, when we'd all finished work, and we would talk and argue about all sorts of things until dawn."

I remember that I need to work a moral into this story.

"Of course, some of them were in a bad way," I say. "People were drinking lots of wine and other stuff: brandy, whiskey, a weird, really strong drink called absinthe – they also called it the green fairy – and some of those people were killing themselves with alcohol. There were also people taking drugs: cocaine, opium, all sorts of horrible things, and you could see them wasting away before your eyes, and some of the artists couldn't work anymore, their brains were so fried. Their faces were grey and their teeth were falling out."

"Gross."

"I didn't touch any of that. I didn't want to be sick and, you know, addled."

"What about Hollywood?" she asks.

"Ah yes, Hollywood. Well, one night a group of Americans came into one of these cafés I've been talking about, and they sat at a table for a while watching me and my artist friends. We were having a lively discussion, in French of course, about Communism and the Soviet Union – at least I think that's what it was about.

"Anyway, this older American man came over to me and said, 'Excuse me mademoiselle, but my friends and I can't get over how much you look like Moira Ray.'

"I had no idea who Moira Ray was, but it turned out she was a Hollywood actress who was very popular at the time. She was in a lot of B-grade action films where she was always having to jump out of speeding cars and climb onto the wings of aeroplanes and hang off cliffs. You know the sort of thing?"

"Um . . ." She looked a bit bewildered.

"Now," I go on quickly. "I haven't told you the worst thing that happened about this time. I hadn't seen Alexander, the count, for a few days, when a little boy knocked on my door. He had a note from Alexander, saying he was really sorry but he had to go back to Transylvania with his mother. By the time I got the note he had already gone, because they did a midnight flit. That means . . ." I can see her mouth opening to ask the question. "That means they sneaked out of the hotel at midnight when no-one was around because they couldn't pay the bill."

"Didn't the hotel have their credit card?"

"People didn't use credit cards in those days."

"And so he just left without saying goodbye?"

"Yep. You can't count on a count.

"I was planning to stay in Paris, but the American wanted to know if I would come to Hollywood and be Moira's stunt double. A man in a wig had been performing her stunts, but it was pretty obvious. If they had someone who actually looked like her they could do a whole lot more, the man said.

"Well, if I heard that now I'd understand that he meant they could do a lot more dangerous things, but I didn't get that at the time. I was still only seventeen! I probably wouldn't have cared about the danger anyway. I just thought it sounded like fun.

"I didn't even ask what they were going to pay me, and I wouldn't have believed it if he told me. It was much more than I'd ever earned.

"So off I went with them to Hollywood, on a plane, which was a big first for me."

"Did you do a midnight flit?"

"I did not. The production company gave me an advance, so I paid up my debts, thank you very much."

Julian comes to the door which is open by now, Henrietta stretched across the threshold enjoying the sunshine.

"Is Claire with you? Ah, there she is."

"I'll tell you what happened in Hollywood next time," I promise Claire.

I'll have to rack my brains for the next few days to think up the next chapter of my story. Can I think up some really off-putting story about drug-taking without scaring her too much?

30

I think Stella's a bit annoyed with me because I haven't been putting in my usual hours in the past week, and I still haven't finished the last job she gave me. Well, I don't think – I know she's annoyed.

Starting early on Monday morning, I put my head down and work fiercely until after two o'clock. Now that I know Claire has choir on Mondays I don't have to worry about being home for her, so I can stay out for as long as it takes.

The bus to the city is unbelievably slow and there is a long wait for the train to Burwood, the nearest station to Abigail's house. I sit on the platform, my stomach knotted with frustration, and by the time I get to the school gate the main crowd has already gone, with just a trickle of stragglers.

I walk all the way to the house without seeing Abigail or any other schoolgirls. The house is inscrutable, and I worry about hanging around there in case she sees me. Later, when I make my move, it wouldn't do for her to recognise me and get suspicious.

I search in the other direction, then through the shopping centre, but after a while I have to admit defeat and head for home. My mood is dark and I think fleetingly of visiting Paul, whose gentle good humour is starting to feel like the brightest thing in my life; but I can't see him while I've got this on my mind, imagining his horror if he could read what I am thinking.

As I'm hovering on a street corner, tossing up whether it will be quicker to walk to the bus stop or the station, a car pulls up beside me and I hear the whir of a window winding down.

"Linda!"

Round face, blonde hair teased up, a toothy smile. For a moment I'm completely flummoxed, then I recognise Stephanie from the party.

"Would you like a lift?" she says. "I'm just on my way home from work. You're staying with Stella and Richard, right?"

"Yes, thanks." I climb in gratefully, already racking my brains for something to talk about other than Mount Wallace.

"Terrible traffic," she says. "On a good day I'd be home by now. But I've had to do a detour to drop off something for my father. Is that okay with you? It's just a couple of blocks from here, and I'll only be five minutes."

"Of course," I say. "That's fine."

She turns in through a wide gate and parks in front of a low, pleasant red-brick building.

"Why don't you come in?" she says, pulling a bulging plastic bag from the back seat. "He'll be really chuffed, if we can get through to him who you are. The doctors say it's really good for him to see people from the past. It stimulates his memory."

I'm a little nervous about this, but if Paul mistook me for Linda what do I have to fear from a demented old man? I follow her through dim, carpeted corridors redolent of disinfectant, air freshener and urine. She taps in a code at an unmarked door, and halfway along another corridor she gently opens a door labelled "176 Mr G Carey".

The code was 4321. Hardly the most secure choice, I think.

An old man is sitting hunched in a chair next to the single bed, his head bowed, thin strands of white hair straggling across his speckled scalp. He is skin and bone but his bones seem too big for him, giving the impression that he is coiled up inside the ghost of a larger, more vigorous man. He looks up at his daughter with watery blue eyes.

"I've got your new pyjamas here, Dad," she says loudly. "And I've washed your other ones. They're in the bag."

He says nothing. His eyes stray around the room and rest on me.

"Look, Dad," she shouts. "I've brought someone to see you. It's Linda."

I step forward with an encouraging smile and he squints up at me.

"Who's that?" His voice is hoarse.

"It's Linda, Dad. Linda! You remember, from Mount Wallace, the grocer's shop?"

"No!" He flaps a hand, as if waving me away. I smile nervously.

"It was a long time ago, Dad," says Stephanie, stooping down and putting her arm around him. "Think. You must remember Linda."

"No!" he says. "That's not Linda. I don't know her. Tell her to go away!"

He's shouting now, and I don't dare look at Stephanie to see what she makes of this.

A young man in a short blue cotton jacket pops his head around the door.

"Is everything all right in here? Mr Carey, sit back down in your chair. We don't want another fall, do we?"

I back out as fast as I can. Within a few seconds Stephanie joins me.

"So, that went well," she says ruefully. "Sorry about that, Linda."

We walk back to the car.

"I'm sorry I upset him," I say pointlessly.

"Oh, he goes off like that sometimes. It's part of the illness. He had a go at me once when I was trying to tidy up his bedside drawer. Said I was after his money. To make it worse, he thought I was Mum."

She chatters breezily on the short trip home, talking about people I seem to be expected to know, and I smile and nod and laugh where it seems appropriate. But I sense a slight uneasiness in her, or maybe I'm just imagining it. I wonder if her father gets more lucid than that, and I wonder if they'll talk about me next time she goes to see him.

The third girl was called Lila. I never did find out where she fitted in. She was older than Abby and Claire – about eighteen – and didn't go to school. Abby had known her for a long time because their parents were friends or former neighbours, something like that. She and Abby had planned the Bali escapade together and decided to involve Claire mainly so that they would have an alibi for Abby.

After Bali we grounded Claire. She continued to insist that all they'd done was swim and sunbake and explore their surroundings, and that it was no different from a holiday with the whole family except that they didn't have to do anything boring. But just in those few days away she'd grown thinner. Her hair was stringy, her face had an unhealthy pallor under the tan and she seemed angry a lot of the time.

One day some cash went missing from my drawer. I had arranged for the electrician to come and fix a faulty power point and a few other things that had been mounting up. The day before he was due I had taken the cash out of the bank to pay him, and I came home early from work the afternoon he had agreed to come.

Claire and Abby were sitting in the kitchen in their school uniforms, and they were obviously startled to see me.

"I didn't expect you to be here," I said. "What's happening?"

"Oh, we got sent home early," said Claire.

"Yes, there was a bomb scare," added Abby.

I saw their eyes meet and I could sense a repressed giggle.

"Well, I'm going to make a cup of tea," I said. "The electrician's coming."

"We were just off down the road to get an ice cream," said Claire. "Is that okay, Mum?"

"You're supposed to be grounded, Claire. Just go straight there and back. And Abby, I'd like you to get your ice cream then go home."

The electrician arrived and I forgot about the girls. When he had finished I went upstairs to get the cash out of the drawer and stood there, stupefied. I had been very busy at work, and my first thought was that I had forgotten to get the money out; but I could recall the way it felt in my hand, I could remember counting the notes to make sure of the amount.

I got the electrician's address and promised to drop off the cash later, then I went looking for Claire. Only then did I realise that she hadn't come home. She turned up just as I was putting dinner on the table, and I couldn't bring myself to tackle her in front of Richard and Julian. Later, I went up to her room while she was getting ready for bed.

"Claire, I had some cash in my drawer and it's gone. Did you see it, by any chance?"

"No. Why would I look in your drawer?"

"I just thought, you know, you might have borrowed it?"

"Do you think I stole your money?"

"Of course not. It's just that you and Abby were in the house, and I thought . . ."

"You think we stole your money! Abby's rich, Mum. Why would she want your stinking money? Why don't you accuse Julian? He goes into your room all the time."

I went downstairs, shaking with rage and frustration.

"What's wrong?" asked Richard, looking up from the newspaper.

"Some money's disappeared from my drawer – the money I got out to pay the electrician. I think Claire and Abby took it."

"Claire? Jesus, Stella – I know she does some stupid things, but she doesn't steal from us. You must have put it somewhere else and forgotten about it."

A few days later, when I turned the corner into our street, a car drove towards me and somehow I got the impression it had just started up. Maybe it was accelerating. All the windows were open and loud music was blaring – if you want to call it music, that aggressive rap sound with "motherfucker" this and "motherfucker" that. I glimpsed three or four young men with prison haircuts and tattoos, wearing the expensive sporty clothes that were fashionable among their ilk at the time – clothes that seemed to scream "Okay, I stole it. Whaddya want to do about it?"

Claire was in the hall, just putting her schoolbag down.

"Did you see those guys in the car outside?" I asked suspiciously.

"No. Why?"

"They looked like they were driving away from here. You didn't know them?"

"I told you, I didn't see them. Don't you believe me?"

That became her mantra, her challenge. "Don't you believe me?"

The only honest answer was "No, I don't." But I couldn't say it.

31

On Tuesday afternoon I take a taxi, determined to get to Abby's school in good time. I'm waiting outside when the school bell rings and there she is, coming out with the main rush. She sets off alone, her stride purposeful. Today she's carrying her violin case.

I hang back, confident I know where she is going. At the station I buy a ticket to the city and peep cautiously onto the platform.

She's sitting on one of the long seats, looking down, swinging her legs. There are only a couple of other people on the platform.

I withdraw and walk around the block a couple of times. When I get back to the station she's gone, and another city train is due in ten minutes.

My heart is going faster than it should and my palms are damp. I sit on the train taking deep breaths and gazing out the window, trying to calm myself by counting houses, disused carriages, railway bridges.

Once in the city, I wander through the Queen Victoria Building, distracted, and stop at one of the open cafés for a coffee, which only increases my agitation. The sensible thing to do would be to go home now and come back another day – Thursday or maybe next Tuesday, at six o'clock. That's when she'll come back to Town Hall Station to catch the train home.

But I can't do it. I can't break the invisible thread that binds me to her now. I wait.

After the Bali episode we saw less of Abby, and Claire seemed docile, but I still felt things were not right.

Towards the end of August Claire was invited to a party organised by another girl in her class, Jasmine.

"I've never heard you talk about Jasmine," I said. "Are you friends with her now?"

"Sure. She's great. You'd approve of her, Mum. She's our class captain."

"I don't know. When is the party?"

"Saturday week."

That would be Saturday 8 September 2001. The day after that, the ninth, Claire would turn sixteen.

"But I was thinking we'd have your birthday dinner on that Saturday."

"Can't we have it on Sunday, Mum? It would be so good if I could go to the party and get to know Jasmine a bit better, and all her friends. She's got some really nice friends."

"Will Abby be there?"

"I suppose so. It's the whole class."

Of course I let her go, as she knew I would. We even went shopping for something to wear. The dress was stunning: black taffeta, with a close-fitting bodice and a full skirt. It was dramatic but still modest in its cut: perfect, in my view, for a young girl.

I drove her to the house, a mansion in Strathfield, and watched her walk up the path to the front door, the dress swishing against her long, slim legs, her shining hair cascading down her back. She had blossomed into a beautiful young woman.

The door opened. I wanted her to turn around for a moment, not so much to wave goodbye as to let me glimpse her face, the whole effect. But she slipped inside without looking back.

Richard was to pick her up at eleven, but some time before that she called and asked if she could stay the night.

"Lots of the girls are staying," she said. "They've got this huge space in the attic with piles of mattresses. It'll be such fun, Mum. And Lucy's staying too, so I can get a lift home in the morning with her parents."

I let her stay. The next morning wore on into lunchtime and I hovered uncertainly between the kitchen and the dining room, where her birthday presents sat on the table, wrapped and beribboned. We had filled her room with flowers and there were more on the dining table with the presents, their perfume wafting through the house.

"Call them," said Richard.

"I haven't got the number. She must have given it to me at some point, but I can't find the piece of paper."

Leaving Julian at home, in case she turned up, we drove to Strathfield. A woman answered the door, a face of pleasant enquiry.

"We've come for Claire," I said. "Is she still here?"

"Claire?"

"She came to Jasmine's party, and we agreed that she could stay."

The woman turned and called out something. Presently a tall, thin girl with glasses appeared.

"Jasmine? I'm Claire's mother," I said. "Is she here?"

"Oh! No, sorry. She left."

"Are you sure?" I said stupidly, my brain refusing to function. "Maybe she's still up there with the girls who stayed the night?"

"All the girls who stayed have gone home," said Jasmine.

"What?"

"Claire left the party early. I think they were going clubbing."

"They? Claire and who else?"

"Claire and Abby. Someone was picking them up – I didn't see who it was."

I walked back to the car and got in. The car smelt of flowers too, because we had brought a spare bunch to give Claire as soon as we saw her. We had all viewed her sixteenth birthday as something really special, a rite of passage.

"I don't know what to do," I said on the way home.

"We just have to wait," said Richard. "It's her birthday. She'll turn up for the dinner, and we'll deal with all this afterwards."

Lauren and Phil came by at about six to wish her a happy birthday. I was in the kitchen cooking the meal, all Claire's favourite dishes.

"She's out," I said. "I'm sorry you missed her."

Lauren knew something was wrong and she knew I didn't want to talk about it. Phil gazed into the distance. He had started to behave oddly, and she was too worried about him to think much about anyone else.

At the dinner table Julian ate silently, but Richard and I sat looking at each other, unable to touch a morsel. I had tried Abby's house, and Donna had breezily told me that Abby was staying the night with her father. When I tried the number she gave me for him it rang out.

"I'm going out to look for her," said Richard.

"Where? How would you know where to look?"

"I can't just sit here." He took the car keys and a few seconds later I heard the door slam.

Julian got up, came over and put his arms around me, leaning down awkwardly to where I still sat. He rested his head on mine for a moment, then he quietly cleared the table and I could hear him in the kitchen, washing up.

Richard was out for most of the night. I was aware of him crawling into bed just before dawn, and at the usual time he was up again, dressing for work.

"Where did you look?" I asked him.

"It doesn't matter. I didn't find her."

I went to work too. When I got there I rang Claire's school and waited while the roll was checked.

"I'm sorry, no, she's not here," said the cheerful voice.

"Tell me, has she missed many days this term?" I asked.

"Did you say you were her mother?"

"Yes, I'm Stella Lannigan."

"Well, we have your note here, for the chronic fatigue."

"The what?"

"Your note says she's been diagnosed with chronic fatigue syndrome. She's missed . . . what . . . fifteen days so far because of that. We're still waiting for the doctor's certificate."

"And what about Abigail Kincaid? Has she also been taking days off school?"

"I'm sorry, I can't give out information about another student."

Donna insisted that Abby was not missing. She was staying with her father and they might have gone away for a few days, Donna wasn't sure. I asked her to check with the school to see if Abby was attending and get back to me, but she didn't call and she stopped answering her phone.

We contacted the police on the second day. At the police station we answered all their questions and the young female constable wrote everything down and tried to reassure us. She said she would call us every day with an update, but we never heard from her.

Every night followed the same pattern. We would wait, we would start preparing for bed, then Richard would stop, grab his coat and the car keys and go out. We had mobile phones by then, and I insisted that he take his and call me if he found any trace of her. He never called.

At dawn he would crawl into bed, exhausted, and I would put my arms around him and hold him until he was asleep. I don't think I slept at all.

I stayed in the living room, usually at least until midnight, with the television on and the sound muted. Whenever a news bulletin was announced I watched for the images I was dreading, and turned on the sound to hear if it was anything even slightly related to death, crime, the police. Most of the channels showed news at about the same time and I would flick through them, but the stories were nearly always the same as they had been earlier in the night.

On the Tuesday night the soundless news bulletin I was watching switched abruptly to images of a skyscraper building which appeared to be exploding. Debris and clouds of black smoke erupted silently into a clear pale sky. As I watched a plane floated into the frame and was swallowed by the adjacent building, and I suddenly recognised the twin towers of the World Trade Center in New York.

Thinking the channel had returned to some disaster movie while I wasn't paying attention, I switched to another channel, only to see the same images. I thought I saw bodies flying from one of the buildings.

I turned the sound up, but I couldn't make sense of what I was hearing. Nor could I feel anything.

I fell asleep in front of the television that night. When Richard got home he led me gently to bed and curled against my back with his arms around me. He seemed to know about the planes crashing in New York but he didn't say anything, and neither did I.

On the first anniversary of 9/11, a year later, he said, "I'm glad I didn't see the footage that night. Apparently they edited it afterwards to spare people."

"I saw it," I said.

"I know."

That was the first time we spoke about it to each other.

Late on the fourth night the landline phone rang. It was Abby. Her voice was thin and quavering.

"She's in an alley off Riley Street. It's near McDonald's – there's a yellow fence at the end. I've called an ambulance."

"Are you with her? Can she talk? Let me speak to her."

"I have to go. Please don't tell them my name."

My hands were shaking so much it took several attempts to dial Richard's number, then I fumbled for a coat and shoes and got myself out into the street and ran all the way to the taxi stand.

When the taxi arrived at Riley Street, Richard came out of the lane as I paid the driver, scattering notes everywhere.

"Don't go down there," he said, gripping my arm.

"Let me pass."

The cobblestones were dark with mud, rain and filth. The alley smelt of vomit and urine. She was lying on her back, her eyes open and staring at the sky, a streak of yellowish saliva trailing from the side of her mouth. Her hair was damp, lank and slick with mucous and vomit. There was a dirty rag tied around one arm and a thin trickle of blood.

She was wearing clothes I'd never seen before, cut-off shorts and a skimpy top, her bare midriff streaked with bloodied scratches. I found myself wondering where her beautiful black dress had got to. It seemed to me that if she still had her black dress on she would be all right.

I was screaming but I'm not sure any sound came out. I thought if only I could scream properly she would hear me and wake up.

32

Long before six I position myself near the entrance to the station, watching all the approaches in case Abby comes from a different direction.

This time she's late. She doesn't hang around waiting, she doesn't look at the timetable displays. She slips through the barrier and dashes for the escalator.

By the time I reach the crowded platform she's halfway to the end. I fight my way through, glancing at the arrivals board. The train is due in one minute.

She stops with her feet on the yellow line, gazing like everyone else towards the tunnel. There's a faint vibration underfoot as I move rapidly into position behind her. People elbow me aside and I push my way back to where I'm close enough to reach out my hands and touch her.

She's holding the violin case protectively against her chest. My mind focuses on the violin case, the image of it crushed and springing open, the unseen violin inside splintering, exploding into a thousand pieces, the strings whipping around like wounded snakes.

All eyes turn to the tunnel where the headlight of the train winks as it comes sliding towards us. I steel myself and take a step closer.

"Wait for me!" A voice rises above the hubbub. Abby and I turn our heads as one. A woman in a trim black suit is struggling along the platform, holding a briefcase with one hand and waving with the other.

I can see Abigail's face turned towards the woman, her delighted smile.

Her mother. The resemblance is striking.

I'm confounded, paralysed, and the train glides harmlessly into the platform and stops.

Her mother. All I've ever known about Abby's mother is that she died in a car accident a few years before Abby and Claire met. So she will, then – but not yet.

This doomed woman was on the edge of seeing her daughter die at my hands. If I had done it, that is. I had practised the action over and over in my mind, I had seen in my imagination the flurry of girl, train, violin case. I had convinced myself it was justified.

But then suddenly it wasn't just my girl against this stranger girl, this monster. There was also one mother over another mother. I might be spared the filthy alley, the agony of that pallid face; but this mother's scream would echo through the rest of her life. She would see the girl's plaits whipping around as she turns, spots her mother, smiles; then a terrible absence.

In that moment I could not be sure I had the right to choose myself over her.

They have disappeared onto the train and it has gone with a rush, and still I stand on the platform. Something has left me. My bright, sharp resolve is dissolving and I have to get it back.

33

When I get home Stella is in the kitchen, still in her work clothes, her briefcase on the bench. The picture is clear: she has arrived home late and found me not there and nothing prepared for dinner.

"Let me help you!" I say hastily.

"Don't worry, it's all done. I think Claire's looking for you – she's got a bee in her bonnet about something."

Claire is in my room, sitting on the edge of the bed. Henrietta is purring at her ankles, but Claire is ignoring her. Her face is a picture of misery.

"Marika wrecked your computer," she says.

"Wrecked it? How?" I glance at the old computer on my work table. It appears to be intact.

"She had this stuff on a CD she wanted to show me and Julian was using the one upstairs, so we came here and she pulled out your CD."

"Okay . . ."

"I don't know what she did . . . She closed your file and opened it and tried to do something and closed it again, and I kept telling her to stop and she wouldn't listen."

"My file? That work I was doing?" In my haste to go after Abigail I must have left it open.

"She's deleted it. It's all gone."

"Let me have a look." With a sinking feeling I explore the file system. It looks like she's right, up to a point.

"She's a bitch." Claire has tears in her eyes. "She said horrible things and I said horrible things, and she's gone now. Are you going to tell Mum?"

"Shhhh." I put my arm around her. "It's not so bad. I do backups every day on another CD. Look, I've got the one from yesterday." I open the top drawer and show her. "It's only the last little bit that got wiped, I can soon put that stuff back in."

"Are you sure?"

"Yes, don't worry. Go and get yourself ready for dinner."

I'm eaten up with guilt. Something tells me this was the last straw in the relationship between Marika and Claire, and now the rift is final. This is my fault. If I had been here instead of chasing after Abigail it wouldn't have happened.

I have also realised, in my quick glance at the CD in the drawer, that my last backup was yesterday morning, so I have lost two full days of work.

After more than one disaster in my working life I know that the best thing is to get back to the keyboard as quickly as possible and start reconstructing the missing work. It's amazing how much pops out of the memory in those early hours, so the work goes much faster the second time.

Consequently, I slip away from the table as soon as we've eaten and install myself at the desk. I work for most of the night, until my fingers are numb and my eyes smarting with exhaustion.

When I finally get to bed I can't sleep, but now and then I slip into a doze in which I see that terrible cascade of girl, train, violin as though it had really happened. I hear the anguished screams of the witnesses around me, feel heavy hands falling on my shoulders.

Just before dawn a new and terrible thought assails me. What if that girl was not Abigail? I have not succeeded in following her to Abigail's house. I don't recall that Abigail had ever played the violin. I had thought that Abigail's mother would be dead by now, with Donna in residence at the house.

What if I had pushed an innocent girl into the path of a train, right in front of her mother?

Even if I had got away with it and fled, the terrible realisation would have smacked into me before I was out of the station. My memory would have served up its usual torture: Claire in the alley, her sightless eyes. Nothing would have changed.

34

I need to know. This time, as soon as I have got my work back into shape, delirious with exhaustion, I make my way to Abigail's house and walk up and down the street until it dawns on me that there is a small park further down the street, with wooden benches where I can sit.

It's still early, so I stretch out on the grass, cradle my head on my jacket and fight sleep for a while. I could easily wake to find myself here after dark, my excursion pointless, so I drag myself up and sit on one of the hard benches, my eyes on the front fence of Abby's house.

Of course we told the police Abigail's name, and she was dragged in for questioning. Since the Saturday night of the party she and Claire had been in the houses of various "friends", where they had been taking as much heroin as they could get with the last of their money. Abby gave the police the names and addresses of some of these friends in return for immunity from prosecution, and to cover herself further she maintained that it was all Claire's idea and she had just gone along with it.

If I had had the chance to kill Abby in those days I may well have followed through.

From what she said, it seemed they had started taking heroin well before the trip to Bali. They had imagined themselves to be occasional, social users and congratulated themselves on their ability to handle the drug, but it quickly, inevitably took hold of them.

Richard and I only managed one meeting with Abigail and she was evasive, giving ridiculous answers to our interrogation and refusing to look us in the eye. When she and I were alone together she didn't try to keep up her indictment of Claire, but confided that they had both been led astray by Lila.

I asked Abby precisely what her relationship with Lila was, and I asked her what Lila's last name was and where I might find her, but Abby clammed up. When I pressed her, she insisted that Lila was Claire's friend, someone she had known before she met Abby.

On that last night Abby and Claire had procured one shot, all they could afford, and agreed to share it. At that time there was a consignment of unusually lightly cut heroin on the streets.

In their ignorance they perceived no danger and instead were excited about the drug's "purity", thinking it would give them an even better high.

Claire went first. The plan was that she would empty half the syringe then pass it to Abby. As her thumb depressed the plunger, Abby told me, their eyes locked, then Claire gave a little sigh and pushed it all the way down.

Abby screamed abuse, slapped her, pushed her into a sprawling heap on the cobblestones and finally ran off, leaving her crawling in the mud.

"She wasn't trying to hurt herself," Abby told me. "She didn't know what it would do. She just wanted it all for herself."

Abby roamed the area, strung out and dizzy, her brain half blotted out. Eventually she crept back, desperate enough to scrabble for the needle in case there were any last drops. She saw Claire, fell to her knees and vomited until her body was empty of everything except pain; then she found a public phone and called me.

A low-slung car passes me, slowing down, a convertible of some sort with the roof down. I hear an insistent tooting, look up and realise it has stopped outside Abigail's house.

The car is blocking my view so I get up and walk slowly along the street, watching the house. The door opens and the woman I saw on the platform at Town Hall station steps out. So the girl with the violin really is Abigail, this is Abigail's mother, and she is still alive.

The mother is young, small and fine-boned like Abigail, with long dark hair like Abigail, and dressed in expensive casual clothes. Despite the warm spring sunshine she is donning a scarf, a long, floating silk scarf printed with a swirling wash of colour. She flings a trailing end over her shoulder as the man in the car leans across to open the passenger door, grinning his appreciation of her.

I stop right in their line of sight with my wind-blown greying hair, my shabby op-shop jumper too thick for the balmy day, my ill-fitting jeans and clumpy shoes that my mother didn't want. The arrogance, the obtuseness of this woman who doesn't imagine she is in mortal danger, the recklessness that she has passed on to her daughter, ignites a spark of fury.

The woman looks up, unfriendly.

"Can I help you?"

"No," I say. "You can't help me, but maybe you should help yourself. Look at you in that stupid scarf! What do you think's going to happen with that, flying around in the traffic? Haven't you heard of Isadora Duncan, you stupid woman?"

She gets into the car and slams the door, glaring at me, but she does gather up the end of the scarf and tuck it into her jacket. The man glances at me and murmurs into her ear, something that makes her give a little snort of laughter, and they drive off without looking back.

I watch the car recede into the distance, laughing too. What a crazy old lunatic I must have seemed to them! Bag-lady indeed. Something is shifting in my brain, like gears changing. Thoughts seem to slide through and slip away but I can't grasp them, like dreams when you try to remember them upon waking.

I walk back to the station and wait for a train to the city. I'm not even sure what I'm doing in this suburb. The train I catch is going through to the North Shore and I stay on it, my mind empty and strangely calm.

I get off at North Sydney and walk mechanically to Paul's door at Crows Nest.

"I'm sorry," I say. "I'm really sorry."

"It's okay." He puts his arms around me and it feels so natural I hardly notice. "I was worried . . . I was mainly worried because I didn't know how to get in touch with you. I thought I'd never see you again."

I separate myself from him gently as we walk to the kitchen.

"Have you eaten yet?" he asks. "I've got some bits and pieces here."

"That'd be nice, thanks." I watch as he pulls plates and containers out of the fridge.

"How was the concert?"

"Sublime." He hands me a program, pointing out a few interesting details in the notes. There's a piece by a composer I haven't heard of, with a marvellous name.

"That was really something," he says. "The composer's Finnish. The Finns are pretty extraordinary, musically."

"Yes, I heard a wonderful Finnish cellist playing there a while ago," I say incautiously. "He played *The Swan* from 'The Carnival of the Animals' and it was heart-rending."

"At the Opera House?" He's frowning. "What concert was that?"

"Oh, maybe it was somewhere else." Damn it. The cellist in question is no doubt still a schoolboy, back in Finland.

My thoughts wander unbidden to Abigail and her violin. Why was I so interested in that girl? I can't think of any reason now.

We eat little sandwiches and a quiche, the pastry as light and flaky as any I have tasted, and we wash it down with ice-cold riesling.

"Did you make this pastry?" I ask.

"Indeed. I've had plenty of time to practise, and I was determined to get it right."

"Well, you've got there. This is brilliant." I remember not to mention *MasterChef*.

"How is it that you have time to perfect pastry? Are you still working?"

"I just do locums, three days a week. I dutifully enrolled in medicine to please my mum, but I never could work up any interest in being a specialist. I found I really liked being a GP, just helping ordinary people with their ordinary problems, and that's what I did."

"I should have thought 'my son the doctor' would be enough for most mothers."

"It should, and my son the doctor agrees. Though he is a skin specialist – not quite glamorous enough for his grandmother, I suppose, but she died before he was born."

"I'm sorry to hear that. She must have died young."

"She was fifty-one. Poor Mum. I never forgave her for interfering so much in my life, and I don't think she really cared. I was just a disappointment to her. But I wished later that I had reconciled with her, just in my own mind, while she was still alive."

"I got on pretty well with my mother, so I didn't have any reconciling to do," I say. "But I still feel privileged that I was with her when she died, holding her hand."

My eyes sting with a couple of stray tears. I feel even more privileged that I have been able to see Anne again and spend that time I never managed while she was alive. But do I have to go through her death again, I wonder.

He puts his hand over mine.

"I've witnessed a few ends like that," he says softly. "A loved one with a loving family. It's one of the reasons I like being a GP."

We sit for a moment, his hand over mine. I look down at it.

"I have ..." I start, but in the same moment he says, "I just ..."

We both laugh. "You first," I say, withdrawing my hand.

"Okay. I just remembered something Linda said to me, that night, when she was trying to get me to run away with her."

"Yes?"

"She said something like, 'I've had enough of this town. I've had enough of dirty old men looking over fences at me.' It struck me as odd, because her house was a bit isolated, you know? And the side fence was too high for anyone to look over."

"That's right," I say. "I knew the house."

"Just one of those mysteries," he says. "Now you – what were you going to say?"

"Yes. Well. I have to go away."

"When?"

"I don't know. Pretty soon. It might happen in a way I have no control over. But I just want to say ... I'm sorry if I don't get to say goodbye."

I look up at him, and he's looking gravely at me. I know he's being careful not to say what he's feeling, and that this is hard on him.

"If it happens, don't look for me," I say. "There's no point looking, you won't be able to find me."

"You'll be unreachable?"

"Yes."

"With your unreachable husband?"

"Possibly. But listen, if you can wait twenty years, I'll come and find you again."

"Twenty years!"

"I know, I know. You'll be really old. But you should be okay. You have to look after yourself and stay healthy. You have to be here when I come back."

He laughs. "You'll be really old too. How are you going to get here?"

"Don't worry about me. When you see me again you'll know what this is all about, I promise."

"Do I really have to wait twenty years to find out?"

"'Fraid so. But look, I'll give you something to go on with. Let me write down some stuff." I look around. "Where can I write a list so you'll have it for the next twenty years?"

"On the wall?" he suggests. "If I have to repaint I'll paint around it."

"You might want to put this where no-one else can see it."

"Inside the cupboard in my bedroom?"

"Sounds good. Now, have you got a good indelible pen?"

We go into his room which is spartan and neat, the bed made and a towering pile of books on the bedside table. He opens the wardrobe door and I write carefully on the inside:

Columbine High School
9/11
Buddhas of Bamiyan
Boxing Day Tsunami
GFC
Black Saturday
MH370
Je suis Charlie
Brexit

I wish I could think of other things, apart from disasters, but that's what I remember. Racking my brains, I add a bit more:

Eric the Eel
Makybe Diva × 3
Will and Kate

"Well, that's pretty cryptic," he says. "What am I to make of all that?"

"You'll have some idea by the end of the twenty years," I say. "Whenever one of those things makes sense to you, tick it off. Then, when you see me, if you see me, you might believe what I say."

"You certainly are an enigma," he says. "I like that. Now, let's go and finish our supper."

Over cocoa – his idea of supper is novel, but it suits me – he returns to the subject of his mother.

"The real problem was that I convinced myself pretty quickly that she knew all about Linda, and she was making sure we never saw each other again."

"Did she know?"

"There's nothing to say that she did. But once I realised Linda had really left, I assumed she would write to me. I figured she'd gone somewhere, probably Sydney, and was going to wait there for me. Every day when I got home from school I'd rush to the hall table, where my mother used to put any mail that had arrived; but there was nothing.

"After a while I had an epiphany. Of course, I thought, my mother was opening my mail.

"I wasn't game to confront her about it. Whenever she went out – which wasn't often – I would search in her room, but I couldn't find anything."

"Would she have kept the letters?"

"I thought so. She would have relished waving them in my face if we'd had a big blow-up. I felt she was somehow daring me to mention them.

"Then we moved back to Sydney, and I was desperately worried that Linda's letters wouldn't reach us at all. I kept nagging my mother about mail forwarding. She just said I should tell my friends my new address, and I thought she was playing cat and mouse with me."

"Did you ever find any letters?"

"Never. After Mum's funeral I made an excuse to come home early, by myself, and I scoured the house from top to bottom. She got sick and went downhill pretty quickly, but I suppose she could have had time to burn any letters she'd been keeping."

"But in all the years since then you still believed Linda was alive, and that she would turn up eventually?"

"Sometimes I did, sometimes I didn't. At first I thought she loved me so much she would find her way back to me eventually, then when she didn't I thought it must be because she was dead. But as I got older I understood that people can move on. I thought for Linda I might be just a nice memory, and she'd gone on with her life and not looked back."

"As you did?"

"Yes. Well, sort of. Ah, I don't know. It's as though she slipped into another universe."

"Or maybe time travelled to another century?"

"Yes, some nonsense like that. Is that what you're going to do?"

"More or less." I stand up. "Time for me to go."

"You could stay," he says tentatively.

"I don't think I could, but it is a nice thought."

He helps me on with my coat and wraps his arms around me for a moment. I lean into his shoulder.

"I'm sorry I'm not Linda," I murmur. "I think that would have been the best outcome."

"I don't know," he says. "I think I'm glad you're you. Matilda, or whoever you really are."

I'm anxious to get back home, but by the time I get there everyone is in bed except for Julian, whose light shines out of the side window of the house. I resist the urge to go up and knock on his door. He needs me and there's something I have to tell him. I keep forgetting to tell him, and I must remember. It's something about Paris.

Claire needs me too. I've got more stories to tell her, morality tales to tide her over when I'm not here. In my head I turn over Hollywood fantasies, gleaned from God-knows-what autobiographies I have read over the years.

My mind keeps coming back to Alec Guinness and his wonderful memoir, where he describes having dinner with James Dean then going out to the carpark with him to see Dean's brand-new convertible. I know that frisson he experienced at the sight of the car. That's what I felt when I saw that woman, the flying scarf, the grinning companion. Cold horror.

Alec Guinness warned James Dean not to drive his new car, and he was ignored. I wonder if this woman will ignore my warning or if it will have some effect on her, a tiny effect like a butterfly's wing, enough to change her destiny.

I wonder why I warned her in any case. I'm not sure exactly why I was there. I must have had some purpose or other, but it has slipped my mind.

I take time off to do some cooking the next day, and we sit down together to a real family dinner. Richard eats and, when prompted by Stella, thanks me for the food.

He seems preoccupied, and once more I sense strongly that I need to get out of here and leave him in peace.

"Did you see the agent?" asks Stella, eager to engage him in a neutral subject.

"Yeah. We can put down a holding deposit, then we can buy off the plan when they get approval and a start date. It's not a bad idea, because we'll avoid stamp duty that way and lock in a decent price."

Claire looks up dreamily. "I have no idea what you're talking about," she announces.

Stella laughs. "It's those flats they're going to build in the old engineering works. Daddy's found out what we can do about buying one."

"No, no, no, you can't buy one of those."

"It's all right, darling. Maybe when the time comes we'll be able to afford it without selling the house."

"No, it's not that. Those people are going to wreck the beautiful cottages. They're going to lie and say they didn't know. Don't give them any money."

"What cottages?" asks Stella, still smiling. "What is this?"

"Beautiful fairy tale cottages hidden inside the old sheds." Claire is getting upset. "They're going to smash them up late at night, when no-one's looking."

"Where did you hear that?"

"Aunt Linda told me."

They all look at me.

"Uh ... I heard some people talking about it," I say weakly.

"Well, I'm sure it's all going to be done properly," says Stella, frowning at me. "There are laws about this kind of stuff, Claire, but people do like to spread silly rumours."

I withdraw as soon as I can, feeling slightly shaken. I really do have to watch my mouth. If I'm not careful I might actually put them off buying our lovely flat, where my Richard, the non-grumpy one, is even now waiting for me to come home, frozen in the future, waiting for time to catch up.

As I settle down at my desk for another marathon session, redoing the rest of my lost work and trying to get the wretched job finished, I wonder why I persist in thinking of either version of Richard as non-grumpy. Just the other day the older Richard, my Richard, came inside complaining about the way the other tenants had put out their wheelie bins for the rubbish collectors.

"Half of them are the wrong way round, and it's nothing like a straight line," he said. "I had to step out onto the road to get past."

"But there's no traffic down there," I said. "You could walk down the middle of the road and not see a car."

"But they should line them up properly on the edge of the footpath!" he said.

"What does it matter?"

"This country is going to the dogs." He sat down at the big dining table and buried his nose in Facebook on his computer. "Hey, listen to what that moron in Bendigo said to my comment! If he's not denying climate change

..he's bloody well insisting we should make new immigrants renounce the Koran."

"You said you were going to unfriend him."

"Ah, he makes me laugh."

But I haven't seen Richard laugh much lately.

35

I wake up freezing in a tangle of clammy, sweaty sheets with a memory, like an after-image, of the twelve-year-old Claire lying on a railway track with worms pouring out of her mouth. Her eyes were blank but she was trying to say something. I try to go back to sleep and dream myself scooping her up and wiping her mouth, but it's futile.

I blame Lila. I wish I knew where to find her in this earlier world, but I never even knew her last name. She was older than Claire, so she would be at high school already, but I don't know which school or even what area she would be living in at this time.

Lila. Just thinking her name makes me clench my fists, fingernails digging into my palms. If only I had realised what she was when that name started cropping up in Claire's conversation. If only I'd seen through the network of lies Claire told in order to get out of the house and spend time with Lila and her cohorts.

If I could find Lila now I would grab her by the throat and threaten her with every punishment I could think of if she ever even considered befriending a girl called Claire. I would assure her that I would be watching from some hidden vantage point, and that I would be quite prepared to rip her eyes out.

They met through that other girl, Abigail, who was Claire's first friend at her new school. Abigail seemed like a nice girl, ideal best friend material, and I wished they had spent more time together, but after a while Claire pronounced Abby boring.

It's true that Abby spent a lot of time on her music. She was a talented young violinist and also played piano and sang in a choir. I was a little envious. I had always wanted my children to be musical, but Claire flatly refused to practise the piano that we briefly owned, and Julian just listened to standard pop music until he developed a passion for something called techno and then psychedelic trance, which I found truly mystifying.

I think the key to Abby's success was her mother, whom I met a couple of times. She was a lawyer or something like that, a glamorous divorcee, but she also found the time and energy to be intensely focused on her daughter. As long as she was around, Abby was never going to stray from the path, much as she might have been tempted.

Because Abby did have some questionable friends, and Lila was one of them.

They must have met at Abby's sixteenth birthday party, a couple of months after Claire started at the school. Claire went off in a pretty, lacy dress that she had had for a couple of years and barely worn. We had arranged – I groan now at my naiveté – that I would pick her up at eleven.

At ten-thirty, as I was digging out the car keys, she called me on my mobile.

"Mum, some of the girls are going to an after-party at Lila's. Please, please can I go? Francesca's boyfriend can drop me at home afterwards. I won't be too late, I swear."

Alarm bells rang in my head and I stood staring at the phone.

"What is it?" asked Richard, already in his pyjamas.

"She wants to go to another party. An after-party."

"Jesus. Should we let her go?"

"Someone-or-other's boyfriend is going to bring her home."

"What the hell? Who holds a party for young girls at this time of night? Tell her she's coming home."

"Claire, you stay right there," I said into the phone. "I'm coming to get you now."

When I arrived, she was standing at the front gate of the house, furious. There was a stain on the front of her dress that looked like red wine. While she was getting into the car a couple of other girls came out, laughing loudly and staggering against each other. One of them was wearing what looked like lurex shorts with knee-length boots, and the other was tugging at a skin-tight glittering dress that barely covered her ample backside.

"Had those girls been drinking?" I asked with feigned innocence on the way home.

"No! God, Mum!"

Even when she was talking to me again, a day or so later, she wouldn't tell me anything coherent about the party, but she was in rhapsodies over Lila.

"She's two years older than me. But she's fantastic, Mum. We think the same way about nearly everything."

Soon Lila was spending time at our place, even on school nights, though she was considerate enough not to stay late. She was an attractive girl, quiet and polite to me and Richard, though I could hear plenty of talking and laughter from Claire's room when they disappeared upstairs. As she was older it seemed reasonable that they should go out together on Friday and Saturday nights, to movies and the odd concert, then inevitably Claire started staying out.

"Lila wants me to go to her house after the movie and listen to some records. I could stay the night, Mum, then you won't have to come out and get me."

After a while it started to feel wrong to me. Claire was thinner, bad-tempered and had dark circles under her eyes, but when I suggested she curb the late nights she flew into a rage.

"For God's sake, Mum, I've just got a virus. Everyone at school's got it. Why do you always want to spoil everything for me?"

"If you've got a virus stay home tonight, go to bed."

"I'm over it now. Please, Mum. Things are going so well for me. And Lila's got some fabulous videos she wants us to watch together."

Lila was not working or studying – apparently she was on a gap year. She lived in a luxurious house in Glebe with her father but I found out later that they moved around constantly.

There were a lot of things I found out later.

36

I deliver my work to Stella after breakfast the next morning, and she takes the CD up to her study to check what I've done.

I wash up and tidy the kitchen, trying to soothe away the slight feeling of guilt that makes my hands shake. It doesn't make sense that I can feel so disquieted about my relationship with myself.

But that is the trouble. From my side, as the so-called Linda, there is no subtext in this relationship. Every negative thought Stella has about me flares like a beacon before my eyes. Every attempt she makes to hide her feelings behind a mask of politeness makes me more uncomfortable.

From her point of view I am an increasing problem, bland in the way I present myself but worryingly contradictory. I am remembering more and more about this episode in our lives, about the false Aunt Linda – at this point I suspected her to be false, but whenever I raised the subject with Mum on the phone she would energetically reassure me: "No, darling, she's definitely Linda. I know my own sister!" And I also remember Richard's increasing pressure on me to send her packing, and Claire's increasing fascination with Linda's clearly fictitious account of her life.

Of course Claire was breathlessly passing all the stories on to me, and my anxiety grew with every word. I felt, obscurely, that the stories were harmful for Claire, and I was starting to have grim thoughts about the false Linda's motivation.

I know all this, but how can I, the false Linda, mollify her?

When she comes downstairs I sense a new uneasiness in her. I'm not the only one who's feeling guilty here.

"You've done great work, as usual," she says. "I'll get some cash out of the bank and pay you this afternoon, if that's okay."

"Yes, sure. Is there another job you want me to do?"

"Um . . . we've pretty much got everything covered at the moment." She won't meet my eyes, and no wonder. She's never got everything covered. I know what this is. Richard has been telling her to disentangle me from her working life and she sees the sense of that, even though she could still use my help.

"Okay," I say brightly. "I'll have a bit of a break, then." I slip out of the kitchen before she can ask if I'm planning to go away. Maybe it's time, though. This can't go on much longer.

A little later the phone rings, and after a moment I hear Stella calling me. I pick up the receiver with a sense of dread. It's Stephanie.

"Oh, Linda. I'm so sorry to disturb you, but I'm a bit worried about Dad. Ever since he saw you he's been really off the planet and the nurses can't get him settled down."

"I'm really sorry about that," I say. "I don't know how I —"

"They want to give him injections, you know, to sedate him. I really wish they wouldn't. He gets so dopey and he falls over, and you know that's really bad at his age."

"Yes, well I —"

"I know it's a lot to ask," she ploughs on, "but I was wondering — well, they think it's a good idea too — I was wondering if you could come to see him again, and bring your ID?"

"My ID?"

"Yes, you know, like your driver's licence. I know it sounds crazy, but he keeps raving on about you not really being Linda, and maybe this would settle it for him."

"But do you really think he's in a fit state?"

"Maybe just seeing you again might do the trick? You could talk a bit about Mount Wallace when you were there, the old shops and everything? He's living in the past anyway. I hate having to ask, Linda."

"Okay," I say helplessly. "Look, I'm a bit tied up at the moment, but maybe next week?"

"Sure, or could you manage Sunday? It's a bit easier for me, with work and everything. Could you do that?"

"I'll see," I say. "Give me a call over the weekend, okay?"

We hang up and I sit there for a moment, stupefied. If I try hard I'll be able to come up with an excuse for not having ID, but can I pull off the rest of it? Even Stephanie is going to get suspicious before too much longer.

Desperate for something to do, I catch the bus to the city and explore every antique and second-hand shop I can find, looking for Linda's bracelet. I take the train to Newtown, where I remember seeing more possible shops, then work my way back through Glebe. There are no charm bracelets, and none of the shop owners can recall when they last saw one.

After school, Claire finds me reading in my room. I've been browsing through Stella's books, among which I found a biography of Grace Kelly, who became Princess Grace. It must have been a present and I'm sure Stella has never opened it, but it has given me some ideas for the next phase in Linda's colourful life.

As a result, I have some rough ideas ready when Claire deposits herself on my bed, reaching for the purring Henrietta.

My hand snakes into my bag. I find my phone and turn it on.

"What's that thing?" asks Claire as I draw the phone out and hold it up to my face, my fingers stabbing the icons.

"It's a sort of calculator," I say. "I'm just checking something."

She lays her cheek against Henrietta's neck, and the little cat struggles to escape.

The battery light is flashing red, so I close the camera app and turn the phone off. I wonder if it recorded. Sometimes, when the battery is really low, it won't co-operate.

"I suppose you want to know about Hollywood?" I say, stuffing the phone back out of sight.

"Yes, please."

"Well, it was fun for a while, especially for me because I had no idea at that time how they make films. For a start, it's very slow. A scene that lasts five minutes, if it's a big scene, can take days or weeks to film.

"Some of the action stuff I did looked quite exciting in the films, but it wouldn't be so great if you saw it these days, because it's so obviously fake. For example, if you're sort of balancing on the wing of an aeroplane, or running along the roof of an express train being chased by bad guys, the plane would be on the ground, or the train wouldn't really be going. It wouldn't be a real train, anyway. The most they would do would be to shake it up a bit. Then, after they'd filmed it, they would add film of the moving background, to make it look like the train was moving. Do you see?"

"Ummm."

"Anyway, even though it was safe they usually got me to do that stuff, just in case the main actress fell off and sprained her ankle or something, which would hold up the filming.

"I also got to jump into quite a few lakes and rivers, and off boats into the sea, because they didn't like the star to get wet and ruin her hairstyle. All that was fun, except when it was cold. I had to teach myself not to shiver."

"It turned out that Moira Ray's career didn't last long. Moira Ray, the actress I was originally hired to stand in for? She looked quite good but she had absolutely no talent, so they stopped giving her work. Then she got into booze and drugs, and she would hang around the studio shouting abuse at the producers and begging the directors for work. It was really sad to see."

"I suppose so." She's not really interested in these kinds of stories.

"Just always remember, people get tempted to drink and use drugs, but they ruin your life. You'll remember that, won't you, Claire?"

"Sure." She jumps up. "I have to do some homework now. Will you tell me some more later?"

"Of course." I watch her go, chewing my lip. It's pointless telling her all that stuff at her age. I need to be here when she's older, maybe fourteen.

I get up, close the door and put the Grace Kelly book back on the shelf. I was going to have Linda go back to Paris as a stand-in when they made *To Catch a Thief*, but that can wait.

Hang on, though. Was the cat burglar in that film played by Grace Kelly or someone else? Damn it, how did we look up things like that before we had Google?

Paris. Julian. When he comes home I'm in the kitchen, preparing dinner.

"You need to go to Paris when you're older," I tell him abruptly.

"Oh. Why?"

"It's just one of those places you have to go to, like Berlin. Just make sure you go out and see the world when you're old enough, and take Claire with you."

"Okay." He smiles and wanders out again. To be honest I don't know why I think it's so important for him to go to Paris. It's just a feeling I have in the pit of my stomach. The feeling is more like anxiety, a fear that he won't go.

After dinner a golden opportunity falls into my lap. Claire is helping me to clean up. I scrub at the pots, determined to get years of black marks off them, and she stands with a tea towel, waiting to dry each one.

"We were reading palms at school today!" she announces brightly. "Did you know this is my lifeline?" She holds up a hand and my heart stops.

"Do you want to see? Look, there's a break in it, quite early." She traces the line with a delicate finger. Sure enough, there is a noticeable break, surely just where she turns sixteen. Of course it's all nonsense.

"It starts again, though." My voice is husky.

"Oh, sure. Let's see yours."

It turns out my lifeline has a similar break in it, also at about sixteen. I have to remind myself that I'm not Linda.

"Let me see yours again," I say, taking her hand. "I knew an old fortune-teller in Istanbul, Claire. Let me see the minor lines."

"What, these?"

"Yes. Hmmm. You're going to have a very eventful life."

She chuckles. "Sarah says this one shows I'm going to have four children."

"Oh, at least four. But look here, look at this wiggly line."

"What is it?"

"It's your danger line. It sort of works off your lifeline. Oh dear."

"What?"

"I've seen this pattern before. Oh my. It's the Lila fork."

"Lila?"

"It means you'll be in particular danger if you have anything to do with anyone called Lila."

She shivers, enjoying it. "I don't know any Lilas."

"That's just as well. You must steer clear of Lilas, all your life. The danger will always be there."

"Okay." Her eyes are wide with delight. "No Lilas."

When we've finished the dishes I retreat to my room. I can hear the television going in the living room and occasional laughter, but I'm afraid my presence would cast a pall.

Stella has left an envelope on my bed with a wad of money in it. It's a generous amount for what I did. It's enough to get me away somewhere, but I can't think what I could do when I get there.

With Linda's birth certificate I can make a serious effort to get myself an identity, and with that I might be able to get a place to live and a job, or even a pension. Or by putting in the applications I might flush out the real Linda, if she is alive. That would be something.

I wonder what the real Linda would think of me. I imagine we'd get along very well. I imagine us exploring the city together, arm in arm, two peas in a pod, cackling at each other's jokes. But that's not really me and it's not really her. I can't separate her from the fantasies I've woven about her, for me and for Claire.

The real Linda might know what to do about Claire. She would scoff at my feeble attempt to put Claire off Lila. She would hunt down Lila and deal with her.

We did try to dampen down Claire's relationship with Lila. We wondered why a girl of eighteen would want to spend so much time with someone like Claire, not yet sixteen and young for her age. We tried to steer Claire towards girls her own age, her classmates at the new school.

When Claire asked to go to Jasmine's birthday party I was dizzy with relief. I had been very nosy about Claire's classmates, trying to find out which ones would be suitable replacements for Lila, and I knew that Jasmine was a serious, studious girl, and the class captain.

"That's great, darling. When is the party?"

"Saturday week."

"We were going to have your birthday dinner on the Saturday night." I could see her watching me, scarcely breathing. "I suppose we could make it Sunday."

I drove her to the house, a big place in Strathfield with a long front path leading to a tessellated tiled verandah. To her chagrin, I walked to the front door with her, hoping to meet Jasmine's parents.

Jasmine came to the door, a tall, thin girl with glasses. She greeted Claire in what seemed to be a friendly way. Before I could ask about the parents Claire gave me a little push and waved me away.

"See you later, darling," I said, resigned. She gave me a brief hug and I could smell the perfume of her freshly washed hair. Then, as she followed Jasmine inside she turned for an instant and gave me a little private smile. I do love you, Mum, it said. I just have to look cool in front of Jasmine.

Claire looked ravishing that night in an elegant black taffeta dress that we'd bought just for the party. She was turning sixteen the next day, and I walked back to the car thinking how she had weathered the awkwardness and chaos of childhood and emerged like a butterfly.

Before I got home she called and asked Richard if she could stay over. He agreed, knowing how much I wanted her to make friends with these girls. He didn't think to get any details, such as the phone number, so we drove back together the next morning to pick her up.

The car was full of flowers for her. I can't have fresh flowers in the house any more: the smell makes me nauseous and brings on panic attacks.

No, Jasmine said, Claire had not stayed the night. In fact, she had left the party early.

"She left? Who with?"

"I think it was Lila."

"Lila? Do you know Lila?"

"Oh, yeah. Lots of the girls know her."

Putting it together later, with what I discovered about teenage behaviour and the epidemic of drugs, I realised that Lila must have been dealing – supplying many of the girls in that expensive school.

We drove straight from Strathfield to Lila's house in Glebe and pounded on the door. An old lady popped her head out of the decrepit neighbouring house.

"I think he's away, love," she said.

"Are you sure?"

"Yeah. I seen him getting into a taxi yesterday. He goes away a lot, business trips I suppose."

"What about the daughter, Lila?"

"Oh, she's not there. She comes and goes."

We came back several times over the next few days and nights. The house was dark and uncommunicative, but we didn't know where else to look. Richard went out searching every night. He didn't tell me where he went and I didn't ask.

I found Abby's number and called her. She insisted that she hadn't seen Lila for a long time and didn't know how to contact her.

It was the police who called me, and by the time I saw Claire she was in the morgue.

37

I have to face the fact that so far I have achieved precisely nothing. My memory keeps serving up that image of Claire in the morgue, her colourless skin, her face as smooth and cold as a marble statue.

They pulled aside a corner of the green cloth so I could identify her. Richard had insisted that it was his responsibility, but at the door he had stopped, his hands over his face, shaking uncontrollably.

"I'll do it," I said.

"No, you can't . . ."

"She's my daughter. I'll do it."

They spared me her ravaged body, her wounded arms. Her hair was dark with moisture, but they had smoothed it back from her face, which they had washed clean.

"Where's her dress?" I murmured.

"Pardon?"

"Her clothes. What happened to them?"

They gave me a plastic bag with some clothes, but I couldn't open it. There was something denim, something with lurex, all the things in the bag damp and streaked with mud. I couldn't look.

A week later I was sitting alone in the living room, watching yet another endless post-mortem of 9/11, illustrated by black smoke and planes disappearing and debris flying, over and over, unable to feel anything. I heard a car stop outside for a moment, then drive off again.

I went to the door and opened it. A big green garbage bag sagged on the step and I was, for a moment, terrified. It seemed to be related to the objects exploding out of the shattered upper storeys of the two buildings.

I peeped into the bag, put a cautious hand inside, felt the slippery surface of the black taffeta dress.

When they finally released her body we cremated her in the black dress, and I wish we hadn't. Whenever I see or touch anything like taffeta I imagine it exploding into flame in my fingers.

38

The next morning is Friday. I give in and set off for Crows Nest to see Paul. I haven't trusted myself to visit him, because I'm afraid I will break down and ask him to take me in.

In the event it doesn't matter, because he's not at home. He did tell me that he works three days a week, so I suppose this is one of those days.

When I get back at about midday Stella is in the kitchen, and I can see immediately that this means trouble.

"Oh, hi," she says. "I'm just making some tea, would you like some?"

"Yes, thanks." I think I should say no, but an awful weakness comes over me.

"How do you have it?" she asks.

"Same as you." Should I just tell her? How would she take it?

"The same as me? I have it super-strong with a dash of milk. Most people find it a bit much."

"No, it's fine. I like it that way."

She bustles around, getting mugs out and visiting the fridge more than once. She's got something to say and she's putting it off.

"Listen, I've been here too long," I say, trying to forestall the inevitable conversation.

"No, no, you're always welcome here."

"It's okay, really," I say. "I've pretty much sorted myself out, and I think I'd better get back to where I came from."

I wish.

"So you're going back to Perth?"

For a moment I've forgotten what I said when I arrived.

"Oh . . . uh . . . yes. Perth. I'll miss all of you."

She hands me my tea, relaxing a little.

"Well, you know where to find us now. Come back and visit. You'll come back anyway, won't you, to see Anne?"

"Of course. And I'd love to stay in touch with all of you. Especially Claire."

"Yes." She frowns a little. "Look, I know you meant well, telling Claire all those stories, but I'm not sure it's good for her. Sooner or later she'll realise it's all made up."

"Yes, but . . . This is hard for me to explain, but I'm actually telling her morality tales."

"Morality tales!"

"Yes, like Aesop's Fables, and most of the fairy tales. You know what I mean."

"Claire doesn't need morality tales. We've brought her up with a perfectly good set of values. She's got a very healthy sense of right and wrong. What on earth are you putting into these stories to call them morality tales?"

"I'm trying to warn her." Now that I have embarked on this path I'll have to try and make Stella understand. "There's trouble ahead for her, serious trouble. If I can't be there with her in the future, I'm trying to warn her now. To forearm her."

"Are you saying we can't look after her ourselves?"

"Of course not."

"Because we're her parents. Who are you?"

It's a rhetorical question, so I don't have to formulate an answer to that, but I am getting desperate.

"Stella, something bad is going to happen to Claire. Something really bad."

I remember this conversation now. It comes flooding back. This crazy old woman who had somehow been taking advantage of me and worming her way into the hearts of my children.

She was standing in the middle of the kitchen, wild-eyed, her greying hair askew as I looked at her in growing dismay.

Why had I let this person into my house? Why had I let her spend so much time with my daughter, my beautiful, vulnerable Claire?

"Are you threatening my daughter?"

This is going badly. I can't seem to find the words to make her listen to me.

"You have to understand. In the future, she's going to have problems, big problems. I'm trying to give her ... reference points ... so she can deal with what's going to happen. I'm trying to save her life! If I'm not here to do that, you have to do it, and you have to understand what's going to happen."

"We don't need you! I'm doing just fine, bringing up my children and looking after them. Claire is safe with us."

"She's safe now, but there's going to be awful pressure on her when she's older. She'll change schools – don't send her to St Monica's – and she'll make friends you won't like, and she's going to lie to you and steal from you and start taking drugs."

"How dare you! Claire would never do any of these things. Who do you think you are?"

"I'm you, Stella. I'm you in twenty years' time. I've come from the future to warn you, to tell you about Claire."

That was the moment when I realised she really was mad, a lunatic who had talked her way into my home, into my mother's home. On her own admission she was not

Linda, and in some part of my mind I had never believed she was Linda.

"I don't know who you are, but you'd better pack your things and go."

"I'm going, I'm going, but first you have to listen to me."

"I don't have to listen to anything!"

"I'm you, Stella. I had a stuffed dog called Loco and I couldn't sleep without him until I was thirteen. There was a monster with red hair and green lips that I thought was lying under my bed, ready to grab my ankles, so I was too scared to get up and go to the toilet. I had a gollywog, for God's sake, that Dad called Black Sambo. I've never told anyone these things, you know I haven't."

I put my hands over my ears. How could she know all this? She must have been stalking me, worming information out of my mother.

She was still talking and I could still hear her. "When Julian was born I was paralysed with terror for the first three months. I had this fantasy that his fingers or toes were going to drop off because I'd been careless. Every time I unwrapped him I had to count them."

I thought I'd never told anyone that. I must have told Mum.

"A little while ago, I think it was last summer, you had a big argument with Richard and you decided to leave him. You changed your mind when Claire found a dead kitten in the street and you watched him burying it for her and comforting her."

Claire had told Mum about the kitten, but I'm sure no-one knew that I had contemplated leaving Richard. I would never have told Mum that.

"Stop!" I said. "That's enough. Please go now."

She seemed defeated then. Her shoulders sagged. She turned and went out the back door while I stood trembling in the middle of the kitchen.

She won't look at me as I come back through the kitchen, my sparse belongings hastily shoved into the cheap overnight bag, my coat over my arm.

"Please just remember our conversation," I say as I pass and our eyes meet. Our identical eyes.

"You're sick," she retorts. "I should be calling someone to come and take you away. And don't you go near my mother again!"

I suddenly remember the notebook. I left it hidden in the drawer, under the other notebooks. I turn to go back for it.

"Go!" she hisses. "Just go!"

"Goodbye, Stella," I say sadly.

Maybe she won't find it. She's got no reason to look in the drawer, under the unused notebooks. If she does read any of that stuff it will confirm her view of me. Of course she wouldn't believe any of it. She can't. She believes in logic, in a rational world, and there's no possible, logical way that I could be here, that I could be her.

I can see it differently because I am here, because it might be impossible but nevertheless it is happening.

In twenty years' time she'll know the truth. In twenty years she'll understand that I was making one last effort to set things right, and that I knew it would be fruitless.

I forgive you, Stella.

After the fake Linda left I tried to work out how she had known all those things, but I found I couldn't trust my memory. She must have drawn some things out of Mum, I thought, and then maybe my mind raced ahead and imagined all the other, private things she might have said if she really was me. She couldn't have really said those things.

It was so disturbing I wanted to forget it, to forget her, and I pushed it all out of my mind. With a huge effort I forgot what she had said about me, and I forgot what she had said about Claire.

I – Stella – will find the notebook, but not for a long time. When we were packing to move, years later, I emptied out the drawers of the old desk. The pristine notebooks were a rebuke to me, an affront. I hadn't used them and I never would.

I took the notebooks into the living room, where Richard had lit the fire and was burning some old papers.

As I threw the bundle onto the fire one of them fell open and I saw writing in there, my writing.

I couldn't remember ever writing in any of these notebooks. Individual words flickered as the pages curled and were consumed. *Julian . . . Françoise . . . Abigail.*

Then a scrap detached itself and floated up towards the chimney, the words on it still faintly visible: *Claire will die.*

It was too late to snatch the pages back; the fire was too hot, the flames crackling.

Afterwards, it was easier to think that I had imagined the whole episode.

39

My plan, such as it is, is to go back to Crows Nest and sit outside Paul's house until he comes home, then plead with him to take me in; but by the time I get to Town Hall station I have regained some self-control.

The person I really need to see is my mother. Of course, by the time I get there Stella will have already called her and urged her to throw me out if I show my face. I hope Anne won't try to convince her that I really am Stella. I don't think she will. If I am remembering correctly, Anne was maddeningly bland.

"I know, dear, it's all right. I knew from the start that she wasn't Linda."

"Then why didn't you say something? She's an imposter! Why did you let her into your house?"

"I like her company. We've grown very close. In a lot of ways it really is like having Linda back."

"She's taking advantage of you! She's insane, Mum. She says she's me."

Mum just chuckled. "She's more like you than you'll ever know."

The train trip is as long and tedious as ever. I look out the window and try to gather my thoughts.

All I can do in Mount Wallace is say my goodbyes to Anne. I don't know where I'll go after that, but it will have to be somewhere far away. Melbourne, I suppose, or Adelaide, or even Perth. I've got enough money to get to any of those places and live for a while.

Strangely, I'm not really worried about where I'll be and how I'll survive. It doesn't seem to matter. But if I can find a way to keep myself, wherever I go, I'll come back in three or four years and secretly, invisibly, watch over Claire.

The warmth is leaching out of the spring day when I step onto the platform. It has been so balmy this past week that I've taken to wearing my original clothes. I stop for a moment to add my trench coat, then hook the overnight bag onto my shoulder and walk out to the street. A shadow looms beside me and a voice hisses in my ear.

"Linda!"

I turn with a start. It's the fat, slovenly woman I saw on my first day in Mount Wallace.

"Oh! Uhhh . . . Iris?"

"You recognised me!" She is thrilled. She drops a heavy hand on my arm. "Linda, it's so good to see you!"

"Well, it's nice to see you too, Iris." I start to edge away.

"Come and have a cup of tea with me. Please, look, we're just over there. You remember Mum's old house?"

"Um – I don't think I ever . . ."

"No, of course you've never been inside, have you? But we've always lived here, the Woodridges. Please come in, just for a minute."

She has a firm hold on my elbow and she's already steering me towards the front gate. I acquiesce.

"My brother was a bastard," she says cheerfully, throwing open the unlocked front door, and for a moment I'm unsure whether she's commenting on her brother's character or divulging a family secret.

"I hardly remember your brother," I say. I think I'm on safe ground there. Anne mentioned him, and she said none of the girls liked him.

"I'm sure you don't." We're in the small, dark kitchen now. It's a perfect time capsule, with skimpy old kitchen cupboards, cracked and worn Laminex, a too-large dark veneered dresser. The wood stove is alight and it's stifling.

"He was a bastard, anyway. All those years he let me think . . . Well, I can't say what he let me think. How do you like your tea?" I'm jolted by her change in direction, and stare at her with my mouth shut.

"I could make coffee instead..." She picks up a jar of instant coffee, its label faded. I can see that the contents have half solidified.

"No, tea's fine thanks. I like it strong."

"Oh, that's good." She takes a steaming teapot from the back of the stove. I assume it's been brewing there all day, so the tea will be strong, all right.

"Yes," she says. "I bet you didn't know that after you'd gone, John, that's my brother, used to say you were his girlfriend?"

"Well, what a nerve," I say.

"But it was worse than that, and that's why I'm so happy to see you."

"Yes?"

"Please, have a seat." She gestures to a chair at the old pine kitchen table. Resigned, I peel my coat off and sit down.

She puts a thick white china mug of tea in front of me and plonks herself down opposite. There's a small jug of milk on the table, covered with a beaded doily. I don't want to sniff it while she's looking, so I pour a dash into my tea and hope for the best.

"You might not know what happened after you left," she says, "but they were searching for you, around Mount Wallace, like."

"Were they?"

"Yes, they put posters up and everything. Posters saying 'Missing', you know. And one day when we walked past they was dragging the lake, and John, he said, 'Well, they won't find her in there.'"

Something prickles at the back of my neck.

"And I said, 'What do you mean? How would you know?' And he just laughed and said, 'Like I'd tell you!'

"Well, he never said anything else at the time, but I started to get worried. You just never knew with John. He seemed harmless, never got into any real trouble. They said he had learning problems, but he always seemed smart enough to me. Cunning.

"Time went by and you didn't come back, and it seemed no-one had heard from you. I asked him about it another time, when he'd had a few drinks. I said to him, I said, 'John, what do you think happened to Linda McCutcheon?' and he got real shitty. He said, 'Why the hell are you asking me? Mind your own bloody business.'

"Well, that didn't make me feel any better, but I sort of forgot about it. But then we had that real hot summer, about twenty years ago, I suppose, and we was sitting out in the backyard because it was too hot to go inside. We was like an old married couple, me and John, always squabbling. Neither one of us got married and we both just stayed in the house after Mum died."

"Is John still around?" I ask.

"No, love, he's ten years dead. But I'm getting to that. This hot summer's night, as I was saying, I said, 'This is like that time Linda McCutcheon went missing. It was real hot then, day and night. Maybe she did go for a swim in the lake and drown. You could drag that lake for weeks and still not find someone, it's that big.'

"And he said, 'That'd be a funny sight, her swimming in them fancy city clothes she had on.' And I said, 'What city clothes?' and he said, 'That suit, sorta thing, like what Mum wore to Dad's funeral.' I said, 'That's how much you know, the posters said she was last seen in a white dress,' and he said, 'That's how much you know, stupid bitch.'"

The prickling is stronger, and I take a sip of the bitter tea to calm myself.

She goes on. "And then I said, 'Well, maybe someone killed her and threw her in the lake. I don't reckon they'd ever find her.' And he said, 'That'd be stupid. There's better places than that.' And I said, 'Like where?' And he said, 'There's all that bush on the Big Mountain. There's places in there no-one ever goes.' And I tell you, the way he said it, it made me shiver."

"Did you ask him how he knew what I was wearing?" My voice comes out a little hoarse.

"Not really, because he was starting to get shitty again and all that worry was starting up again inside me. He got off work late, though, that night, so I suppose he could have seen you somewhere, on your way out of town, like."

"I suppose so."

"What was you wearing, anyway, that night?"

"I don't remember." I don't want to alarm her. She's got more to say.

"He was pissed that night, of course," she says. "He and his boss used to get on the piss after work, and that night they was painting until midnight, trying to get it done, and I reckon they had a few after they finished. His boss got into trouble from his missus for working so late. I heard John get home about one or two o'clock, revving outside and slamming the door. He had the van from work – had to drop off the painting gear, he said. Mad.

"So anyway, he got the cancer, and it was one of them bad ones, and he went downhill that quick. Ten years ago next week, it was, when he died. He was in the hospital in Sydney, they took him up there but even those specialists couldn't do nothing. The last few days I stayed with him all the time, and towards the end I said, 'John, if you've got anything on your conscience you should say it now, before the end. It'll make you feel better when your time comes.'

"And he said, 'Anything I've got to say, I'll say it to the priest.' And I said, 'Please, John, just tell me once and for all. Did you do something to Linda McCutcheon? You've let me think things all these years, you know you have. You were just teasing me, weren't you?' and he said, 'Forget about that bitch. She got what was coming to her.'"

She gives a little sob and pulls out a tattered handkerchief.

"Sorry, Linda, but those were his words." She brightens and looks up at me.

"But the bastard was teasing, right to the end. Because here you are!"

"Here I am."

"I can go to my grave now, knowing I'll be with Mum and Dad again on the other side, and him too."

I must look as uncomprehending as I feel.

"I thought he might be in Hell, you see," she explains gently. "But he wouldn't go to Hell just for teasing me, would he?"

"He told lies about me, too," I remind her.

"He confessed that to the priest, at the end," she said. "Well, he didn't say they was about you, but he confessed to telling lies. I think he'll be all right."

"So you heard what he said in his last confession?"

"Yes. I wasn't supposed to, but I just stayed in the room. He was whispering, but I could still hear."

"And did he say anything about me?"

"No, it was just the usual things, like what everyone says. Well, but you don't tell the priest the really bad things, do you?"

I need time to process all this. I stand, a little shakily.

"I'd better go, Iris. Thanks for the tea, and for what you told me."

"There's one more thing. Just wait there." She whisks out of the room and I feel weighed down by dread.

"Here." She presses something into my hand and I barely glance at it. I know what it is.

"This is yours, isn't it?"

I nod mutely.

"I found it when I went through his things after he died. You must have dropped it, right? He would have picked it up off the road?"

I nod, not trusting myself to speak, and somehow I get myself out of there. When I'm well away from the house I open my hand.

The bracelet is just as Anne described it, and there's also something familiar about it, as though I have seen and handled it before. The charms are neatly spaced, the original gold ones interspersed with the silver, and the little turquoise bird is there. Next to it is an extra gold charm that Anne didn't mention. It's a heart with some tiny letters engraved on it, and I hold it up to my eyes and squint in the evening light to read it.

P loves L.

40

Anne opens her front door with a smile.

"I thought you'd be on your way here," she says.

"Stella called you?"

"Yes. She said if you turned up I should give you short shrift. I don't think it was a good idea to tell her who you really are."

"No, it just slipped out."

We go into the living room and it feels warm and safe.

"Well, like I said, dear, you can come and stay with me for as long as you like."

"I won't, Mum." I turn and give her a hug, and she pats my shoulder.

"I'm going to go away. If I stay here it'll just make trouble between you and Stella."

"I can handle Stella," she says.

"Don't forget that I'm her too! No, if I stay around it'll be bad for her, for you, for the whole family."

"Oh dear. I'll miss you."

"You'll have me. Stella is going to start visiting you a bit more often."

I've just remembered that. I was quite shaken by the visitation of the false Linda, and I started to worry more about Anne being on her own. I'd forgotten until now why that was. I resolved to make a habit of coming down every second weekend, and I persuaded her to come to Sydney more often, too. Claire loved Anne dearly, and was delighted to be seeing more of her. Maybe as a result of that, Claire . . .

But no, the vision is still there. The alabaster face.

And now there's another vision: Linda walking along the road in her good suit, marching with determination down the hill towards the station, unaware of the van creeping past her, stopping just ahead, the door starting to open.

If I am to be transported again, before I go back to my time and my real life, let me find myself here in Mount Wallace in January 1950, on that hot Saturday night. Let it happen now, tonight, so I'll be in the right spot: outside the old school yard, in the shadows of the tall trees. I will watch Linda heading to her meeting with Paul and then, after a short while, emerging, stumbling a little, carrying her bag. She will start down the hill and I will fall into step beside her.

"Excuse me," I will say.

Only then will she look at me, her face streaked with tears.

"Is this yours?" I will hold out the charm bracelet.

"Oh! I must have dropped it. Oh thank you, thank you very, very much."

"I'm glad you got it back," I will say. "Where are you going?"

"Down to the station. I'm going to wait for the morning train."

"I'll walk with you."

The van that was crawling along behind her will accelerate, pass and disappear in a cloud of dust.

Or maybe she comes out of the school yard and turns the other way.

"Is this yours?"

"Oh, thank you so much."

"Where are you off to?"

"Just going home. I was going to leave town, but I've changed my mind."

"Let me walk with you."

"You seem really troubled, dear," says Anne. "I'm going to get you a glass of sherry."

As she disappears into the kitchen I call out to her, "Get yourself one, too."

Sherry is her last-resort cure for everything stressful. I pull myself together with an effort and, when she returns, sip delicately at the little glass, then put it down on the side-table.

I still can't decide what to tell her. The bracelet burns in my coat pocket.

"Let's drink to Stella," I say.

"Let's drink to all our beautiful girls," she says. "To both Stellas, to Linda and Claire."

"And yourself," I say, my eyes moist. We clink our glasses together and drink.

Over dinner, I ask Anne about our family history and she happily rattles off a string of names and relationships, starting with the convict couple who might or might not be my great-great-grandparents, depending on whether the spelling of a name was changed. I struggle to commit it all to memory, wishing I could use my phone to record her.

Afterwards she is obviously tired.

"We can talk some more in the morning," I say. "I'll leave before lunch."

She hugs me and kisses my cheek.

"We'll have a nice cup of coffee together," she says.

"I'm going out for a walk now," I say. "I've been sitting all day and I really need to stretch my legs."

"It's dark out there, and it's getting cold. Are you sure you'll be all right?"

"I'll be fine, Mum. You go to bed. Lock up, and I'll use the spare key to get back in."

Naturally she keeps a spare key under a pot plant beside the back door.

"Goodnight, then, dear."

Wrapped in my coat and scarf I walk briskly up the hill to the old house. It's barely nine o'clock but the streets are deserted, just as they would have been on that hot Saturday night. All the shops are closed and there are only a few cars parked in the main street.

Somewhere on the other side of town there'll be a service station open, selling lukewarm pies and soggy chips to the desperate. There might be a few teenage boys there, playing pinball. Apart from that the whole town is tucked up behind locked doors.

When I get to our old house I stop and linger by the front gate. The windows are dark. That's how it would have been. I wouldn't see her at first, because she would slip out the back door and round the side, then suddenly she would be in the street, close to where I'm standing.

I step back into the shadows and imagine her walking to the corner and crossing the road. The site of the old Catholic school is very close, just in the next street. It's gone now, the buildings demolished and a cyclone wire fence around the whole block. I walk to where the school gate was, willing it to reappear, fingering the bracelet in my pocket.

Of course, if it were possible to time travel at will I wouldn't be here at all. I would have gone home long ago.

I imagine her running back out the gate after her meeting with Paul, upset, possibly crying, then she stops and pulls herself together.

Which way did she go?

The sensible thing would be to turn back towards her house. The whole point of leaving had vanished, and there was no need for her to cut herself off from everyone she loved: her family, especially Anne, and Paul.

She turns the corner back into our street just as the van comes gliding along. He stops and opens the door.

"Going somewhere?"

"Just going home," she says stiffly.

"I'll give you a lift."

"It's only in the next block."

He would have had to get out of the vehicle and force her. Did he hit her? Knock her out?

No, she wouldn't have headed for home just yet. She was upset, angry, defiant. She marched down the road towards the station, maybe hoping that Paul would change his mind and run after her.

The van came gliding down the hill, swung wide to pass her, then stopped. He stuck his head out the window and she looked at him in disdain. John Woodridge, the town creep. All the girls despised him.

"Going somewhere?"

"None of your business."

"That bag looks heavy."

"It's not."

"Here, I'll give you a lift."

If he forced her into the van, wouldn't she have screamed and fought? Wouldn't someone, tucked up in their bed, have heard her?

Maybe she accepted. She was a strong, popular girl and he was the town nobody, a loser. Maybe she was confident she could handle him. Where was the harm in riding down to the station with him? Or maybe it occurred to her that he could take her to Bowral, where she could catch the other train.

Maybe he drove up the Big Mountain with her. She probably wasn't used to driving around the area, was unfamiliar with all the roads.

"Is this the way to Bowral? Shouldn't we be on the highway?"

"It's a shortcut. Don't you worry, I know my way around here."

Did he stop up there, maybe on the dead-end road to the lookout, and reach for her? Maybe she tried to run, but he was faster. She stumbled on the rough path. Linda, you should have fled into the dense bush, crouched down and hidden.

He might have knocked her out with a branch, or a tool he'd brought from the van. I'd rather he knocked her out and she never knew what he did to her after that.

Or it could have been an accident. She was walking down the middle of the road and he, drunk, not looking, drove straight into her. He stopped, gasping and panting with horror, then bundled her body into the back, intent on hiding his deed. He knew where to take her.

Every time he passed that spot on the road, for the rest of his life, he saw the smear of blood, even years after it had worn away. Nobody else ever noticed it. Every time he passed that spot he relived the horror, for the rest of his life.

Maybe she died instantly, her head full of thoughts of Paul, and never knew what hit her.

I walk down the road towards the station. It's cold and quiet and there's no-one around. It could be 1997, or 1950, or 2017. There's still time.

But it's not a hot night in 1950. The closed and shuttered shops are exactly as they were when I passed them on the way up.

I let myself into Anne's flat and sleep fitfully, oppressed by black roads and shadowy figures. I wake up in the middle of the night gasping and flailing, driving off an image of Claire's body being dragged out of a lake, trailing dead reeds and the slimy tendrils of a shredded white dress.

41

I drag myself out of bed quite late, and I know Anne's been up and about since dawn. Washed and dressed, I go around the corner and get takeaway coffee, a cappuccino for her and a short black for me, and some coffee scrolls from the bakery that I know she likes.

"So, where will you go?" she asks, sipping her coffee.

"I'm not really sure, and it might be better if I don't tell you. Just so you can tell Stella you don't know where I am."

"Will I hear from you?"

"If you don't, it will be because I've gone back to my own time. Be glad for me, if that happens."

"Of course." She's sombre. "I thought . . . I suppose I was hoping I'd see you before I die. You know, just before."

"You will." I take her hand. "I'm Stella, remember."

"So you will be there?"

"Yes."

"I know it's silly," she says tremulously. "I know you can't tell me, and I shouldn't be asking, but . . . will I suffer?"

For a moment I don't know what she means, then I understand the fear in her eyes.

I struggle to compose my answer. "Mum, no. When you die it will be peaceful and easy. You're not going to suffer. And I'll be with you, holding your hand, all the way to the end."

"Are you sure?"

I laugh, and she laughs too. "I suppose you are sure."

"Listen," I say. "It's the other Stella who'll be with you, but she is me. If she whispers something that you can't hear, what she's saying is, 'I love you, Mum.' And you'll mumble something back, and she'll never know for sure what you said."

"I'll be saying 'I love you, Stella. My dear girl.'"

We smile at each other, dab our eyes in unison and sip our coffee. I reach into the pocket of my coat, draped over the chair behind me.

"Mum, hold out your hand."

She obeys, and I give her the bracelet. She sits gazing at it for a long time.

"Oh, dear," she says.

"I'm sorry."

"No, it's . . . I'm glad. I knew she was dead. I could feel it. And . . . I know it's selfish, but what if she was alive, all this time, and she never bothered to contact me?"

"I wish she wasn't dead, though," I say. "I've always imagined her alive somewhere, and so has Claire. I'd rather Claire didn't know."

"I suppose you're right. Maybe when she's older?"

"Yes, maybe then. She wouldn't know if I hadn't come back like this and found the bracelet. You wouldn't know. I think it's better to keep things the way they were."

"You're probably right." She fingers the bracelet again. "So you searched for it?"

"I did. I looked in every shop I could find." That's not a lie. And now the moment has passed, and I haven't told her what I know. She doesn't need to be burdened with that knowledge. She doesn't need to imagine, as I will for the rest of my life, what Linda went through. She doesn't need to see Iris Woodridge in the street and know what her brother did, and Iris Woodridge doesn't need to know either.

Anne stands up, holding the bracelet.

"There's an extra charm here. I wonder what that means. I suppose it's been through a few hands, though, since she had it."

"I suppose so." Her old eyes aren't good enough to make out the inscription. I keep quiet about that too.

She drives me to the station, and we do a last circuit of the town on the way. Driving from our old house back down the hill, I ask:

"Where was the grocery shop where Linda worked?"

She slows down and stops in front of a cluster of townhouses.

"Right here," she says. "It was still going when you were a little girl, then the supermarket opened down by the station and all the shops gravitated towards that."

"I think I remember. There was a big old boarded-up shop next door, wasn't there? Was that the furniture store?"

"That's right. Very fancy in its day. The Careys did it up that summer, the year Linda went. Big plate glass windows, beautiful new sign and they painted it all, inside and out, and had a grand opening. Then a few months later they were gone. Packed up and left town."

She starts up the car again.

"They were painting?" I repeat. "Who did the painting?"

"Gil Carey did it himself. He was always tight with his money. And that John Woodridge, who was working for him at the time. They were in there day and night, up till midnight by all accounts, all the lights blazing. I reckon in the end he paid John more than it would have cost to have it done. In any case, John Woodridge was splashing money around the town for weeks afterwards."

John Woodridge. So Gil Carey was his boss. They were painting until midnight, Iris said that too, then John came home in the van, arriving noisily in the small hours.

"Here we are." We're pulling up outside the station and Mum gets out before I can ask her not to.

"Let's just say goodbye here," I murmur.

She hugs me briefly, then turns and goes back to her car. We both hate long, lingering farewells. The train arrives and I step onto it in a daze.

42

The stations tick by in the familiar order, and I gaze out the window at the blur of bushland. I still don't know where I'm going – I'll decide when I get to Central.

John Woodridge had his boss's van. They were painting until midnight. The boss got into trouble with his wife for getting home late. The boss was Gil Carey.

So after they had finished and had a few beers, John was sent off in the van to drop off the painting gear somewhere. He must have been cruising round, just as I thought, when Linda came striding down the road with her good suit and her bag.

But that can't be right. Linda and Paul had met at the old school at ten, and by his account they didn't spend much time together before she stormed off. It can't have been much later than ten-thirty. The two men were still together at the shop, painting.

If they were ever asked, John Woodridge and Gil Carey could have provided each other with an alibi for that night. In a way, they did. They seem to have made sure the whole town knew where they were.

Gil Carey. They thought he was just raving, but I'm convinced that he knew I was not Linda. Could he have really known her well enough to pick the deception, as my mother did? Paul knew Linda as well as anyone, and he thought I was her.

But Gil Carey was certain. What if it was because he knew for sure that Linda was dead?

Gil Carey wanted Linda to work for him, Mum said, but she wouldn't, she took a lesser-paying job instead. He was right next door to the grocery so he would have seen her often, the girl who refused to come and work for him. Paul said she was upset about "dirty old men" watching her over fences. Had she caught Gil looking on when she and Paul had their little trysts in the back yard of the shop?

And another thing: Gil Carey put all that money and effort into doing up his shop that summer. He had his grand opening, then a few months later packed up and abandoned shop, town, everything. Could something terrible have happened there, something so terrible he could not live with the daily reminder of it?

What if they didn't work until midnight? What if they finished by ten that night?

I picture the two of them sprawled on the couches displayed in the front of the shop, looking out through the brand-new plate glass windows, opening their beers with a sigh of pleasure.

No, it was a hot night. Surely they wouldn't be sitting inside in the stifling heat with the smell of new paint. Maybe they dragged some chairs out the front and sat there surveying the empty street.

She comes walking down the middle of the road. They call out to her. There's no-one around. The town is dark, silent, closed up for the night.

If they invited her over or offered her a drink she wouldn't have accepted. She had made it clear she didn't want to have anything to do with either of them. But there were two of them, and there was no-one else around.

Afterwards, John Woodridge could have bundled her into the van and driven her up to the Big Mountain. He was well paid for his efforts. They could count on each other to keep quiet, a hellish pact.

The images click round and round in my head, keeping the rhythm of the train wheels.

Something is building inside me, pressing hard on my brain, a feeling I don't recognise at first. That's because I'm not thinking about Claire, about what Lila did to her, about the people with whom she spent her last days. I'm not thinking about her, and yet that same feeling is mounting inside me: pure, hot fury.

THE LOST GIRLS

At Central, I cross the platform and step onto a train that takes me to Burwood. It's a five-minute walk from the station to the nursing home.

It's late afternoon and there's no-one around. I guess the old people are having a snooze before their dinner, which will be quite early. As for the staff, it's Saturday so there won't be many on duty, and I don't suppose they'll be vigilant.

I tap in the code, easily remembered from last time, and slip through the corridors to Gil Carey's room. He's alone, sitting in his chair like last time as though he has grown roots there.

He looks at me, his eyes blank.

"It's me, Mr Carey," I say softly. "It's Linda."

"No." He shakes his head vigorously. "No. Go away."

"I'm not going anywhere," I say, looming over him. "You don't get rid of me that easily."

"No," he says. "You're not her. She's gone. She's six feet under."

"I am Linda. I've come back. You're going to pay for what you did, you and John."

"He said they'd never find you. Six feet under, he said."

"You think he'd dig down that far?" I scoff. "Lazy, good-for-nothing John Woodridge? I've come back."

"The gravel pits! He said the gravel pits. It was easy, he said."

"Tell me what you did, Gil Carey. Say it!"

"No! No!" He reaches up with gnarled old hands and catches me by the throat. I pull away but he's shockingly strong. His bony fingers dig into my neck and I feel myself gagging, gasping for breath. With a supreme effort I grip his hands and prise them off me.

He's screaming incoherently now. The door clicks open and an ancient face peers in, then another.

"Get her away from me!" he screams. "Help!"

"Help!" quavers a voice. "Help!" There's a chorus now, a tsunami of pale old faces pressing into the doorway. I hear hurried footsteps. I squeeze through the old people to get out the door, shaking off feeble skinny fingers that claw at me. A different attendant is coming down the corridor, an Indian woman.

"What's happening?" she calls. "Excuse me! Could I have your name, please?"

I retreat as fast as I can, stab in the code with shaking fingers, and flee. At Burwood station a train is arriving and I jump onto it, scanning the platform anxiously as we leave. Nobody comes panting after me, shouting for the train to stop.

I'm pretty sure this is one of those trains that go to Central then on to the North Shore. I can get to Paul's place this way. I need to tell him everything.

If I am obliterated from the planet, or cast into the distant past or the unimaginable future, someone needs to know. Paul can be the guardian of the secret, and when he thinks the time is right he can help them to find her and give her a proper burial. As far as I know the old gravel pits halfway up the Big Mountain are still there, undisturbed, even in my time.

I scour my memory. Did they find her? Apparently not.

Maybe it will be me. If I never go back to my own time, if I find somewhere safe to keep myself, to watch and wait, I can be the one to inform the police. It's not in my memory yet because it hasn't happened yet.

But the other things in my memory haven't happened yet either. I still can't quite grasp how this works, and my brain goes weak when I try. If I could stop myself remembering what happened to Claire could I stop it from happening? Could I force our lives onto a different path?

I still think I would have to take direct action. Lila. I need to find Lila, if not now then sometime in the next four years. When I find her I can threaten her, or bribe her or, if necessary, kill her. My soul – which I don't believe in – will be damned to Hell – which I don't believe in – if I kill an innocent girl, but if it's a choice between her and Claire then I won't hesitate.

Lila. I'll kill her in those few months after Anne dies. I'll have to come back to Sydney in 2001 and start watching that house in Glebe where she lived – will live – with her father.

They will probably catch me and publish my photograph. Stella will recognise me as the madwoman who pretended to be Linda, and they'll lock me up somewhere.

It doesn't matter. Claire will be fine, and Stella will live happily until that day in 2017 when she will disappear. Or maybe she won't disappear after all? Her life will be so different that she won't be in that precise place at that precise time, ready to fall into whatever wormhole or portal or time warp led to all this.

But if that doesn't happen to me, how can I have saved Claire? I must disappear. I will have to make sure that on that day Stella will set out from the apartment, just as I have already done, and go to the city and see that film, just as I did. I will write her a letter from my prison cell and plead with her one last time.

And what about Richard, waiting fruitlessly in our apartment for Stella to come home from the city? I will need to tell Richard why she can't come home ever again.

I try to visualise him, sitting in his favourite armchair by the window, looking out over the water. Does our apartment have a view over the water? When I try to remember it seems to fade, like a photograph produced on film in the old way, the image swimming into view in the developing fluid then gradually dissolving again because my hands are paralysed and I can't reach out to rescue it.

43

As the train pulls into Central there is a garbled announcement on the speaker system. I can't make out what they're saying, but people start to get off.

I stand by the door and listen as the announcement is repeated. Something about there being a problem with this train, and we should change to the train on the opposite platform. I scurry across and get a seat close to the door. The train sits for a while, as though waiting for something.

I think of Paul with a mixture of trepidation and pleasure. He will welcome me and urge me to stay. I will decline, but I am comforted by the knowledge that he'll always be there, offering me a haven.

The news about Linda will be heartbreaking for him, but at the same time it will be the indication he yearns for that she didn't stop loving him, that she would have found him again if she could.

I'll tell Paul that I saw the charm he gave Linda, but that I felt Anne was the rightful owner of the bracelet. It's up to him when he contacts the police – whether he gets them to arrest Gil Carey, or whether he agrees that it's better to wait until Anne has gone and Iris has arrived in Heaven, disappointed to find that her brother is not there waiting for her. Stella will organise a funeral and he can go. Stella will have the bracelet, and he can ask to see it and show her the golden heart.

Is this going to happen, though? My memory tells me nothing about it.

The train jerks into life and I press my forehead to the window as we glide out of Central towards the city. We'll be travelling above the ground for just a minute before we enter the underground system, from which we will emerge just before crossing the Harbour Bridge.

The sun is about to set, a glow on the horizon as I seek out the green skyline of Belmore Park, just visible on the left. Close to the railway line there is a glorious mature jacaranda tree in full bloom, and I see more smudges of hazy electric blue dotted through the green treetops of the park.

Then my eyes take a few seconds to adjust as we plunge into the dimmer light of the tunnel.

It's too early in the spring for jacaranda.

I look around at the other passengers in my carriage. No-one is looking at me. They are all intent on the phones they are holding in front of their blue-tinged faces.

My fingers freeze, then I grope for my own phone and try to turn it on, but it's completely dead.

There is nothing special about the appearance of the train. It looks neither very new nor very old. If there was anyone reading a newspaper I would ask to see it, so I could check the date, but there are no newspapers. People are wearing business clothes, even though it's supposed to be Saturday.

We stop at Town Hall, start again. We stop at Wynyard. There are people pouring onto the train, people coming home from work. At Wynyard I crane my neck to read the destinations board. Yes, this is one of the peak-hour trains that go all the way to Wyong.

I look around the carriage for clues. People are dressed in much the same way as they've always dressed, though there are fewer men in business suits than you would expect in 1997, and more women in hijabs and burqas.

Of course I know what this is, but I'll know for sure at Chatswood. They completely rebuilt the station around 2008.

We pass through Wollstonecraft, and from the window I can see a lot of new development around the railway line. I think there used to be a green gully in this spot, but I can't be sure.

Next comes St Leonards where I should get off if I'm going to Paul's, but I don't get off. I have an irrational conviction that if I leave this train now I'll step back into 1997 and I'll never escape again.

The train slips into Chatswood station, and now I know. The new platforms and escalators are already looking a little worn.

I settle back in my seat, stunned. I know this train well. I commuted on it once or twice a week for a few years, after we moved to the Central Coast.

So I am really here where I started, travelling home to our house in the rainforest valley where you can faintly hear the surf at night if it's really rough. It will be after dark when I get there and my cats, Henry and Jazz, will be waiting anxiously just inside the back door.

Home, my retreat from the world for the past ten years.

44

We got a letter from the developers a month after Claire died, and I tossed it onto the hall table with all the other unopened mail.

A few weeks later another letter arrived with a red sticker marked "Urgent", and Richard opened it.

"They want to know if we're going to exercise our option," he told me.

"What option?"

"The apartment. They're getting ready to start work on the building, have you noticed?"

"No."

We didn't discuss it, despite the arrival of another red-stickered letter. At that time we didn't discuss anything.

One night, late, Richard came into the bedroom where I was pretending to sleep.

"Put your coat on," he said. "There's something happening down the road."

The old engineering works was flooded with portable lights and a monstrous machine, some sort of bulldozer, was at work. A few neighbours were standing around shouting objections, their voices drowned in the din. Fred, from the waterfront house at the bottom of the hill, was yelling into a mobile phone.

"Look!" called his wife, Deirdre, as we approached.

The machine was at the back of the building, scooping up sandstone blocks and tossing them into the tray of a waiting truck with other indiscriminate rubble. Another truck stood in the street, piled high.

"That's hand-cut sandstone," said one neighbour. "Look, you can see the marks from the stonemason's tools."

Against the water view now revealed behind the building you could make out the outline of a gabled stone wall with gaping window holes, but as we watched it melted into nothing.

At breakfast the next day, Richard looked directly at me for the first time in weeks.

"Claire told us that would happen, didn't she?"

I knew he was talking about the stone cottages.

"She did. She was quite upset about it."

"Wasn't it the witch who told her about it?"

"Yes, but I still can't imagine how she knew."

Richard went over to the sideboard and picked up the latest letter.

"I'm going to tell them to shove their apartment," he said.

"I think we have to," I said.

Sometime later, I don't know if it was days, weeks, or months, Richard said:

"You know, we've got that money we were going to use for the apartment. Why don't we have a look at the Central Coast?"

He had talked on and off for years about getting out of the city. I had encouraged the Central Coast idea because I didn't want to go back to Mount Wallace, and I did share his love of walking on the beach.

The project saved our sanity. On weekends we would drive up to the coast and explore, often staying overnight in a bed and breakfast somewhere. After a few months we found a place we liked, a few kilometres inland with a vast, neglected garden, then it took almost two years to plan and complete a renovation of the tumbledown farmhouse.

Julian said he liked the idea, but he politely declined when we asked him to come up with us to see the place we had decided on. I only realised afterwards how isolated and uncommunicative my poor boy was in that period. After Claire died he withdrew from everything, including his university studies which he had almost finished, but the next year, with no help from us, he dragged himself back and completed his final year. During that time he lived at home, but he didn't seem to want our company.

Julian didn't object when we told him we wanted to sell the house so that we could be financially free. He helped us to pack up, but none of us, including him, could go into Claire's room to sort out her things.

Lauren said: "I'm sorry, sweetie, I can't do it either, but I know this great charity shop. If you're sure you want to give it all away they'll come and pack it up."

Two refined elderly ladies who must have been sisters, if not twins, spent a couple of hours in the room, then directed operations as a meek young man carried out a succession of boxes. At the end of the exercise one of them handed me a thick envelope and a small carved wooden box.

"We thought you might want her photos," she said, indicating the envelope. She placed the box in my hands without comment.

When they had gone I opened the box and puzzled over its contents. Claire had had it since she was about eight and she always kept her treasures in it: some junk jewellery along with a handful of comparatively valuable pieces: a marcasite watch that Richard's grandmother had owned, an antique gold-plated brooch that someone had told her was worth a bit, which she had picked up at a market, and the silver chain Anne had given her for her twelfth birthday.

Those things were all gone, and I realised with a sick feeling in my stomach that she must have sold them to buy drugs. In their place was a charm bracelet with gold and silver charms, and one turquoise bird.

I looked at it without recognition. I had an uneasy feeling that she had stolen it and not yet managed to sell it, and my instinct was to throw it away; but driven by an irrational feeling that the rightful owner might turn up one day, I put the bracelet back in the box and put it in the back of my underwear drawer in the new house.

It's still there, and the first thing I am going to do when I get home is to take it out and drape the bracelet over my hand one more time. Anne must have given it to her shortly after my last visit.

"This was Linda's," she might have said. "Don't say anything to your mother, she's a bit upset about Linda turning up and then disappearing again like that."

"Didn't Linda want it back?" Claire might have asked.

"No, she had no more use for it. She wanted you to have it."

I might give the bracelet to Paul, if I find him, if he's still alive. I believe he is. In fact, I believe I saw him, only a few weeks ago. Only now do I understand what happened.

I had gone to a concert in the City Recital Hall, mainly because one day, when I had been idly browsing the net, I came across a story on this particular orchestra illustrated with photographs of the various musicians. There was a young female violinist who looked just like Claire's friend for a short time, Abigail Kincaid. I couldn't find her name on the website, but they were to play a couple of my favourite Mozart pieces, so I went.

I bought a program and there, in small print, was Abigail's name with a short biography. It seemed she was doing remarkably well, and I felt a flash of irrational pride.

The concert finished just in time for me to catch a train back home to the coast, and I was struggling to get out of the hall behind all the geriatric patrons with their walking frames when I noticed a tall, elderly man on the other side. He was waving, apparently to me, with a look of astonishment on his face.

The man was a complete stranger who had obviously mistaken me for someone else. He was making gestures that clearly indicated that I should wait for him outside, but I hurried away, wanting to catch my train and anxious to avoid embarrassing him further. He had a nice face, I thought.

Strangely, when he opened the door to me in Crows Nest I had no sense of having seen him before. I still don't understand how all this works.

45

We had a number of good years in the new house on the coast. Happiness may be too strong a term, but we were calm and purposeful, and we learned to talk to each other again.

I reorganised my work so that I did less, and more of it from home. Once things were settled I only had to go to Sydney one or two days a week, always by train.

Richard kept saying he was going to do the same, but every week he seemed to have a different reason for needing to drive down and back almost every day – close to an hour and a half each way. After a while I concluded that he liked the solitude of the drive.

At weekends we planted and tended a garden. Julian visited now and then, and went for long walks by himself.

In the spring of 2008, on the day that would have been Claire's twenty-third birthday, we drove to Sydney together, walked into the alley where they told us she had died and laid a bunch of yellow roses, as we did every year. Then I went to a meeting in the city and Richard went to his office.

I caught a train after my meeting and was home by mid-afternoon, just as a ferocious storm broke, lashing the young trees we had planted so that they bent almost double, rain thundering on our roof. The temperature dropped and I stood by the window wrapped in a blanket, waiting for the central heating to kick in, watching massive hailstones hitting the stone paving and bouncing a metre into the air.

My phone rang and I could hardly hear it.

"I'm heading home now," came Richard's faint voice. "It might be a bit slow in this weather."

"Is it raining there too?"

"Cats and dogs."

"Listen, don't drive in this weather. Come later, if it eases off, or stay until tomorrow."

"What? I can't hear you."

"Don't drive in this weather!" I yelled into the phone.

"I've got to get home. It's Claire's birthday."

"Don't!" I shouted, but the line was dead.

At about eleven I got ready for bed, persuading myself that he had seen reason and decided to stay over after all. Julian had a convenient couch in his one-bedroom apartment, and he never minded us just turning up. Richard's phone battery was probably dead, and that was why he hadn't answered my calls.

I lay under a blanket on the couch in the living room so that I would see the headlights of the car sweeping across the window. Sometime after midnight I was woken by a pounding on the door.

At Hornsby the daylight is almost gone, and birds are returning to roost in the tall trees by the station. The air is filled with their mournful cries.

The train glides into the bush of the national park, lights winking on the Hawkesbury River below. Tiny townships slide by, accessible only by train and river. In half an hour we will arrive at Gosford and I'll find my car, if I can remember where I parked it so long ago, and drive home in the velvety darkness.

Everyone thought I would move back to the city after Richard died, but I have found peace in our old farmhouse and I prefer to be on my own. Even when I travel down for a day to shop or see a movie I don't always tell any of my friends. That way I don't have to see anyone.

Of course if Julian were still in Sydney I'd visit, but Julian lives in Paris now. I have already booked my flight there for Christmas, and I feel a little surge of delight at the thought of that.

But I will come down to the city again soon to seek out Paul, and like the first time I will arrive unannounced. That thought also makes me smile. I have been imagining his growing astonishment and wonderment as the events

I recorded on his wardrobe door happened one by one, especially if I got them in the right order. When he saw me at the concert, looking much the same as our first meeting twenty years ago, it must have cemented the only possible explanation.

I hope he's not too disappointed that he is now twenty years older than me. The age difference doesn't matter to me, but I do hope he has followed my directions and kept himself healthy. We need to tell the police where to find Linda in the old gravel pits, and we need to bury her together. Then we can resume our pleasant, easy conversation, and I want it to last for a lot more years. I'm not going to give up my solitary life, but we can visit and cook for each other. I think he would like the rainforest house and garden.

If I had to be sent back in time like that, I wonder why I couldn't have gone back ten years, to Claire's twenty-third birthday. Surely I could have done something to stop Richard getting in that car.

But if I had saved Claire, I would also have changed everything that happened on that day. We wouldn't have walked into the alley and laid the yellow roses. We wouldn't have separated and set off for home, each alone. We might not even have moved to the coast. Maybe we'd still be in our old house, or maybe we would have gone ahead with our original plan and moved into a flat in the old engineering works.

If we were living on the coast, maybe we would have taken Claire out for dinner then stayed the night in Sydney, with Claire and whomever she was sharing her life with; a couple of girlfriends, or a fresh-faced young man who was to become the shadowy husband who would worship her, who would eventually give her that brown-eyed baby who always appears in my dreams.

Or Claire and I might have prepared her birthday dinner together at her house, from ingredients I had brought from home: fruit from our trees, fragrant bunches of herbs and vegetables from our garden. Rocket. Coriander. Lemons.

The storm would have broken, and we would have looked out the window, marvelling at the ferocity of the thunder and lightning.

"Has Dad got an umbrella?" she would have asked.

"I don't think so. I wish he would take better care of himself."

I still don't know why I couldn't stop what happened to Claire. I suppose it was because I never knew how. Not then, not now. There was no magic path into her mysterious mind.

46

Julian surprised me, a year after Richard died. He had been coming to stay with me, like a dutiful son, every second weekend. Over dinner one Saturday night he suddenly said:

"Would you be very upset if I went away for a while?"

"Away? Where would you go?"

"Europe, I thought. I can get six weeks off from work. In fact they're going to make me take six weeks, because I've got too many holidays mounting up and it upsets the accountants."

"I'd love you to go and see a bit of the world. My biggest worry about you is that your life seems awfully . . . constricted."

He gave a little smile.

"Not much of a life at all, eh? Well, that's what I thought. It seems kind of selfish to waste all those chances that Claire and Dad didn't have."

He rarely mentioned them, and I knew it was because he wanted to spare me anguish. I could feel tears coming to my eyes, and I jumped up and took our plates to the sink to hide them.

"I don't think you're selfish, darling, but I agree," I said, rinsing the plates, my back to him. "There's a big world out there and lots of stuff that could interest you and make you happy."

"I might go to Italy and do a short course in Italian at Perugia," he said. "But first I have to go to Paris."

"Paris would be a good start," I agree.

"I've sort of got to go there," he said. "I promised Claire. We had a deal that as soon as she was old enough we'd go together."

He got up, came over to me and turned off the tap.

"She thought she'd be old enough when she turned sixteen. I said no, we didn't have enough money, and also – I suppose the real reason was I didn't like the way she'd been acting."

His voice broke and I put my arms around him.

"Don't imagine any of that was your fault," I murmured. "Your father and I wouldn't have let the two of you do something like that anyway. We all did everything we could for Claire, everything we knew how to do. It was no-one's fault."

"I know, but I keep going back to that time again and again, thinking there was something I should have seen, something I could have done."

"Going back?"

"In my mind," he said.

"Do you know why she was interested in Paris?" I asked. "Maybe it was because she was learning French, and she really took to it."

"There's this big department store she wanted us to go to. It's got the name in giant letters on the roof, and you can go up there and see all of Paris from the top."

"Samaritaine?"

"Do you know it?"

"Yes, it's just down from the Rue Rivoli, by the river. Your father and I went to France and Germany when we were first together, before you were born. We went up onto the roof of Samaritaine, and it's just like you said. I don't remember ever telling Claire about that."

"Maybe you should come too, Mum?"

"Not this time," I laughed. "If you're finally going to get out and see the world you don't want to bring your mother along."

So he went. Samaritaine was easy to find but it was closed, the building sealed up and abandoned.

He stood on the river bank gazing up at the proud façade, picturing himself and Claire up there looking down between the letters. An elderly man stopped for a moment next to him.

"*C'est dommage, n'est-ce pas?*"

"I'm sorry, I don't understand you," said Julian. "*Je ne comprends pas*. Do you know when it's going to be open again?"

"Never, I think. They say it will be fixed. One year, three years. But I think never."

Julian was about to walk back up towards the Gare du Nord, to the cheap hotel where he was staying, but the Pont Neuf drew him in the opposite direction. He decided to have a try at seeing the stained glass in the Sainte-Chapelle, near Notre Dame. I had told him about Sainte-Chapelle, and warned him that it's hardly ever open.

Indeed, he found it closed, but he kept walking, and crossed to the Left Bank on the Pont Saint-Michel looking for the next landmark he had heard about, the Shakespeare and Company bookshop.

A young woman was walking in front of him on the Quai Saint-Michel, her shining brown ponytail swinging languidly. There was something familiar about her.

What tiny, arbitrary coincidences shape our lives. How many decisions, large and small, led to Julian being on the Quai Saint-Michel at that particular moment in time.

He crossed the road and ran a little way, then crossed back so that he was walking towards her. She had paused to search for something in her bag, her head down, then she looked up and her dark eyes met his.

"*Je sais tu*," he said, with great effort.

She laughed. "*Vous me connaissez?*"

Her name was Françoise and she did remember, vividly, her short stay in Sydney on secondment for the BNP, years before; but not that fleeting smile exchanged with a lanky young man in the financial district one lunchtime.

This time he asked her to have a coffee. She accepted and led him to a little bar in a narrow lane, and they have been together ever since. She came back to Sydney with him for a while, then they moved to Paris just before their little boy Guy was born.

Every second year I go there for Christmas and every other year they come here, and in the northern summer we all travel around Europe together: Spain, Poland, Slovenia, the Dalmatian Coast. Guy is five now. He calls me *Grand-mère*, and speaks perfect English with a charming French accent.

Julian has been hinting that he has something to tell me, and Françoise has been staying in the background during our video chats, but I know she's looking a bit pale and wan. They've got my hopes up. If Guy had been a girl they told me they were going to call her Marie-Claire, Mimi for short.

We have lost enough girls in our family. Maybe if fate is kind enough to give us one more I will find myself restored too.

Woy Woy is behind us and the train is slowing down again. People are gathering their possessions as we glide into Gosford station. I get off the train mechanically and find my car without thinking about it.

At home, I plug my phone in and turn it on. The battery is still so flat its icon is red and the phone gives a long unhappy beep, then cuts out. In that instant of life an image flashes onto the screen: a shy smile showing a mouth full of metal, the struggling little tortoiseshell cat with her fur on end as usual, the background of white walls and a darkened leadlight window.

The phone won't turn on again until it's nearly charged, and when I check again the image is gone.

ACKNOWLEDGEMENTS

I want to thank my agent Lyn Tranter for taking me on, and my former agent Gaby Naher for her support and understanding. Thanks too to Lyn and Kirsten Tranter for their insightful constructive feedback on my first draft.

Thanks to my champion Fiona Henderson and all the wonderful people at Simon & Schuster for their enthusiastic support, especially Dan Ruffino, Jo Munroe and Michelle Swainson; and to Christa Moffitt of Christabella Designs for the beautiful cover and book design.

I want to thank my beautiful grandchildren Sigrid, Ariana, Jemima and Hemi for keeping me grounded and showing me how boundless love can be.

Finally, thanks to my husband Bruce Spence for putting up with me, believing in me and being the first and most challenging reader of all my work.

ABOUT THE AUTHOR

Photographer: Jacalin King

Jennifer Spence has worked as an English teacher, a scriptwriter of soap operas and a technical writer. She is the author of three children's books and a crime novel. She lives in Sydney.